## MISTLETOE AND KITTENS

"Hello, Derrick," Claire whispered, starting forward.

At the sound of her voice, old pain knifed through the captain's heart. Yet at the exact moment his boot inched forward, the gray kitten suddenly leaped straight down from the wooden chandelier above him onto his gold braided epaulet.

The captain rebounded high into the air.

Startled as well as enchanted by the surprise, Claire began to laugh.

"Well, I have met your midshipman, Derrick," she at last declared, her voice warm with mirth, "but what is this one's rank?" she completed, reaching out to carefully disengage what seemed to be hundreds of tiny claws from the braid, then drawing the rumbling creature away to cuddle it close to her black woolen bodice.

"Stowaway," the captain responded gruffly while he brushed composure back into his uniform, his lips, too, quirking into a half-grin in spite of his determination for it not to happen, his brows losing their downward slant.

Once more the viscountess's smile blazed. "And what is this?" she again inquired, fingering the makeshift collar around the kitten's neck.

"Mistletoe, my lady," Derrick replied, giving the kitten a stroke. "Mistletoe . . ."

from The Rose and Shadow, by Jenna Jones

# WATCH FOR THESE ZEBRA REGENCIES

**LADY STEPHANIE** (0-8217-5341-X, $4.50)
by Jeanne Savery
Lady Stephanie Morris has only one true love: the family estate she has managed ever since her mother died. But then Lord Anthony Rider arrives on her estate, claiming he has plans for both the land and the woman. Stephanie soon realizes she's fallen in love with a man whose sensual caresses will plunge her into a world of peril and intrigue . . . a man as dangerous as he is irresistible.

**BRIGHTON BEAUTY** (0-8217-5340-1, $4.50)
by Marilyn Clay
Chelsea Grant, pretty and poor, naively takes school friend Alayna Marchmont's place and spends a month in the country. The devastating man had sailed from Honduras to claim his promised bride, Miss Marchmont. An affair of the heart may lead to disaster . . . unless a resourceful Brighton beauty finds a way to stop a masquerade and keep a lord's love.

**LORD DIABLO'S DEMISE** (0-8217-5338-X, $4.50)
by Meg-Lynn Roberts
The sinfully handsome Lord Harry Glendower was a gambler and the black sheep of his family. About to be forced into a marriage of convenience, the devilish fellow engineered his own demise, never having dreamed that faking his death would lead him to the heavenly refuge of spirited heiress Gwyn Morgan, the daughter of a physician.

**A PERILOUS ATTRACTION** (0-8217-5339-8, $4.50)
by Dawn Aldridge Poore
Alissa Morgan is stunned when a frantic passenger thrusts her baby into Alissa's arms and flees, having heard rumors that a notorious highwayman posed a threat to their coach. Handsome stranger Hugh Sebastian secretly possesses the treasured necklace the highwayman seeks and volunteers to pose as Alissa's husband to save her reputation. With a lost baby and missing necklace in their care, the couple embarks on a journey into peril—and passion.

---

*Available wherever paperbacks are sold, or order direct from the Publisher. Send cover price plus 50¢ per copy for mailing and handling to Penguin USA, P.O. Box 999, c/o Dept. 17109, Bergenfield, NJ 07621. Residents of New York and Tennessee must include sales tax. DO NOT SEND CASH.*

# *CHRISTMAS KITTENS*

## *Lynn Collum*
## *Jenna Jones*
## *Judith A. Lansdowne*

Zebra Books
Kensington Publishing Corp.
http://www.zebrabooks.com

ZEBRA BOOKS are published by

Kensington Publishing Corp.
850 Third Avenue
New York, NY 10022

First Printing: November, 1997
10  9  8  7  6  5  4  3  2

Printed in the United States of America

# CONTENTS

# A Purrfect Christmas
# For The Marquis

## Lynn Collum

# *Chapter One*

A sudden gust of cold wind whistled down the old nursery chimney, causing the orange flames to dance in protest. Neither of the young ladies seated before the fire looked up, for they had grown used to the sounds of Westwood Park during their year of residence.

Karis Lockhart pushed her needle through the pink tulle fabric, then eyed the silver leaf she'd stitched with a critical gaze. Satisfied with her work, she tied the thread and clipped the end. The dress for her cousin, Dorinda Westwood, was ready for the Christmas Ball at Medford Hall. It was an event the Lockhart sisters had heard repeatedly extolled over the past month. Their cousin was determined to make a conquest of the duchess's grandson who was to attend.

Glancing to where her sister sat opposite her, Karis smiled at the look of concentration on the nine-year-old's pretty face as she cut a paper star to add to the decorative greenery placed about the room. Karis had tried, in some small way, to recreate the traditions from their small cottage in Oxford here at Westwood, but her efforts were confined to the small nursery.

A soft meow in the corner drew her attention away from her sister. A large orange cat's head appeared over the rim of a wooden box before the animal noiselessly leapt from the makeshift bed and padded across the floor. The large feline, called Mrs. Damon by her owner, purred loudly as she rubbed her head on the woolen fabric of Anthea's skirt.

Karis frowned at the appearance of the cat. It had been a near thing, with Aunt Flora wanting to ban the animal from the premise when they'd first arrived. But the sisters had prevailed with promises that Mrs. Damon would be no bother.

Unfortunately the cat had presented them with an unexpected litter of seven kittens in October. By some miracle Karis and Anthea had been able to keep the kittens' existence a secret from their aunt, but the rambunctious lot were getting harder and harder to contain in the nursery. Karis knew she could no longer delay the subject with her sister, for the tiny animals were eight weeks old and ready to leave their mother.

Looking back at the busy girl, she could see the tip of Anthea's tongue locked at the corner of her pink lips as she maneuvered the scissors back and forth making sharp points on the paper. When the excess vellum, painted silver for Christmas, fell to the table, the child held up her creation and crowed, "I did it. Look, Karis, it is as good as the ones you make."

"So it is, my dear," Karis prevaricated, eyeing the somewhat misshapen star and giving her sister a smile of encouragement.

Anthea rose and skipped across the room to the windows, making her reddish blond ringlets bounce. She tucked the paper luminary into the branches of fir which nestled on the sill, then stepped back to survey the display. "I shall make some more to make it look just right."

"To be sure. There is plenty of paper."

Anthea returned to her seat and began cleaning up the bits of paper from the last star before she started work on another.

Feeling an absolute coward, Karis continued to delay mentioning the kittens to her volatile little sister. Instead she made small talk. "It is dreadfully cold today. I am surprised that Aunt Flora and Dorinda decided to make morning calls."

An angry glint appeared in Anthea's hazel eyes. "I am glad they went, for now you might spend the morning with me instead of running and fetching for Dorinda, and reading for Dorinda, and drawing sketches of Dorinda—"

"Now, Anthea, you know that we owe Aunt Flora a great deal for taking us in after Papa died. I do not mind—"

The door opened, interrupting Karis. One of the house maids who'd befriended them entered the room carrying a coal scuttle.

"Good morning, Miss Lockhart, Miss Anthea, I brun' you some extra coal when no one was watchin'."

"Mary, you mustn't get in trouble on our account." Karis rose and went to take the scuttle from the little servant.

"Don't worry about me. Miss Dorinda and Lady Westerly returned and the young lady's in such a rare takin' that no one is payin' attention to anythin' but makin' miss 'appy."

Anthea picked up her scissors and paper to begin work on a new star. She'd grown used to her cousin's tantrums and exhibited only the mildest interest. "What has made her peevish this time?"

Mary grinned and winked at Karis. "Seems 'er Grace's nephew done sent 'is regrets for the party next week. Miss Dorinda says it ain't worth 'er time to deck 'erself out if there ain't goin' to be no one present above the rank of baron. And her a baron's daughter.''

Karis made no comment for she was not one to gossip with servants. She made up the fire, wondering how she and Anthea would survive until their cousin was married and safely gone from Westwood.

Miss Dorinda Westwood was the most beautiful young lady Karis had ever seen. The seventeen-year-old was blessed with raven black curls, pale blue eyes and the face of an angel. Unfortunately she was also vain, arrogant and spiteful, characteristics she was often able to mask from the casual acquaintance with a cloyingly sweet manner. Karis knew she would be in for a day filled with useless errands to appease her cousin's foul temper.

Lost in her worries about her cousin's temperament and with her back to the open door, Karis didn't see the small tan pug waddle into the nursery. Only Mrs. Damon, who'd been busy cleaning herself, took note of the dog's entry and destination. The orange cat darted across the room and positioned herself in front of the box where her kittens lay sleeping.

Dorinda's pampered pug rarely came to the upper floors, but with the commotion below, she'd followed a passing servant in hopes of finding a treat. What Princess discovered after her long journey excited her interest. The animal continued towards the box. Curious about the strange scents emanating from the region and oblivious to the bristling mother cat, she drew closer and sniffed.

Mrs. Damon arched her back, her eyes rounded in fright. A low moaning began in her throat, then with a lightening swift motion she lunged forward, striking the advancing enemy on its ugly flat nose.

Princess issued the loudest yowl ever in her life and dashed for the door as fast as her short legs would take her. She ran straight into the outstretched arms of her mistress, come in search of her cousins.

Miss Westwood scooped up her howling dog, making kissing sounds. "My poor baby, my poor baby, what has happened to you?" She glared at Karis as if she'd inflicted the tiny scratch on Princess's nose.

Aunt Flora's voice echoed in the hall behind her daughter, calling for Karis. She arrived on the scene eyeing her two nieces and Mary with unspoken accusation. A plain, large-boned woman with a round face and faded brown eyes, one would never think her the mother of the delicate beauty who stood beside her. "Why is everyone here in the nursery?"

Her question was greeted with silence. The maid looked at the floor and her nieces stood as if they were turned to stone.

As the pug whimpered, Lady Westerly glanced at Dorinda, watching the girl lavish kisses on the fat dog. Losing patience, the baroness snapped, "I declare, Dory, you spoil that animal far too much."

"Spoil! No such thing, Mama. I warned you having dogs and cats in the same house would come to no good end. That dreadful Miss Demon creature wounded my Princess."

Anthea jumped to her feet. "Her name is Mrs. *Damon*. It's from Greek mythology which you would know if you read anything but ladies' magazines. As for my cat, she was in her room and Princess was the invader. Aunt Flora, you cannot punish her for she was only defending . . ." The child trailed off realizing she mustn't tell her aunt why the cat was in front of the box.

Karis stepped to her sister, placing a restraining hand on her shoulder. "We are truly sorry, Dorinda, but surely it is only a small scratch and we have kept the cat away from the dog as we promised."

Before Dorinda could comment a din of tiny meows emanated from the box. The disturbance had awakened the kittens and they wanted out to play. Karis and Anthea exchanged a look of defeat.

A disapproving frown appeared on Lady Westerly's round face. "Is that what I think it is, Karis Lockhart?" When her niece nodded in the affirmative, Aunt Flora shook her head, her graying brown curls, which hung in great ringlets from under her cap, brushed her lace collar. "I am greatly disappointed in you for taking advantage of my hospitality in this way. I agreed for Anthea to keep her cat, not to start a breeding farm up here."

"Aunt, we have taken care that they did not disturb anyone and I have already made arrangement with Mrs. Shelby to take the litter to Whiteoaks."

"Take them to Whiteoaks!" Anthea protested. "In this weather! But they are just babies. Aunt Flora, they are no trouble, please let them stay until they are older."

"Posh! Dorinda has had enough upset this morning without adding to her distress. Either your sister must take them to Mrs. Shelby today or I shall have Daniel get rid of them some other way." Westwood's head groom gave the appearance of hating man and animal alike.

"That won't be necessary, Aunt," Karis insisted at once, for she suspected Daniel would simply do away with the kittens. "Mrs. Shelby is quite lonely in that big old house and would welcome the company."

"Very well, Karis, but see that this sort of thing does not occur again."

Karis gave a sigh of relief. Mrs. Damon was to be spared even if her kittens were now banished. "I shall see to the move at once. Perhaps Anthea might go down and play something soothing on the pianoforte which would calm Dorinda's shattered nerves." Feeling her sister about to protest, Karis's fingers tightened on the child's shoulders in warning.

Lady Westerly cautiously eyed her daughter, not wanting a repeat of the scene enacted in the carriage after learning of the defection of Medford's heir. Pasting a smile on her face, she said, "Why, that is just the thing to soothe one's nerves, is it not, Dory dearest?"

Dorinda's eyes glittered maliciously at the sisters, but her tone was utterly sweet as she cooed, "Yes, I should like Anthea to play for me and, Karis, pray, don't dawdle at Whiteoaks, for I have some errands that must be finished before we dine this evening."

"Well, that is all nicely settled. First we shall see to your precious little Princess's nose. I believe a little ointment will do the trick nicely." Lady Westerly's voice was full of relief as she urged her daughter out of the nursery. She called over her shoulder, "We shall expect you in the drawing room in ten minutes, Anthea." Then the ladies disappeared down the hall, the sound of Dorinda speaking baby talk to her pug echoing back to the nursery.

"Why did you do that, Karis? You know how I dislike playing for Dorinda. She chatters and laughs the entire time and never listens." Anthea glared up at her sister. At nine she had an extraordinary gift for the instrument, but knew her skills were wasted on the likes of her cousin.

"Because, my dear sister, I didn't want any more talk about Mrs. Damon and her kittens. I would not put it past Dorinda to insist that your cat should leave as well as the litter."

Mary spoke up. "Listen to your sister, Miss Anthea. Miss Dorinda be a spiteful little creature. Don't be wise to be givin' that one excuses for doin' you a 'arm. Lady Westerly 'twould do near anythin' the chit wants to save a scene."

Anthea's eyes grew round. "I am sorry, Karis. I always speak before I think. I shall go down and play until my fingers hurt. Pray, get the kittens safely to Mrs. Shelby and ask her if I might visit them tomorrow."

The child started towards the door but halted at the sound of her sister's voice. "Anthea! No funeral dirges, please. I think you delight in playing only the gloomiest tunes for our relatives.''

The girl grinned at her sister. ''I do, for it makes Dorinda's face pucker in the most dreadful way. But this time I shall be good and play only Christmas music, I promise.'' So saying, she tripped down the hall.

''Mary, can you find me a large basket?''

''That I can, miss.'' The servant hurried out of the nursery.

Karis quickly went to retrieve her heaviest cloak and bonnet. Whiteoaks was nearly three miles through the woods and aunt would never think to offer her a carriage. Returning to the nursery dressed for outdoors in a sturdy gray wool cape, Karis found Mary waiting with a large old basket that was narrow but deep. They made a bed from an old blanket. Then they settled the seven protesting kittens inside—three orange, two black and two multicoloured. Karis covered the basket with a wool scarf, hoping to protect the young animals from the bitter cold.

Within ten minutes, she was well into the wood, shivering as the bitter wind whipped her cape around her ankles. The swaying of the basket on her arm appeared to have put the kittens asleep, for they'd grown quiet after a noisy beginning. She walked quickly, as much to hurry as to keep warm. Soon she could see the peaked roof of Whiteoaks through the trees and she hoped Mrs. Shelby was at home.

As she approached the lovely old Tudor house, she wondered why the estate's owner left it abandoned. Despite its run-down condition, the half-timbered structure had character. The heir had left it in the capable hands of Mrs. Shelby and her husband ten years ago. But the housekeeper's spouse was dead these two years hence and the property had slowly fallen into ruin. There had been no extra funds forthcoming for Mrs. Shelby to hire additional help, a fact that the woman made clear to all and sundry residents of the neighborhood who dared lament the condition of the once beautiful property.

Karis picked her way through the overgrown garden at the back of the house. Arriving at the kitchen door, she knocked. While she waited for the friendly housekeeper, she peeked in at the kittens nestled in a pile in the center of the blanket, sound asleep. She hoped the cold journey had done them no harm.

After several minutes passed without an answer, Karis bit at her lip wondering what to do. She couldn't return the kittens to Westwood or her aunt might have Daniel do something dreadful to them. It was too cold to simply leave the basket beside the door, hoping Mrs. Shelby would find it.

Karis deemed it unusual for the housekeeper to be from home. Perhaps the woman was merely somewhere deep inside the house, for she did her best to maintain the interior alone. If she were upstairs she couldn't hear the knock. Karis tried the handle. The door swung inward. She stepped inside the warm kitchen and closed the door behind her. "Mrs. Shelby, are you here?"

The room smelled of spiced apples and Karis saw a pie cooling on a table beside the large old fireplace. Clearly Mrs. Shelby was somewhere near. Karis made her way to the door that led to the main hall, then opened it and called, "Mrs. Shelby, are you here?"

Still there was no answer. Karis hesitated a moment for she had never gone beyond the confines of the kitchen. Knowing there would only be Mrs. Shelby about, Karis ventured into the narrow passageway that led to the Great Hall.

Stepping into the large antechamber, she paused in awe. Unlike the more modern Westwood Park or the small cottage in Oxford where she'd grown up, Whiteoaks was huge. The cavernous hall was filled with suits of armor and old iron candlestands. The walls were covered with beautiful tapestries and ancient weapons. It was like taking a step back in time.

Remembering she was an intruder, she again called "Mrs. Shelby, it is Karis Lockhart. Are you here?" Her voice echoed back at her, but there was no other sound. About to return to the kitchen, she noticed a door open on the far side of the hall.

Going to the portal she peered in and discovered a large, well-stocked library. She was only vaguely aware of a fire crackling in the fireplace, for her interest was centered on the books. It was a room that she thought existed only in her imagination.

Realizing the library was unoccupied, she hesitated only a moment. She gently placed the basket of sleeping kittens on a table in the hall then entered the room. Taking a deep breath, her lungs filled with the wonderful scent of old books. Sheer heaven, she thought, for the thing she'd missed most about her life in Oxford was her father's extensive library. That had been sold to pay their debts.

Karis knew she shouldn't be here. Aunt Flora would disapprove of her ogling the vast literary treasure. She had declared that both Karis and her sister, having been raised by only their Greek scholar father, were well on their way to becoming bluestockings. She had forbidden both girls the use of the small library at Westwood, saying they would be wise to use Dorinda as their model and pursue more feminine arts.

Looking guiltily over her shoulder at the empty Great Hall, Karis decided Mrs. Shelby wouldn't object if she took just a moment to inspect the books. What harm could there be in that? With an unladylike eagerness, she advanced on the shelf directly in front of her.

Derrick Kenton, tenth Marquis of Marsden, tied the reins of his horse to the rear of his carriage. Walking round the vehicle he called to the coachman. "Jock, how much farther?"

The coachman pulled the red woolen scarf from over his nose and mouth saying, "Recken it's another twenty miles, milord."

Marsden noted the red nose and watering eyes of the fellow. It had been a cursed cold journey into Warwichshire and he didn't want his servant to pay for his fit of temper against his grandmother and her infernal matchmaking. "Do you need to stop at an inn to warm yourself?"

"Not I, sir. I'll wait till we get to Whiteoaks." Jock repositioned the scarf to protect his face and tugged his cap to the marquis.

Marsden entered the carriage quietly so as not to disturb his sleeping daughter. Settling with his back to the horses as the coach lurched forward, he inquired, "How is Lady Rosalind?"

The young nurse, a pink-cheeked country girl of barely twenty, hesitated a moment before she answered her new employer. "Been sleepin' most of the way, milord. But she seems right 'appy to be away from Marsden 'ouse. Says she ain't seen much of your lordship since her mama up and died."

Guilt washed over the marquis. He knew he'd indulged his anger after the death of his wife last year. "No, she hasn't, but that will all change, Binx."

He'd wrapped himself in a cloak of indifference to cover the humiliation of having his wife run off with a wealthy prince of foreign birth. Rachel had always done the least expected thing. But the ill-fated flight had cost the pair their lives when their ship had gone down during a storm.

His youthful marriage had been a mistake from the beginning. Rosalind was the only good thing to come from the union, but he'd forgotten that for a time.

With Bonaparte safely exiled for a second time, Marsden had wandered aimlessly about on the continent for a nearly

a year, hoping to avoid the whispers of Society. On his
arrival in London at the end of the summer, his grandmother had convinced him to let Lady Rosalind remain
with her where the child had resided during his absence.
He now realized the woman was only interested in giving
him the freedom to reenter the social whirl, to do his duty
and remarry.

In October, he'd returned from the country and made
the attempt to get back to his old life. But he'd been
besieged by every match making mama in the *ton*. No fewer
than three young ladies had made the attempt to get him
alone and declare themselves compromised. One had actually come to his town house and tried to gain entry. Now
by December, he'd taken to avoiding the company of any
unmarried female below the age of thirty.

Even worse, his own grandmother engaged in deceit of
the worse kind. Harriet, Dowager Marchioness of Marsden,
was determined to see him married again. His man, Elsworth, had fortunately stumbled upon the plot to force
him to propose to the daughter of their neighbor during
Harriet's Christmas house party. The dowager knew he
would not miss being with Rosalind for the holidays and
would be in residence.

But Marsden was not a man to be manipulated. He'd
warned his grandmother to stay out of his affairs when
she pushed several young ladies in his path over the past
months but she'd only reminded him he had no heir. Why
did all Society think he must be married? After all, he was
only thirty.

Looking at the pale face of the sleeping child, he realized
just how much his daughter needed him. He would never
again surrender her care to another relative. He knew his
grandmother must have been furious to return from her
morning visits to discover that he'd fired the governess
she'd employed and whisked his daughter away from her
rigidly run household. Angry at her machinations, he'd

left no word about their destination, only his apologies that he wouldn't be staying for her Christmas house party. With the help of Elsworth, the marquis had arranged to slip away to the one place no one would think to look, Whiteoaks, his late wife's abandoned home, leaving the valet behind to misinform all who inquired about his direction.

Lord Marsden had no intention of rushing back into marriage. He'd barely been twenty-one when he'd wed the first time. He'd been completely bewitched by a pretty face and spent the next nine years paying the price for his foolishness. He didn't need a wife at this period in his life. There was time enough to worry about an heir later.

His unexpected isolation from his family would give him time to concentrate on getting Rachel's old home in order. It was his daughter's legacy from her mother. He was certain Rachel, who'd retained possession of the estate in the marriage settlements, hadn't spent a farthing on the place in years. He needed to use this time to get reacquainted with his child as well.

"Hello, Papa. I did not know you had joined us." The child's voice startled him from his contemplate of his life. A pair of sky blue eyes looked at him from a thin, pale face framed by dark brown curls. The dowager had cut the child's hair fashionably short, but the style only emphasized her thinness.

What bothered him the most was that Rosalind spoke to him almost as if he were a stranger, but then hadn't he been for the past year? Well, no more. "Good afternoon, Rosebud."

A grin brightened Lady Rosalind's countenance and she lurched forward in the rocking carriage to throw her arms around her father's neck. "Oh, Papa, I have missed you and missed being called Rosebud."

Pulling the child onto his lap, he kissed her. Her unexpected display of affection warmed his heart. "And I missed you. Can you forgive me for being away so long?"

"I forgive you. But promise you won't go and leave me with Grandmama again, Papa."

"I promise and will seal the bargin with a kiss." Holding his young daughter felt so right.

Lady Rosalind gazed lovingly up at him, absently asking, "Where are we going to spend Christmas, Papa?"

"I am taking you to Whiteoaks. Your mother left it to you and I want you to help me fix it up."

"Can it be like it was when I was young and you would come to see me and take me for rides?"

The marquis told her he had much to do in Warwichshire, but he promised to take her with him when weather permitted.

Father and daughter talked as the carriage rumbled through the countryside. Derrick kept the tone light, enlivening his daughter with amusing tales about his journey, for she seemed to have lost much of her old spirited enthusiasm for life. He wanted to see the sparkle back in her blue eyes.

At last the vehicle slowed to make the turn up the drive to Whiteoaks, passing between two stone lions blackened with age and barely visible beneath the encroaching ivy. The marquis felt a sinking in his stomach at the state of the small gate lodge. Clearly they would be in Warwickshire until the spring, if the house was in such disrepair.

The carriage rolled up the weed-infested drive to the house. Beyond the glass he could see the gardens were an over-grown jumble of brambles and weeds choking the surviving plants. As the carriage turned on the circular drive, Derrick got his first look at Whiteoaks.

What a fool he'd been to drag his daughter out to this desolate ruin and expect her to enjoy her Christmas. His only hope was that Mrs . . . er . . . Shelby, that was it, had gotten his hastily sent message and was prepared for them in some small way.

The carriage drew to a halt. The marquis exited, then helped his daughter and her nurse down. The trio stood gazing up at the sinister-looking manor, reluctant to enter.

"Papa, the house looks angry," Lady Rosalind innocently remarked.

The marquis laughed. "Angry? I think I would call this unbounded fury."

Placing her hand in her father's, the eight-year-old wisely observed, "Then we will make it very happy by living here."

Smiling down at the child, the marquis realized that the house wasn't important only them being together. "Shall we go in?"

Thankfully the door was unlocked. They stepped into a Great Hall that was excessively dark, but the clean smell of beeswax and turpentine pleasantly filled the air. At least the inside had been maintained, he thought with relief. While Nurse and Lady Rosalind stood observing their new surroundings, Lord Marsden strode to the open door to the left end of the Hall.

He immediately checked at the portal. Sitting in front of the fireplace was an unknown young woman pretending to read one of the books. Certain this lovely creature was not the aged housekeeper, he mentally cursed. How the devil did a designing female find out he was coming? Could he not escape the pursuit of marriage-minded ladies even here in the wilds of the country?

"Madam, who are you, and why are you in my house?"

Karis started guiltily from the chair. She hadn't heard anyone enter, she'd been so engrossed with the story. Now she found herself being glared at by a tall aristocratic gentleman with mahogany brown hair, an angular face and dove gray eyes full of hostility. "I beg your pardon, sir. I am Miss Lockhart from Westwood Park come to find Mrs. Shelby. I-I did not think the owner was in residence."

"And did you think Mrs. Shelby was hiding between the pages of that book?"

"Sir, I know this must seem strange, but I was looking for the housekeeper and became . . . distracted by your extraordinary library."

Marsden's gaze swept the room and even he had to admit it was an impressive collection. His wife had spoken of her father's intellectual pursuits, but he'd never met the gentleman since he'd been long dead before she'd come to Town. Still, the marquis was suspicious of this young woman proclaiming an interest in books. His experience had proven that the prettier the face the emptier the head.

His gaze came to rest on the intruder whose cheeks now flamed red. There was nothing of the fashionable chit about her. Her green woolen gown was rather plain and unstylish. Rich auburn hair was parted in the middle and pulled into a neat chignon and a few wisps of curls had escaped to frame her heart-shaped face. By the *ton's* standards she couldn't be called beautiful, for her mouth was too generous. But her deep green eyes were definitely an enticing feature.

"And what was your business here at Whiteoaks, Miss Lockhart?"

Karis's shoulders sagged. Suddenly, she realized that if the owner, whoever he was, had arrived then Mrs. Shelby would not be able to keep the litter of kittens. "Well, sir, I . . . er . . . that is I brought—"

Childish squeals of delight interrupted Karis's rather disjointed explanation. In the hall, she could now see a girl no older than Anthea pointing and laughing at a spot beyond her view. Karis dashed past the glowering gentleman and turned to discover that all seven kittens had awakened and escaped from the wicker basket.

Two climbed up the tapestry behind the table. One was settled lazily in an empty cut glass bowl intrigued with his own tail. Another was climbing down an embroidered table runner to join the three who scampered loose on the marble floor, making their way determinedly towards the young child. Clearly by the grin of delight on her thin face, the girl was enjoying their antics.

"Oh, dear, I am sorry." Karis ran forward and tugged the two kittens from the tapestry, placing them back in the basket. Then she went in pursuit of the three scurrying across the floor. She grabbed up two of the three by the nape of their necks and took them back to join their siblings. But this time, the first two in the basket had again climbed out and were running down the table away from her. She stuffed the captive pair from the floor into the basket, then went after the two escapees. Grabbing them before they started down the runner, she took them back to the basket only to discover it was again empty. Slowly, she started collecting the kittens, keeping them in her arms this time.

Lady Rosalind laughed delightedly as she watched the young lady chase down the lively kittens only to return each time and find the basket again empty. Finally the woman gathered them all in her arms, until she held all seven.

"Do they belong at Whiteoaks, Papa? Can we keep them?"

Arms overflowing with squirming kittens, Karis turned to the gentleman whose eyes had softened as he smiled at his daughter. A ray of hope for Mrs. Damon's progeny and something else undefinable shot through her. "Sir, it would be a great favor to my sister if the kittens could remain at Whiteoaks, for my aunt has ordered them gone from Westwood."

"Papa, please may I keep all the lady's kittens?" Lady Rosalind ran to her father, tugging excitedly on his hand.

Marsden knew he couldn't resist Rosalind's request, for

he liked the spark of happiness he saw in his daughter's eyes. "Very well, Rosebud, you may have them all."

The child ran to Karis. "Do they have names?"

"Yes, but I fear you will have to ask my sister what they are. I cannot keep them straight. Would you mind, Mr . . ." Karis paused, hoping to learn the name of their cat's benefactor.

"I apologize, Miss Lockhart for not making proper introductions sooner. Allow me to present my daughter Lady Rosalind, and I am the Marquis of Marsden." A hint of a smile lightened the gentleman's features, making him appear quite handsome.

Karis gave an answering smile. "Would you mind if my sister came and paid the kittens a visit, my lord?"

Marsden's hand tightened into a fist. No doubt the sister was some ravishing beauty that Miss Lockhart was hoping to promote. Coldly he replied, "As you can see, we are not ready to entertain company at Whiteoaks."

Despite his unfriendly tone, Karis couldn't resist the urge to laugh. "I don't think one nine-year-old constitutes company, Lord Marsden. I thought perchance Lady Rosalind might enjoy some companionship her own age, for I know Anthea would."

The marquis suddenly felt the fool. He was allowing his imagination to run amok. He attempted to recant his statement without appearing too ridiculous. "I suppose my daughter would welcome a visit from Miss Anthea. Would you not, my dear?"

Lady Rosalind looked up from the small, orange kitten she was stroking. "Oh, Papa, this will be the best Christmas ever. I shall have you, my new kittens and a friend of my own as well."

Feeling very content with his decision to come to Whiteoaks, the marquis gave Miss Lockhart a formal bow. "I owe you a debt of gratitude, ma'am, for as you can see, you have made this a very special Christmas for my daughter.''

Karis's heart fluttered in the most unusual way, but she attributed it to relief that the kittens had a new home. It was not likely that she would be attracted to this rather aloof lord, was it?

Suddenly remembering her sister was probably still playing for Dorinda, she thanked his lordship for his kindness before bidding father and daughter goodbye. She knew Mrs. Shelby would know just how to care for the animals.

As she made her way back to Westwood, she wondered in what way Lord Marsden would affect the neighborhood. Despite his reserved manner and with only a simple compliment, he'd stirred something deep within her.

# *Chapter Two*

The following morning Lady Westerly, her daughter and Karis sat before the fireplace in the back parlor at Westwood. It was a small room filled with battered and worn furniture since Lady Westerly thought it foolish to waste money refurbishing a chamber where only the family gathered. Anthea had wisely decided to remain in the nursery, being very much out of temper about the loss of the kittens and not likely to guard her tongue.

Mrs. Hartfield, a neighbor and Clarendon's biggest gossip, had paid an early morning call while they had still been at breakfast. She'd included the Westerlys on her rounds with the fascinating news that Lord Marsden and his daughter were newly arrived to spend Christmas at Whiteoaks.

Karis had deliberately neglected to mention her meeting with the gentleman to her aunt and cousin because the visit involved the kittens, a subject she thought it best not to discuss. Thankfully, her cousin waited until Mrs. Hartfield had departed and they were settled in the parlor to express her views about the marquis's unexpected visit.

Dorinda stamped her satin clad foot in anger. "How could Papa be so disagreeable as to be in Jamaica just when I need him?"

Karis glanced up from the sketch she was drawing of her cousin styled as the Greek goddess, Artemis, with bow and quiver. She suspected that her uncle so often absented himself from Westwood Park just to avoid these kinds of scenes.

Aunt Flora, never looking up from her embroidery, clucked softly. "Now, Dory, you know your father had no way of knowing he would be needed at just such a time. He has promised to be home in time to take you to London for the Season."

"But the Marquis of Marsden is here, *now*, and there is no one to pay a call. How shall I get a chance to meet him? You can be certain he won't be entertaining in that rundown old ruin of a house. I wonder why he allowed the Shelbys to—" Dorinda suddenly stopped her complaining. Turning on her cousin, she demanded, "But you were with Mrs. Shelby at the manor yesterday, did you meet Lord Marsden?"

"I met the marquis and his daughter." Seeing the calculating look which came into her cousin's blue eyes and realizing where the girl's thoughts were leading, Karis added, "But don't think we can trade on that briefest of meetings to promote an acquaintance. There is much to do to repair Whiteoaks. I doubt he intends to entertain anyone during his stay."

Dorinda's face puckered in distress. "It's not fair. Karis, who has no expectations at all, gets to meet the gentleman and I am left a virtual stranger. *I* want to meet him. I *shall* think of a way—"

Alarmed at what her willful daughter might do, Lady Vesterly lowered her tambour and offered a suggestion.

"Then we must give a dinner party to welcome the gentleman to Warwichshire. Now that Karis has met Lord Marsden, there is nothing improper with our sending an invitation."

Mother and daughter were at once in agreement, and Dorinda's tantrum was over as she ran to shower kisses on her relieved mama. The ladies quickly huddled together to begin a guest list which, with the exception of Karis, included no single female but Dorinda. Karis knew they would be forced to include her, for she was their only connection to the marquis.

There was one final moment of discord when Lady Westerly tried to insist they invite Squire Tanner, his wife and eligible son. She soon dropped the notion when her daughter threatened another tantrum. Besides, her ladyship realized, her daughter could not make up to two gentleman at the same time. Should the marquis prove elusive during his stay, she wouldn't want Dorinda to spoil her chances with Roland Tanner. Despite his being a mere squire's son, an income of fifty thousand a year was not to be dismissed out of hand.

When the selection of proper guests was complete, Lady Westerly announced she would write up the cards herself.

Dorinda, now in the best of humors, declared she must ride into Clarendon to purchase new gloves and perhaps flowers for her hair. She rushed from the drawing room, without a thought for anything but how she would look when his lordship saw her.

Karis, finding herself free of responsibilities for a few hours, decided to take Anthea over to meet Lady Rosalind. Only telling her aunt they were going for a walk, she and her sister escaped the confines of Westwood Park.

As the Lockhart sisters made their way through the woods, Karis fielded a barrage of questions from the nine-year-old about Lord Marsden and his daughter. There was little Karis could tell Anthea, except the child had been quiet but friendly. That the father had not, Karis kept to herself.

Karis realized how lonely life had become for her sister at Westwood. The child had not only lost her father and her friends in Oxford, but she'd spent hours by herself in the nursery to avoid Dorinda and her incessant demands.

Hopefully, Lady Rosalind and Anthea would become fast friends, if the girl's father would permit it. That gentleman was a puzzle to Karis with his cool stare and his rigid formality, but there was nothing like a mystery to enliven one's existence.

Dorinda surveyed herself in the large mirror in her room. The riding habit of crimson velvet with black frogging suited her dark coloring to perfection. Her parents were complete fools if they thought she would waste her beauty on a coxcomb like the squire's son, no matter the fortune.

Why, if the marquis were to catch a glimpse of her he would fall at her feet, she thought, as she tweaked a black curl on her forehead. Somehow to look so stunning and not be seen by anyone but perhaps Squire Tanner's son or a lowly farmer on his way to the village infuriated the beauty.

Her mama's party would not take place for three long days. She simply would not wait so long to meet the marquis. Too much time would be wasted, for it was uncertain how long the gentleman would remain next door.

Taking up the hussar style black beaver hat with crimson scarf, Dorinda set it just so over her curls, then smiled at her reflection. She rushed to the stables, for a plan to meet the marquis this very day had come to her.

* * *

Mrs. Shelby opened the kitchen door to find Miss Lockhart and her sister on the step. "Come in, come in, ladies, afore you freeze."

"Good day, Mrs. Shelby. I have brought Anthea to meet Lady Rosalind and to visit the kittens."

"Darlin' things they be and they do brighten up the young lady's face when she plays with 'em. I apologize for not bein' here yesterday, but I had to go to the village what with all them arrivin'." Mrs. Shelby glanced over her shoulder and lowered her voice. "I think the child has been poorly since her mama died last year, but I say a little of my good cooking and some fresh country air will put the bloom back in her cheeks."

Karis liked the cheery housekeeper whom she'd met in the village nearly a year ago while running errands for Dorinda. "No doubt, that is just the thing she needs, Mrs. Shelby."

Anthea, loosening her heavy woolen scarf, asked, "Is she taking good care of the kittens?"

"Aye, she is, wee one. Come along, let me take you to her." The older woman led them through the kitchen and into the Great Hall. Karis looked around, curious where his lordship might be. She wasn't certain why, for he'd been anything but welcoming. She simply knew she'd like to meet the gentleman again, if only to thank him for allowing her sister to visit.

Mrs. Shelby noted her searching gaze, but mistook it for fear. "Don't worry about runnin' into the master. Up early and out on the estate, he was. I'm delighted to say he intends to return Whiteoaks to its former glory. He sent the coachman to hire a couple of sturdy lads from the village to set the stables to rights and told me to hire extra help for the house. There's much work to be done."

Karis merely nodded her head, stifling the swift feeling

of disappoint. She trailed behind her sister as they followed the housekeeper to the third floor. They were ushered into an ancient nursery, devoid of books or toys. Across the room, Lady Rosalind sat beside a window, her chin propped on her hand as she stared glumly out the window. At her feet on a rug, all seven kittens lay sleeping.

Nurse rose from a chair beside the fire, smiling gratefully at the visitors. She'd been at her wit's end wondering how to amuse her rather listless charge who was disappointed when she learned her father had gone out before she'd risen. "Look here, Lady Rosalind, you've got someone come to see you."

The child straightened, then smiled at Karis and her sister. "I am so glad you have come. I should like to know the kittens' names."

Anthea, never shy, removed her wool cloak and bonnet. She immediately went to Lady Rosalind. Karis was delighted to see the girls chattering like old friends within a matter of minutes.

Nurse edged close to Karis and the housekeeper, confiding in a whispered undertone, "Oh, miss, is this not a rather daunting room in which to keep a child? Why, I can't find so much as a toy soldier in the place."

Karis's gaze took in the empty shelves, the yellowed paint on the walls and the faded curtains at the window. Clearly it had been years since a child had resided at Whiteoaks. "Did you not bring any of her playthings?"

Binx lowered her voice. "Never even saw Lady Rosalind afore yesterday, miss. Seems 'is lordship whisked 'er away from 'er grandmother's 'ouse in a thrice without bringin' much beyond a few dresses. She's a dear little girl, but so quiet. I'm 'opin' your sister might cheer 'er up some."

Mrs. Shelby offered, "Perhaps later you might take a look in the attic for some toys. Surely they weren't all thrown out, but then it's been years since Miss Rachel lived here."

There was some mystery surrounding his lordship's unexpected arrival, but Karis knew it didn't truly concern her. Instead, she decided to do what she could to improve the nursery. "I have a suggestion." She quickly recommended that they decorate the nursery for Christmas. She and the girls would cut greenery if Nurse would go to the village and purchase red ribbon. They could get apples and candles from the kitchen.

Nurse was hesitant, at first, not knowing what his lordship might think, but Mrs. Shelby convinced her it was just the thing for Lady Rosalind. Binx informed her charge what they were going to do. She declared she would return as soon as possible and made the child promise to be good. "This shall be great fun."

The servant hurried from the room with Mrs. Shelby following in her wake. The older lady declared she had her own duties to attend.

While Lady Rosalind tied the string to her fur lined cape, she eyed the sisters as if they were foreign beings for suggesting they do what was servant's work. "I have never helped decorate for Christmas. Grandmama says one must always remember one's proper station in life."

"Oh, pooh!" Anthea declared while pulling on her mittens. "There is nothing wrong with doing something you enjoy. Why, Karis knows how to make rooms look very pretty at Christmas time. It is always great fun, you will see." So saying, the child went to her new friend and took her hand as they made their way out of the nursery.

Karis noted that Lady Rosalind seemed infected by Anthea's enthusiasm as she giggled and skipped down the stairs. No doubt the two would be good friends if Karis could but find the time to bring her sister over.

Clearly, the marquis's arrival in the neighborhood had distract Dorinda enough to give Karis some spare time to spend with her sister and Lady Rosalind today. But the thought of her cousin in pursuit of Lord Marsden left Karis suddenly feeling uneasy. She had never known her cousin to fail in achieving something she desired and clearly she desired the marquis.

The gentle mare plodded along the road to Whiteoaks, leaving Dorinda mad as blazes. For the first time in her life, she wished she carried a crop. Never a good horsewoman, she'd adored the fat little bay her father had found for her last year. Nothing about the docile horse had been frightening, but today she was eager to get to the gates of the marquis's estate. Bess, however, was perfectly content to amble along at her usual gait.

At last the horse arrived at the gate and stood patiently as her rider fidgeted on her back. Dorinda strained to look up the drive, but the estate was so overgrown, she could barely see the slate roof of the manor house. Suddenly, she heard the crunch of gravel as someone came rapidly up the drive.

She slid from her horse, allowing Bess's reins to fall free, for there was no danger of the lazy mare moving. Scanning the ground, she found a clump of dead grass to the side of the drive. She wasn't so foolish as to wish to ruin her new habit by reclining in the dirt. She quickly lay down, positioning herself as if she'd taken a fall. Then she waited for her prey. A smile touched her lips as she envisioned his lordship carrying her back to Whiteoaks as he wondered who this fallen goddess might be.

Binx hurried up the drive towards the village, saying a word of thanks to God for sending Miss Lockhart and her sister to them. She was too new at her post to know how to handle Lady Rosalind. Miss Lockhart seemed to know the trick, for the child had positively glowed at the suggestion of a trip to cut greenery.

When Binx rounded the curve of the weed-filled gravel carriageway, she spied a female dressed in a bright red riding habit laying beside the road. The lady's horse stood in the middle of the drive, eyes half closed as if the animal were asleep.

"Upon my soul, where did you come from?" The servant ran forward and stooped beside the fallen lady. She touched the victim, and discovered her to be warm and breathing which was a relief, for Nurse had never seen a dead body.

Binx rose and began to pace beside the injured girl, trying to decide if she should stay with the lady or return to the house. As the advantages and disadvantages of each plan warred in her mind, she heard the sound of a carriage coming up the road. She dashed through the gates and began to wave her arms at the approaching vehicle.

"Oh, sir, can you 'elp me?"

A frail young man dressed in a dark blue greatcoat with large red buttons reluctantly drew his curricle to a halt beside Binx. "What is the problem? I am in rather a hurry, miss."

"Sir, there's been an accident and a young lady's been thrown from 'er 'orse. Can you carry 'er to Whiteoaks?"

"Not Whiteoaks, the manor is empty but for an old housekeeper. We should—"

"The Marquis of Marsden is in residence, sir. We can take care of 'er there."

Suddenly the young man's gaze came to rest on the mare. "Why, that is Lord Westerly's animal." He jumped down from his vehicle and ran to the young lady who'd filled his dreams every night for the past two years. Kneeling, he noted her beauty was not the least diminished by her fall. Taking her hand, he completely forgot himself and called, "Dorinda, Dorinda, my dear, wake up."

Dorinda, laying with her eyes closed, resisted the urge to yank her gloved hand from Roland Tanner's. She despised the squire's son for daring to think she would consider such a mesalliance to someone like him. She had position, fortune and beauty, and she intended to use those advantages to marry well.

It was just her bad luck to have Roland arrive at the wrong time. Still, as she lay in the grass, she held out hope that he and the servant from Whiteoaks would take her to the manor, so she continued to pretend unconsciousness.

Binx watched the young man attempt to wake the miss with no luck. "Sir, I think we must get 'er in your carriage and take 'er indoors afore she takes a chill."

"Yes, I can take her up with me, but her mama would be vexed if I did not bring her daughter to her, for Westwood is just next door and," the young man looked towards the unkempt gardens and manor then added, "I am not certain Whiteoaks is prepared for company. Besides, one is always most comfortable at home."

Dorinda ground her teeth in frustration. Suddenly feeling arms scoop her up, her eyes flew open. "Roland Tanner, take your hands off me, you coxcomb."

The squire's son was so startled by her awakening, he dropped her back onto the grass, causing a loud groan to escape the lady. "Dorinda, you are unharmed."

The lady's backside ached from the sudden fall back to the ground, and she vented all her spleen on the unfortunate Mr. Tanner. "No thanks to you, you clumsy oaf. Go about your business and leave me alone, Roland. And stop calling me Dorinda, you forget yourself!"

Having always called her by her Christian name since they'd grown up together, the bewildered squire's son could only mutter, "But Dor—I mean Miss Westwood—"

Scrambling to her feet, Dorinda marched to her horse and grabbed the reins. She looked back at the blushing young man with disdain. "Well!"

Roland hurried forward and meekly cupped his hands and gave the lady a boost up onto her mare. He watched her guide her horse around his curricle, and ride back towards Westwood, grass sticking to the back of her habit and hat like feathers on a sparrow in flight. He wondered what had just happened.

The little servant from Whiteoaks came to stand beside him. "That was right peculiar, sir. What do you reckon the young lady was about?"

Roland Tanner had long ago given up trying to understand Miss Dorinda Westwood. He only knew that he would worship her beauty until the day he died. Suddenly remembering his errands for his mother in Clarendon, he asked the servant if she wished a ride to the village, and Binx accepted with delight.

The marquis guided his horse though the woods while he made a mental list of all the things he wanted to accomplish before Christmas. He was so lost in his plans that it was several minutes before he realized that the sounds of singing could be heard in the cold afternoon air.

Curious, he guided his animal in that direction. He recognized the song as the Coventry Carol, one he'd sung himself as a child. As he came round the trees into the meadow, he spied his daughter, Miss Lockhart and he assumed the lady's young sister. The lady was cutting greenery as the children danced around the cut boughs of holly, sweet bay, ivy and pine while they sang with great spirit but little talent. His heart swelled with joy to see Rosalind enjoying herself. Whiteoaks would be good for them both. To his surprise, he found himself softly singing the lyrics. "By by, lul-ly lul-lay!"

The tones of a rich baritone jarred Karis from her cutting. Her gloved hand clinched the shears and her heart fluttered at the sight of Lord Marsden seated on a huge black horse, singing the carol. She was delighted to see him, but uncertain how he would react to her taking command of his daughter's care, if only temporarily.

She took heart that he was still smiling as he finished

the verse with the girls. "Good afternoon, my lord. I hope you don't mind that Anthea and I offered to help Lady Rosalind brighten up her nursery with a little Christmas decorating."

"An excellent idea, Miss Lockhart. I am afraid I have been so involved with fixing the house that I forgot it would be nice to decorate it for the holidays." Marsden dismounted and came to stand among the neat piles of branches.

"Oh, Papa, this is such fun. This is my new friend, Anthea. We are going to decorate the nursery. Does this not smell just like Christmas?" Lady Rosalind, cheeks pink from the cold and eyes sparkling, danced up to her father and waved a fir bough under his nose.

The strong scent of the evergreen triggered happy memories of Marsden's childhood. Reminding him of the days when he would come in from the cold to the warm smells of mince pies and pine boughs, adding to his lighthearted feeling. "Yes, Rosebud, that it does. Do you need help? Shall I get a cart to bring the branches to the house, Miss Lockhart?"

"Thank you, my lord. I do believe we have cut enough for now. We shall take the basket of cones and decorate them until the greenery arrives and Nurse comes with the red ribbons."

Karis picked up the basket filled with fir cones, but the marquis stepped forward. "Allow me."

They all started back for the manor. The young girls skipped in front and resumed their off-key singing, leaving Lord Marsden and Miss Lockhart an opportunity for private conversation.

Leading his horse and carrying the basket, the marquis smiled after the children as they disappeared around a bend in the path. "I must thank you and your sister for taking such an interest in Lady Rosalind. I fear I would have forgotten all the traditions of Christmas but for your kindness.''

Karis looked at the gentleman, watching his frosted breath drift away with the breeze as he spoke so earnestly. The cold formality of yesterday was gone and she found herself drawn to this man who cared so much for his daughter. ''We are the ones who should be thanking you. Anthea has been quite lonely since we came to Warwichshire to live with our aunt. Lady Rosalind was just the thing to brighten her Christmas.''

Marsden returned the lady's gaze, and found himself mesmerized by those beautiful green eyes. Miss Lockhart was different from all the other young ladies he'd encountered this past year. She talked to him with no hint of coquetry or artifice. He wondered if that was because she didn't find him attractive. That thought irked him for some reason. Wondering why it should, he merely said, ''Then you must bring her as often as she likes.''

The pair then fell into causal conversation about the cold weather and what the marquis intended to do to improve Whiteoaks. Karis even made a few suggestions. Before she knew it they'd arrived back at the house. The marquis asked Mrs. Shelby to serve hot chocolate to the girls and Karis while he and Jock went to retrieve the cut boughs.

Later, Marsden stepped into the nursery, his arms filled with a variety of cuttings, and he stopped to admire the heartwarming sight. In front of the fireplace, Miss Lockhart and Anthea were showing Rosalind how to paint flour and water on the pine cones to make them appear frosted with snow. The trio were laughing at the kittens trying to bat at the cones and make them roll on the table.

''Where shall I put these?'' he asked, his tone husky with emotion to see his daughter much like her former self.

''By the window, my lord, for the heat of the fire might dry them out too soon.'' Karis told the girls to continue the work on the cones while she made garlands from the cuttings.

Picking up a ball of twine she'd gotten from Mrs. Shelby, Karis took a seat on the window bench. "Won't you join us, my lord?"

His lordship pulled a straight back chair forward and sat down in front of her. He watched as Karis selected a long runner of ivy, then began attaching alternating boughs of fir, box, sweet bay, and privet to create a decorative garland.

She smiled up at the marquis as he watched her nimbly knot the twine. "It will look much better when Nurse returns with the red ribbons, I assure you."

The marquis shook his head, saying, "I have no doubt, Miss Lockhart, that you will transform this grim nursery just as you have transformed my daughter."

"I cannot take the credit, my lord. I believe she is merely happy to have a new friend her own age."

"Karis!" Anthea called, interrupting their conversation, "Where shall we put the cones to dry, for the kittens will be covered with flour if we leave them on the table."

"On the mantelpiece, dear."

Finding himself fascinated with the young woman before him, the marquis remarked, "Karis, that is an unusual name."

"My father was a Greek scholar. He adored all things Hellenic and gave both his children Greek names. Karis means 'grace' and Anthea means 'flowery'. I suppose we should be happy my mother convinced him not name us for the Greek Muses. I am not sure Anthea or I would have been happy being called Euterpe or Terpsichore, those being his favorite muses of poetry and dance."

Marsden laughed. "I believe you had a very wise mother."

Just then the door opened and Binx arrived. Relieved to see her employer smiling, Nurse didn't hesitate to bring the ribbon to Miss Lockhart. "I 'ope I'm not too late."

"We have just begun, but I was beginning to worry you had gotten lost." Karis patted the bench beside her for Nurse to join her.

Binx eyed her charge busily painting cones white, then relaxed onto the bench. "I was delayed, miss. A dark-'aired young lady with the face of an angel took a spill from 'er 'orse right in front of the manor. Me and a gentleman what come along tried to aide 'er, but she wakes up all of a sudden, gets on the mare and rides away. Right angry she was at the young man and 'im only trying to 'elp."

Karis's hand froze. The description closely fit Dorinda but she didn't want to question the girl in front of the marquis. What had her cousin been up to? She wondered if she should warn her aunt that Dorinda was not content to wait until the dinner party to meet the marquis, then realized it would do no good. Aunt Flora couldn't control her daughter and it would only distress her to know what the girl was about.

Pushing thoughts of her troublesome cousin from her mind, she showed Binx what length to cut the ribbon, then set the marquis to tying bows on the garland she'd finished.

Soon completing their task, they set about hanging their creations. By the time they finished with the room, it was draped with the garlands, bows and frosted cones. The mantelpiece, with candles on each end, held red apples nestled among the fir boughs, perfectly matching the ribbons on the garland.

"Oh, Papa, isn't it beautiful and we did it all ourselves."

Marsden was impressed by how a few limbs, pine cones and ribbons made such an improvement to the nursery. "Miss Lockhart, you have created a masterpiece."

Karis blushed at the high praise as she donned her cloak reluctantly, urging her sister to do the same. They were probably late and Dorinda would be wondering where they were. "I enjoyed doing it, my lord.

The marquis was suddenly struck by an idea. "Then

you must do the downstairs as well. We must share your endeavors with all our visitors.''

Lady Rosalind began to jump up and down. "Oh, do please come tomorrow. Anthea and I will help you with all the work again."

Karis bent and kissed the child's cheek, feeling a warm glow flow through her at the marquis's request. "I cannot promise it will be tomorrow. I act as companion to my cousin and my time is not my own."

Lord Marsden stepped forward and took her hand, brushing a kiss on the back that sent a tingling up her arm despite the glove. "Then we will be patient and wait for you to come bring your Christmas magic to the Great Hall."

Karis suddenly found herself wishing her cousin to perdition, then reminded herself that was not in the spirit of the holidays. She knew she shouldn't engage in foolish fantasies about Lord Marsden. As her cousin had so recently noted, she was a lady with no expectations and Society—as well as a titled man as handsome as the marquis—would expect a great deal from the lady he chose.

# Chapter Three

Dorinda coughed delicately several times before sagging back in her chair. "I am not feeling well, Mama. I cannot accompany you this morning."

Karis closely eyed her cousin across the breakfast parlor table. With her rosy cheeks and sparkling eyes, Dorinda exhibited none of the normal signs of illness. But then Karis had never seen Dorinda fall ill at any time over the past year. Perhaps her outing at Whiteoaks yesterday gave her a chill.

Her cousin had made no mention of the escapade at Lord Marsden's gate the night before, but she'd been cross as crabs all evening confirming Karis's suspicion as to who had played the trick. Clearly the resolute miss wasn't content to wait until the party to meet the marquis.

Lady Westerly put her cup down so quickly it rattled the saucer. "My dear, you cannot be coming down with something. Think of the expense of all that wasted food. I have already ordered two legs of lamb and two hams. Do not say you are ill?"

"Ill! It's nothing so serious," Dorinda practically shouted, then in a calmer tone she continued, "I have but the headache. I did not sleep well last night. You *must* deliver the invitations today, only I shall remain in my room and rest." She smiled wanly at her mother as she rubbed her temple with one hand.

Lady Westerly visibly relaxed, then reached over and patted her daughter's hand. There was only one thing she cared about as much as her daughter and that was money.

Anthea, munching on a piece of toast, suddenly asked, "Will you be needing Karis today?"

In a die-away voice, Dorinda replied, "I think only sleep will help me. I don't wished to be disturbed."

Lady Westerly gave her nieces a meaningful warning stare, then said, "Come, dearest, we must get you to bed at once."

Anthea winked at her sister, as Lady Westerly rose to escort her daughter to her chamber. "Since Karis and I shall not be needed, we wish to go for a long walk so as not to disturb dear Dorinda. A *very* long walk."

Aunt Flora was barely paying attention to her nieces. "An excellent notion, my dears. Just make certain you don't return too early for we want Dory looking her best for the party on Christmas Eve."

After hurrying to finish their breakfast, the Lockhart sisters quickly donned their heavy cloaks and bonnets before making their way to Whiteoaks, each looking forward to seeing a different member of the family. The trip through the woods seemed longer than normal due to their excitement.

As Anthea tripped along happily, she suddenly stopped when she spied a particularly lovely sprig of holly. "Do you think that Dorinda caught a chill laying on the ground trying to meet Lady Rosalind's papa?"

Karis's brows rose in surprise. She didn't think her sister

had heard her conversation with Binx much less discerned who the lady on the road was. "It is very possible."

"Do you think she wishes to marry him?"

There was no doubt in Karis's mind, but she merely said, "Dorinda is about to make her come out and she is looking at all the gentlemen to find a proper husband."

Anthea hummed thoughtfully. "Then why is she so dreadful to Mr. Tanner? He is rich, very nice and he likes her in spite of her rudeness to him."

"In Society's eyes, a baron's daughter might look higher for a husband than a mere squire's son, my dear."

Her sister again fell into step beside her, walking in silence for several minutes, smelling the holly branch she'd plucked. Suddenly she tugged Karis arm, pulling her to a stop. "I don't want the marquis to marry Dorinda. She would be as hateful to Lady Rosalind as she is with us."

Seeing the worried expression on her sister's face, Karis hugged the child, then held her at arms' length. "I know you like having a new friend, but we have little say in Lady Rosalind's life. I believe the marquis to be a very good father and you can be sure he will choose an excellent mother for his daughter when the time comes."

They started towards Whiteoaks again. Anthea glanced up at her sister and casually remarked, "You would make an excellent mother, for you take such good care of me."

Karis felt her heart flutter at the prospect, but her rational self soon put the thought to rest. "My dear, titled gentleman do not marry young ladies without fortune or beauty."

Anthea frowned. "But I think you are very pretty. Besides, what good is beauty if it only covers a mean-tempered—"

"Anthea, we should not be discussing either Dorinda or Lord Marsden. We are going to decorate Whiteoaks for Christmas and we should do so in the proper spirit." With that Karis broke into a carol, in which Anthea soon joined her.

Karis didn't like her sister to dwell on their cousin's faults. It only made the child discontent with their life at Westwood, and with their current financial circumstances. Anthea, at least, would live there a long time unless things changed unexpectedly, for Karis knew her aunt and uncle had different plans for her.

They entered the manor through the kitchen door even though the marquis had invited them. That was the way Karis had always come to visit Whiteoaks and it still felt right. After all, she and her sister were little more than servants at Westwood.

Mrs. Shelby greeted them, full of news. She had hired a footman to help her and maid as well. As she chattered excitedly about the changes, she led them to the library where Lord Marsden and his daughter were seated, looking through a book together. The housekeeper then went about her duties.

Marsden rose, liking the way the cold morning air had brought color to Miss Lockhart's cheeks. He took in the drab brown dress beneath her gray cloak and suddenly wondered what she would look like in a fashionable gown. Pushing the unwanted thought from his mind, he cheerfully said, "Good morning, ladies. We were hoping you could come today. In fact, Rosalind and I were trying to look up the Greek god of good fortune to see if he would help bring you."

Karis laughed, feeling a warm rush of pleasure for such a greeting. Then she reminded herself that they merely wished to have their hall decorated in time for Christmas. "I believe you should pray to Hermes for good fortune."

Lady Rosalind went to Anthea. "Papa was wrong. He thought it was Mercury we should pay tribute to."

Karis smiled at the two girls who giggled at his lordship's

error. "Actually, that would be correct as well. Mercury is the Latin name for Hermes."

The marquis beamed at his daughter. "See! Your papa does know a thing or two about Greek gods, or maybe that is Roman gods."

His daughter was now more interested in getting outside than testing her father's knowledge and jumped up and down as she begged, "Can we begin now? Can we?"

"If Miss Lockhart is ready." The marquis smiled at Karis, quite unaware that the simple act made the young lady feel weak in the knees. "I hope you don't mind, but I shall have to leave you and Binx to cut the greenery. One of the new stable hands will bring the clippings in for you. I must go to Clarendon to hire a bailiff for the estate. I promise to return and help with the decorating."

Karis was disappointed, but she assured him they could handle things. As she watched his retreating back, she realized how much she looked forward to his return. Somehow it seemed right for them all to be together.

Dorinda tossed back the covers and hurried to the wardrobe. She'd waited patiently for at least a half-hour, all the while plotting her strategy. Her mother's carriage had just left and she could set her plan in motion.

Pulling out her new burgundy velvet dress with creamcolored lace at the neck and sleeves, she tossed it upon the bed and rang for her maid. The abigail, who thought she'd have the morning to herself, was surprised to see her mistress up. But the village girl merely did as she was bid and helped the lady dress, for Miss Westwood's temper was legendary among the servants.

The process took nearly an hour before Dorinda was satisfied. At last feeling her best in her new dress and with her black hair fashioned just as she liked it with loose curls in the back and around her face, she chose a cream-colored casquet bonnet with burgundy flowers about the tiny flared brim. The helmet-style hat would allow her perfect face to be seen better. Finally she donned a heavy fur lined burgundy cape. Giving the sleeping Princess a final pat, she set off for Whiteoaks with no maid or footman, for that was an important part of her plan.

The journey on foot took nearly three-quarters of an hour, but at last Dorinda stood at the front door of the run-down manor. Patting her curls in place, she excitedly lifted the tarnished brass ring hanging from the lion's mouth and knocked three times.

To her surprise, the door opened in a matter of minutes to reveal a young man in his shirt sleeves, wearing an apron and holding a polishing cloth. He swept her with an accessing gaze. Before Dorinda could utter her well rehearsed speech, the footman announced, "Lord Marsden and Lady Rosalind are not receiving at this time, miss."

In her sweetest voice she cooed, "I have only come to see one of the servants. A young girl who so kindly came to my rescue yesterday when I fell from my horse."

The young man hesitated a moment, then said, "I think that would be Lady Rosalind's nurse you're talkin' about, miss, but Binx is occupied at present."

"I brought a reward for her kindness." Dorinda opened her gloved hand to reveal a shining guinea, resting on the burgundy dyed leather.

In a flash the footman snatched the coin. "The marquis said no visitors, and I reckon he meant the servants as well. But I'll see Binx gets it, miss." Then he closed the door in the visitor's face.

Dorinda Westwood was outraged. How dare the marquis refuse admittance to the daughter of a baron? Just who did he think he was? Viewing the rebuff as a challenge, she decided she would get into that house this very day even if it cost her reputation.

She wandered up the drive, her mind deep in plots and

plans. Turning to survey the weed-choked gardens, she spotted a narrow path which led deep into a hedge-bordered walk. If her childhood memory served her, she thought the path made a great arc back to the west wing of the house. The way was overgrown, but passable since winter had left only the brown leafless stalks of the weeds and brambles. The untrimmed box hedge was still green and plainly visible.

A daring plan entered her brain. Dorinda hesitated only a moment, then she began to fight her way up the nearly impassable path. As the prickly bushes tugged at her cape and her dress, she merely reminded herself that the reward for such a journey could well be the title of Marchioness of Marsden.

Karis glanced at the small clock on the mantelpiece of the nursery. They were nearly finished making the garlands for the Great Hall and still Lord Marsden had not returned. She knew it was extremely foolish of her to wish to spend time with his lordship, but she attributed the desire to the fact that she and Anthea rarely went into company.

No doubt, the marquis had lingered in the village discussing business, for their visit probably meant little to him. He likely knew any numbers of young ladies to amuse him in Town. The thought suddenly brought a tightness to Karis's chest. She pushed her musings of the gentleman from her mind, concentrating on her task. She and Anthea could not spend all day at Whiteoaks, no matter the inducement, for someone was likely to wonder about their long absence.

Tying the last red bow on the final garland, Karis stood and surveyed the great piles of decorations about the nursery. The kittens frolicked among the clutter. Picking up an orange one who was trying to untie a ribbon, she stroked his soft fur as she admired the garlands.

"I do believe we are finished."

Anthea and Lady Rosalind exchanged a secretive glance, then the younger girl rose. "At Marsden Keep we always had a Kissing Bough. The decorations won't be complete without one."

Nodding her head, Anthea held up a small green Spring with transparent whitish berries. "I asked Jock to find us a piece of mistletoe and he did. We must have a Kissing Bough."

Karis smiled at the girls as she placed the kitten on the bench. "But a Kissing Bough is usually made only if you are having a Christmas party."

Both the young girls came forward, each taking one of Karis's hands.

Anthea begged, "Oh, please, it won't be a perfect Christmas without the Bough."

Lady Rosalind added her voice. "Yes, yes, a Kissing Bough. We must have one."

"Very well, but you shall have to paint those remaining pine cones white and I must go to the kitchen to see if Mrs. Shelby has any more candles."

Binx, who'd been enjoying the afternoon making the decorations, rose. "I can do that Miss Lockhart."

"No, Nurse, you stay and supervise the girls so we don't end up with seven floured kittens. I must look around to see what else I might need for the Bough and I won't know it until I see it."

Nurse laughed, then settled into her chair to watch her charge and Miss Anthea.

Karis exited the nursery and walked to the stairs that led back to the Great Hall, mentally listing all she would need to make a Kissing Bough. As she passed one of the large windows which lined the hall, a flash of deep red moving in the garden below caught her eye. She paused, looking down into the untamed foliage. To her horror she spied her cousin fighting her way, in the most determined manner, through the thick tangle of dead weeds, coming towards the west wing.

What mischief was Dorinda about now? Karis knew her cousin was determined to marry a titled man. But why was she so obsessed with meeting Lord Marsden? Her parents intended to give her a Season, or did they?

Over the past year both Lord and Lady Westerly had complained about the expense of going to London for the Season when there were any number of eligible young men in Warwichshire. Each had actually hinted that the wealthy Mr. Roland Tanner would be an acceptable match despite his lack of lineage. Aunt Flora had once confided to Karis that Lord Westerly feared that his headstrong daughter might create some scandal before she brought a gentleman up to scratch. But Dorinda didn't consider the squire's son acceptable. She was determined to do better.

Was that what was driving the girl to pursue the marquis in this most outlandish manner? Karis watched as Dorinda stopped to unsnag her cape from a thorn bush. Once free she set out straight for the house.

Biting pensively at her lip, Karis wondered if she should go down and confront her cousin? She might be able to thwart Dorinda's plot. The only problem was that she and Anthea were not supposed to be at Whiteoaks.

Dorinda would find some way to punish them for what she would see as disloyalty and too often her harshest acts were directed against Anthea. Her cousin knew that hurt Karis far more than any humiliation inflicted upon herself.

Perhaps it would be best to merely secrete herself some place and watch what Dorinda planned to do. That way, Karis knew she could put a stop to whatever it was if the need arose.

Coming to a decision, she hurried down the stairs and entered the library. She went to the tall casement windows and peeked around the edge of the faded green curtains.

Her cousin's cream-colored bonnet was barely visible above the top of the long uncut hedge. Dorinda was making her way towards the very room in which Karis now stood.

As her cousin's face came into view, Karis drew back, wondering if Dorinda was so lost to propriety that she would actually invade Lord Marsden house. The question was answered within minutes when the window creaked and groaned as Miss Westwood pushed it open.

Karis frantically looked for a place to hide. The library was spartanly furnished with few chairs and tables. With the exception of the desk, she could see nothing behind which she might hide. But to step to the huge oak desk would make her clearly visible to her cousin.

Dorinda's leg came through the window, indecorously exposing her silk stocking to the knee. About to be caught, Karis quickly stepped behind the curtain by the window, hoping her cousin wouldn't spy her.

After a great deal of grunting and swearing which was more suited to a groom than a lady of Quality, her cousin pulled herself through the window. She issued another loud groan.

Karis peeked around the edge of the curtain. She saw Dorinda's cape extended back out the window, caught tight on some obstruction, likely a bramble. Her cousin, face distorted with frustration, pulled on the garment with all her might. Suddenly the cape came free, sending Dorinda reeling backwards into a heap on the library floor. Her casquet bonnet flew from her head and landed in the ashes which spilled out on the hearth.

Scrambling to her feet she yanked the bonnet away, but sooty gray stains had ruined the cream-colored surface. Dorinda swore, then tossed the bonnet on the chair. She marched back and closed the window she'd entered through, then returned to the fireplace and removed her cape.

Karis covertly watched her vain cousin pull bits of leaves

and twigs from her black curls, throwing the pieces into the dying fire. The girl muttered angrily to herself, but her words reached Karis.

"Well, my lord marquis, you have put me to a great deal of trouble this cold morning and I shall see that you pay the toll. If I have my way, you shall have a fiancée before I leave this house today."

Karis's heart grow cold. This was no mere attempt to meet Lord Marsden. Dorinda's intent was far more sinister. She was going to try to compromise herself.

The sound of rending fabric brought Karis from her musings. Dorinda had torn the sleeve of her velvet dress, exposing a length of arm. Karis clutched the curtain in horror. She'd never before realized the depth of her cousin's wickedness.

The sound of a door being sharply closed echoed from the Great Hall then the marquis's voice. As footsteps came closer to the library, Karis knew she must do something to protect Lord Marsden from her cousin.

About to step from behind the curtain, she was suddenly struck by the thought that his lordship might think she was somehow involved in her cousin's devious plot to ensnare him. She was filled with uncertainty about what was best to do.

Karis heard the marquis step through the open door and come to an abrupt halt. His familiar voice as cold as the wind outside reminded Karis of her own first meeting with the gentleman.

"Good, God, not another one. Madam, who are you and why are you in my library?"

# *Chapter Four*

Marsden glared at the young woman standing before him. He'd never seen her before but he knew the type—beautiful, spoiled and determined. He'd married just such a woman. There was little doubt in his mind as to why she was in his house.

Dorinda, unaware of his growing hostility, stepped forward. Tilting her head just so, she gazed with a wide-eyed stare so the marquis could admire her blue eyes. In a breathless voice she said, "Thank goodness someone has come. I thought no one had heard my cries for help."

"You were being attacked in my library?" The marquis's voice sounded bored and his face was a mask of indifference.

Dorinda giggled, shaking her head to make her raven locks bounce. "No, my lord, I was coming to Whiteoaks to thank Binx for helping me yesterday. But some large animal, I did not see what, came from the jumble of weeds in the garden and tried to attack me as I walked up the drive. I rushed for the house and came straight in, for I knew I needn't stand on ceremony with my old friend Rachel's family."

His gray eyes were like two bits of stone as they raked her. *"You* were old friends with my late wife?"

"Oh my, yes. I am Miss Dorinda Westwood. My father is Lord Westerly of Westwood Park, the estate next door. Why, Rachel would often come to take me for walks and read me stories, for as you know, she was much older than I." Dorinda had barely seen Rachel Whitehead above two times in her childhood, but she was certain his lordship wouldn't know that since he and his wife had never visited the estate during their marriage.

Lord Marsden allowed his gaze to drop to the bailiff's contract rolled in his hand. If there was one thing he was certain about, it was that his deceased wife didn't have a maternal bone in her lovely body. She'd surrendered Rosalind to a wet nurse after her birth, and barely saw the child after that, being far more interested in her friends and fashions.

Glancing back at the young woman before the fireplace, he took in the torn sleeve, confirming his worst suspicions. She was plotting something, but he would not be such easy prey.

He called over his shoulder to the footman he'd just passed as he entered, "Toby, I believe we shall need Mrs. Shelby at once."

Unfortunately, a knock sounded at the door forestalling the servant from going for the housekeeper. With a feeling of dread, the marquis partially turned and watched Toby open the door. Somehow he knew this visitor meant trouble. It was as if those gods he'd spoken of to Miss Lockhart were punishing him for relaxing his guard over the past few days.

To his surprise, Miss Westwood threw herself at him, pressing close with her hands clutching his arms in a near death grip. "My lord, we must not be found alone like this."

The marquis set her from him. Then he looked up to see a large older woman in a voluminous purple cape with a white fur collar push her way past his footman.

"I have come to see Lord Marsden." The lady, having barely uttered the words, spied the marquis standing in the doorway and without so much as a by your leave, advanced on him. "There you are, my lord. I have come with an invitation—" She abruptly halted upon seeing the gentleman was not alone. Her gaze swept the visitor, then a martial glint settled in her brown eyes. She advanced on the couple. "What is the meaning of this, my lord? Why is my daughter here with you alone?"

The marquis's face grew bleak as the looming marital noose tightened around his neck.

All three of the participants in the little melodrama started when a voice behind them disputed Lady Westerly's claim. "Hardly alone, Aunt Flora, for Anthea and I have been at Whiteoaks all morning."

Karis's knees were shaking as she'd stepped from behind the curtain. She knew she'd pay a heavy price later, but she couldn't stand by and allow her cousin to do such a despicable thing to Lord Marsden. Whatever happened, it would be worth it for the look of thanks reflected in the marquis's eyes as he smiled at her over her cousin's head.

Dorinda's hands drew into tight fists as she stared at her cousin through narrowed lids. Where the devil had the cunning little baggage come from? Karis Lockhart had been nothing but an annoyance for the past year but today she'd ruined everything, Dorinda thought bitterly.

Lady Westerly, an innocent in this dark comedy, appeared at first relieved to see her daughter was accompanied, then curious. "What are you and Anthea doing here?"

Marsden watched as Karis nervously ran hands down the

front of the apron she wore, brushing bits of flour loose while she tried to explain.

"Well, since Dorinda did not need me ... That is, Anthea and I ..."

Seeing the glowering look on Miss Westwood's pretty countenance, the marquis suspected that Miss Lockhart had risked much by foiling her cousin's little ploy. He would not abandon her to the conniving beauty's wrath. "*I* invited your niece to bring her sister, Miss Anthea, for the day to play with my daughter, Lady Rosalind. I hope you don't mind, Lady Westerly."

"Not in the least, my lord," she replied.

That mystery cleared, the lady realized the greater question was why her own daughter was here. The girl was supposed to be home in bed resting. Lady Westerly was suddenly interested in getting Dory alone to find out what plot she was engaged in. Her greatest fear was that the headstrong child would ruin her chances at a good match by doing something outrageous.

When Lady Westerly remained quiet, the marquis wisely continued his efforts for Karis. "I fear my daughter and I have taken advantage of Miss Lockhart's kind nature and artistic talents. She and the girls have been quite busy all morning making Christmas decorations for the Great Hall while I was away handling matters for the estate."

Dorinda laughed. What a great fool her cousin was. She'd spent her time with the most handsome man to come to Warwichshire in ages acting like a nursemaid and servant. No wonder he'd gone off on business. In a sweet voice edged with sarcasm, she remarked, "My cousin does so love getting her hands dirty."

Karis's cheeks warmed, but she merely pulled a pair of scissors from her pocket which she'd been using to cut the red ribbons. "Shall we find needle and thread to repair that tear in your gown, cousin?"

Lady Westerly had failed to note the torn sleeve. "Dorinda Westwood, that dress was new and you have practically ruined it. When I think what I paid that modiste—well never mind. Come with me at once, only Jane has the skill to repair such a fine garment."

"But Mama, what about Karis? We cannot leave her . . . alone with a gentleman."

As Lady Westerly eyed her niece thoughtfully, the sounds of children's laughter echoed in the Great Hall. The girls came down the stairs calling for Karis. The marquis stepped to the door, signaling them to come to the library.

Lady Rosalind entered carrying two kittens. She ignored the unknown ladies, going straight to Karis. "We are done painting the cones. When can we finish the decorations?"

Anthea trailed in behind Lady Rosalind. She also carried a kitten, but halted warily at the sight of her aunt and cousin. A defiant look settled in her hazel eyes. "Good afternoon, Aunt Flora. What brings you and Dorinda to Whiteoaks?"

Suddenly reminded of her purpose, Lady Westerly fumbled in her reticule for a few minutes before pulling out a card. "I almost forgot. Lord Marsden, we are having a dinner on Christmas Eve and you are most cordially invited. It is nothing grand, but I thought you might enjoy meeting your closest neighbors."

Under normal circumstances, Marsden would have refused. He'd come to Warwichshire to repair the house, not to socialize, but just now he knew he should stay in the woman's good graces to try to protect Miss Lockhart as best he could from any reprisals from her cousin. "I should be delighted to attend."

Lady Westerly beamed. "Excellent, my lord. My daughter and I will take our leave. We look forward to seeing you then. We must be off, Dory."

Dorinda wanted to stamp her foot in frustration. *She* was being forced to return home while her mousy cousin might remain. She must leave the gentleman with a lasting impression of her. Her gaze came to rest on the rather frail looking child beside her cousin and Dorinda saw an opportunity to advance herself with Lord Marsden.

"Such an adorable child, my lord." Dorinda went to the little girl who drew back at Miss Westwood's advance. "Don't be frightened for I am an old friend of your dear departed mama's."

Lady Rosalind surprised her father when she sullenly replied, "That is what all the ladies say who are wishing to meet my papa."

Dorinda gave the child a rather sour smile, but quickly rallied. "Can I pet the dear little kittens?"

Anthea would not quietly tolerate such nonsense. "If they are so dear, why did you make me get rid of them?"

Lady Westerly, ever ready to defend her daughter, said, "Anthea, you know it is not safe to have the kittens around a dog. They are far better here at Whiteoaks. Dorinda, it is time that we go for it appears Karis shall be very busy with the girls finishing the decorations."

Dorinda didn't like leaving Karis in the company of the marquis, not that he would look twice at the girl, but she had little choice. Things had not gone as Dorinda had planned. As the marquis coldly returned her stare, she decided perhaps it was best for her to go with her mother. Her cousin would be well occupied with her decorations and the marquis wouldn't likely remain for such domestic business.

Lady Westerly and her daughter said their goodbyes. The lady reconfirming the time for the dinner while Dorinda, in an undertone, reminded her cousin she had duties at Westwood that she should not neglect.

The marquis walked the women to the door, saying farewell and declaring himself delighted to be coming to their dinner. He closed the door with a sigh of relief, knowing what a close thing it had been and knowing he owed Miss Lockhart a debt of gratitude.

He returned to the library, but was offered no opportunity for private speech with the lady. The two girls were again demanding that she help them finish the decorations.

With an apologetic smile, Karis allowed the girls to lead her from the library. She wouldn't dwell on what would happen once she returned to Westwood, but she was certain her cousin would exact some punishment. She decided to concentrate on finishing the Kissing Bough and getting the decorations hung. She called an invitation over her shoulder to Lord Marsden to join them.

Karis's smile broadened and a warmth rushed through her when the marquis fell into step with her and asked what he might do to help as they followed the girls to the kitchen.

On the carriage ride home, Dorinda fobbed her mother off with a lie about going to Whiteoaks in search of her cousins. Then she had been required to sit quietly while her mother rang a peal over her head for being out of the house when she'd been unwell. In truth, she'd scarcely heard a word of the reprimand because her mind had been busy plotting her revenge on her interfering cousin. Just as the carriage drew to a halt in front of Westwood Park, a plan came to her. All she had to do was convince her mother and her problems with Cousin Karis would be at an end.

At last they were settled in the back parlor with a roaring fire. Her mother's mood mellowed by having her feet up and a tray of cook's famous macaroons beside her, Dorinda casually broached the topic. "Do you intend for Karis to make a come-out in the spring at the same time as myself?"

Lady Westerly looked up from the cup of tea she was stirring. "Waste money on a Season for a girl with no fortune and little beauty? I think not, my dear. She and

Anthea shall accompany us to London but continue as they have here, living quietly. It never does to give one ideas above one's station."

"But won't society think it rather strange, nay even mean-spirited of you, to have Karis in your household and not take her about since she is of an age to have a Season?"

A speculative look came into Lady Westerly's eyes. She knew appearances were everything in the social world. But the expense of dressing a young lady other than her daughter was not to be considered. "She will simply have to remain out of sight in Town."

"But Mama, you know how servants gossip. It would soon be all around that you had some niece being hidden away from Society, then we would be thought to be harboring a Bedlamite." Dorinda watched the horror come on her mother's face with satisfaction as she fed Princess bits of cake.

"We cannot have someone thinking there is madness in the family. But I cannot leave the girls here, for I intend to take much of the staff with me to London to save the expense of hiring people there."

Setting her beloved pug on the floor, Dorinda rose and walked to the window. "Was it your intention to provide for Karis and Anthea for a lifetime?"

"Your papa and I had thought when Karis turned one-and-twenty that a position as governess might be found for her. You know she is acting as such to her own sister." Lady Westerly gazed dotingly at her daughter who looked positively angelic in the glow of light from the window.

"Mama, Karis is the cleverest lady I know. You have said yourself she is practically a bluestocking. Why wait and bear the expense of housing her for two more years? I am certain any of your acquaintances would welcome a governess as intelligent as my cousin. As for Anthea, I can set a program of studies for her to follow which would be more fitting than all that Greek and Latin that Karis thinks so important." Dorinda smiled innocently as she looked back at her mother.

Lady Westerly was amazed. Why, for her daughter to be offering to do such for her small cousin warmed her heart. "You would be willing to take on such a responsibility?"

Coming back to take a seat by the fireplace, Dorinda picked up her tea. "To be sure, Mama. Besides, Anthea can take over Karis's duties as my companion. While she is but a child, she could be quite as useful to me as her sister has been."

Lady Westerly nodded agreement. While she liked her nieces she knew what a savings it would be to be rid of her brother's older child. In truth, she'd more than done her Christian duty for Karis. "My old friend, Anne Handley, wrote me that her governess was leaving at Christmas and she would be required to seek another. I shall write to her this very afternoon."

"An excellent suggestion, Mama." Dorinda sipped her tea, relishing her victory. She promised herself she would be present when the news that Karis was to be separated from her beloved sister was broken to her meddling cousin.

A knock sounded at the nursery door, then the housekeeper entered. Her eyes grew round as she surveyed the room cluttered with ropes of garlands. "I do believe you've enough decorations to string from Whiteoaks to Birmingham and back."

The marquis, seated at the table with his daughter and Anthea, watched Miss Lockhart put the finishing touches on the final decorations. He laughed at the older woman's observation. "Binx was just saying the same thing, but her belief was that it would stretch all the way to London."

Karis shook her head at their teasing. "It is not as much as it appears. But we will soon know, for everything is ready."

The housekeeper came forward to look at the Kissing Bough which sat completed on the table. " 'Tis quite lovely, Miss Karis, and very original, if I do say so. You've all been workin' so 'ard that I've made a special treat for your tea."

Karis's gaze flitted nervously to the mantel clock. She was surprised it had grown so late. "Serve the girls, Mrs. Shelby, I have not the time at the moment. Anthea and I shall be quite late returning home as it is and I want to supervise the hanging of the garlands before we go."

"Must we have to leave so soon?" Anthea frowned.

"I fear so, my dear, or we shall be forced to walk through the woods in the dark." Karis, like her sister, wished they never had to return to Westwood, but eventually she would have to face her cousin.

As Marsden watched the Lockhart sisters smile with resignation at one another, he was suddenly overwhelmed with an urge to protect them. While Miss Lockhart had said little of their circumstances, Miss Anthea had innocently made comments over the course of the afternoon about their cousin's demands. He now had a clearer picture of what life was like for them. It was a rather grim prospect.

"Allow me to put my carriage at your disposal, Miss Lockhart." The marquis liked the way her green eyes twinkled with gratitude when she looked at him.

"That is most kind, my lord. But if we start now, while Binx gives the girls their tea, I am certain we shall be able to finish long before dark."

It was soon settled and Mrs. Shelby bustled away to get the tea tray and send Toby up to collect the garlands. Lord Marsden carried the Kissing Bough to the Great Hall as Karis followed. Finding himself alone with the lady at last, he placed the decoration on a small table and turned to speak with the lady. "I want to thank you for what you did this afternoon, Miss Lockhart."

A rosy blush settled on the young lady's ivory cheeks as

she needlessly adjusted a red bow on the Bough, avoiding his gaze. "I am mortified, my lord, that my cousin would have attempted to compromise herself in such a manner."

"Don't fret so about the incident. I have put it from my mind. We, all of us, have things our relations do that we have little control over. No one thinks the worse of one for what others do." Memories of his own humiliation at his wife's hands flashed briefly through his mind, but for the first time he realized he was not responsible for the lady's shortcomings. She'd chosen her own path.

At the moment he was far more concerned with the lady before him. "What I fear is that your cousin might punish you in some way for foiling her plans."

Karis's heart hammered in her chest when she looked up to see the concerned look in Lord Marsden's gray eyes. Eyes she'd once thought so cold, were now softened with kindness. "You needn't worry about me, my lord. Dorinda is clever. She would never do anything to physically hurt me. No doubt her revenge will be of little consequence, and although it will upset Anthea a great deal, it will be nothing I cannot handle, I assure you. Say no more on the subject, I beg of you."

The marquis looked as if he wanted to continue the discussion, but Karis spied Toby coming down the stairs and went forward to instruct him on where to hang the Christmas decorations.

She kept her tone light, teasing Toby when a garland hung crooked or telling humorous stories of former Christmas disasters from her youth. There was no need for Lord Marsden to worry over a matter which might prove to be minor. She even managed to get a laugh from the marquis upon telling the story of Anthea accidently pulling the garland down on the head of their former vicar.

Karis watched with satisfaction as Toby hung the last of the garland through the balusters of the stairs, ending at the ornately carved newel post. Making a few minor adjustments to the ribbons, she stepped back and surveyed the stairway, then the Great Hall.

"That was the last of it, miss." The footman gazed around the hall, thinking the old place vastly improved.

Karis smiled. "Then, we are now finished."

The marquis lifted the Kissing Bough from the table. "Not yet. Toby, lower the center chandelier and I shall attach the Kissing Bough to that."

The servant disappeared into a small door, and within minutes, the wheel-like brass lighting fixture came to within a foot above the marquis's head. He gave a shout for the man to hold, then held the Kissing Bough in place as Karis quickly tied the runners to the light. She was intensely aware of the man as he stood watching her nervous fingers work.

"There, it should hold now." Karis took a step back, feeling like she couldn't breathe at his nearness.

The marquis ordered the footman to raise the chandelier back to its former position. While the Kissing Bough lifted above them, Karis forced her mind away from the marquis. There was no point in wasting her time on dreams of romance. The death of her father had changed her life forever.

With a resigned sigh, she looked about the hall, then back to the rising Bough. Having momentarily put aside her personal regrets, she felt a rush of satisfaction at the job she'd done at Whiteoaks. She knew she had an artistic gift and it gave her pleasure to share it with others. Mayhap she could use her abilities to earn some money, but then where would she spend it? Aunt Flora never took them to Clarendon with Dorinda.

A tremor of fear ran down her spine as she suddenly remembered the glittering menace in her cousin's eyes before she'd departed Whiteoaks. What would be the penalty for an afternoon in the marquis's company?

Lord Marsden intruded on her thoughts when he softly

said, "Miss Lockhart, you have transformed this old house into a home."

Karis drew her gaze from the bobbing Kissing Bough to look at the gentleman before her. His scrutiny was as soft as a caress and she felt a tingling deep in her stomach. She knew dangerous longings were beginning to fill her heart. With a rush she announced, "I believe all is done, my lord. Anthea and I must return to Westwood."

The marquis knew she was right, but on sudden impulse, he leaned forward taking her chin in his hand. "You must allow me the first seasonal kiss under the Bough, Miss Lockhart." He'd only meant to brush her lips briefly as was the Christmas tradition, but when his mouth touched hers, a fever ignited in him that could only be quenched by her responding lips. An impulse as natural as breathing made him draw her yielding body again his chest and he lost himself in her faint scent of jasmine.

At the sound of the footman returning to the Great Hall, Marsden came to his senses and released the bewitching chit. Momentarily speechless, he attempted to control the strong masculine response she'd roused. He watched the play of emotions on her lovely face and knew she had been equally affected by the kiss.

Miss Lockhart's green eyes appeared dazed for a moment as she stared back at him. The chiming of a case clock in the hall seemed to awaken her, for she blinked and looked around as if surprised to find herself at Whiteoaks. Then those expressive eyes became shuttered, locking him from her thoughts.

"It is late, my lord. Anthea and I must be on our way to Westwood. My duties shall keep me from coming again. I would wish you and your daughter a Merry Christmas." Before the marquis could utter his simplest apology, she turned and dashed up the stairs.

# *Chapter Five*

Karis's heart pounded in her chest as she hurried Anthea down the back stairs of Whiteoaks. She knew it was cowardly to slip away unseen, but she couldn't face encountering the marquis again. She couldn't trust herself to conceal her emotions. With one kiss all was suddenly clear. She was in love with the Marquis of Marsden.

She was scarcely aware of her surroundings as they said their hurried goodbyes to Mrs. Shelby, then excited the manor. Anthea, oblivious to her sister's distraction, chattered away about their day while they made their way through the woods to Westwood.

Karis heard little of what the child said. She merely nodded in agreement, her mind still reeling from her folly. She'd fallen in love with a lord who could have his pick of the most beautiful and wealthy women of Society. He'd probably never given a thought to a penniless nobody like herself except as a companion for his daughter. For him the kiss had been a meaningless holiday gesture.

When the red bricks of Westwood came into view, Karis

nearly groaned. Now she must face her vengeful cousin and hope there was little the spoiled girl could do to harm either herself or Anthea. She knew she was in no proper state to deal with Dorinda just now.

The sisters quietly entered the house through the kitchen and managed to make it all the way to the nursery without being accosted. But a maid arrived just as they were removing their wraps with a message that Lady Westerly wished to speak with Karis.

"I must see what Aunt wants. Change for dinner and don't forget to wash your face and hands."

Anthea stepped to her sister, placing a restraining hand on her sleeve. "Does this summons have anything to do with Dorinda being at Whiteoaks today? She means to do something to you because we went without permission, does she not?"

Pushing back reddish-blond curls from her sister's forehead, Karis kissed the girl. "Don't worry about Dorinda. Aunt Flora is foolish, but not likely to be led into doing anything that would harm either one of us."

Leaving her sister with an admonishment to hurry, Karis made her way to the rear parlor, wishing she felt as brave as she'd sounded. Her aunt sat at a table penning a letter while her cousin perused a copy of *La Belle Assembleé*.

When Dorinda glanced up, a smug smile on her lips, she closed the magazine, tossing it to a nearby table. "Mama, Karis has come home at last. Tell her the good news."

Lady Westerly continued with her writing, but called over her shoulder, "Have a seat, Karis. I shall be with you momentarily."

Taking a seat in a chair across from her cousin, Karis was surprised at her aunt's cheery tone. Her aunt seemed gay as a lark, a surprising state considering what her daughter had been about. But then did Aunt Flora truly know Dorinda's reason for being at Whiteoaks? Probably not, for Lady Westerly rarely saw her daughter as anything but the epitome of perfection.

Within minutes she joined the silent girls beside the fire. "My dear, you know it was your uncle's intent for us to find you a position after the formal mourning for your father was at an end."

A wave of apprehension swept through Karis. Was she to become a governess so soon? This was far worse than anything she'd imagined. She would be separated from Anthea, perhaps for years. "I-I thought my Uncle Frederick said I could remain until I was no longer under his guardianship."

"So he did my dear, but we hadn't the least notion of how very learned you were. You and dear little Anthea have been with us for over a year now, and in that time I have come to realize you needn't wait two more years to earn your own keep. You can start at once. An old friend of mine is looking for a governess and I have written to tell her you will come to her in the new year."

Karis clenched her hands into fists knowing her cousin had been behind this sudden change in plans, but before she could protest the arrangements Anthea dashed into the parlor. It was clear to Karis her sister hadn't done as she'd been told since she still wore the same blue wool dress with smudges of flour about the hem. Instead, the child had come down to listen at the door to Karis's conversation with her aunt.

"You are sending my sister away? I suppose we have Dorinda to thank for this." Anthea was close to shouting, her anger was so great.

Dorinda glared at the child and snapped, "You will not speak in that tone of voice. Don't forget to whom you are beholden for the very roof over your head, young lady. You should be thankful to have such a kind family."

"How could I forget with you here to remind us daily? The truth is that we are little better than unpaid servants."

Karis rose and went to her sister, putting a calming arm around her shoulders. She agreed with every word her sister spoke, but they depended on their aunt for their very existence at the present. If she were being sent away she could not allow Anthea to jeopardize her own future here at Westwood. Karis had long hoped that once Dorinda married, that their aunt would take more of an interest in the child. "You forget yourself, Anthea. We have much to be grateful to Aunt Flora for. Please apologize."

The child's shoulder trembled beneath Karis's hand, but she wasn't certain if it was from rage or remorse. The silence lengthened but at last Anthea calmly spoke.

"Aunt Flora, I am sorry . . . that your daughter is a spiteful jade who thinks of no one but herself." The last was said in a rush then the child pulled free from her sister and ran from the room.

Lady Westerly's face grew red. "How dare that ungrateful child slander her cousin so! After all Dorinda has done for you both."

Karis set about trying to soothe her aunt's wounded sensibilities. Unlike Anthea, Karis knew the child would have ended up in an orphanage had their father's only sister not agreed to take them in. "Aunt Flora, please, she is just a child. I know that cannot excuse her bad manners, but I do assure you that once she is over the shock of our being separated she will truly apologize to you."

Dorinda rose haughtily and stood behind her mother. "I think I am the one that deserves an apology."

With resignation, Karis replied, "And so you do, cousin. I hope you will forgive Anthea her show of temper and remember that she has only recently lost her father and is about to be parted from her sister."

Lady Westerly looked back at her thoughtfully. "I had not thought her so emotional but my dear you both act as if I were sending you to the ends of the earth. Mrs.

Handley lives in Coventry. I am sure she will have no objection to your coming to see Anthea on your own time.''

Relief flooded Karis. She would not be completely removed from her sister and would get to see how she went on, even if it was as rare as once a month.

The next half hour was spent appeasing her relatives. She knew she would have to find Anthea and return her to the drawing room for an apology, but Karis wanted the child to have an opportunity to get past her first wave of anger. She even dared hoped her sister might return of her own accord once she realized the magnitude of her insult to their cousin and aunt.

At last, sufficiently certain that Aunt Flora and Dorinda were no longer furious with her sister, Karis excused herself and went in search of the child. Within a matter of ten minutes, however, it became clear that Miss Anthea Lockhart was no longer at Westwood Park.


Anthea paced in front of Binx and Lady Rosalind having just poured out the details of the meeting in the rear parlor. ''I tell you my cousin is despicable. She is making Aunt Flora send Karis away.''

''But why?'' Lady Rosalind looked up at her nurse, puzzled.

Binx returned the girls' questioning stare. She realized, she being the adult, they were expecting an answer from her. ''Well, I can't say why your cousin—what did you say 'er name was?''

''Miss Dorinda Westwood.''

Binx's brows rose. ''The same Miss Westerly what claimed to be thrown from 'er 'orse in front of the manor?''

Anthea nodded her head. ''The very same.''

''Then 'tis clear as glass. Your cousin is a cunning baggage. Tryin' to get Lord Marsden to make up to 'er and she don't want no other female about distractin' 'im. Wasting her time, if you ask me. 'E'd be much better off if 'e married up with your sister."

At first Anthea's face brightened, then her expression grew gloomy. "Karis says that titled gentleman never marry penniless ladies."

Binx sadly replied, " 'Tis commonly true".

Lady Rosalind jumped to her feet. "I wish my papa would wed your sister. Then we would be a family and I should never have to live with Grandmama again. I like Miss Karis immensely, but does my father?"

Binx shrugged her shoulders. "Lord Marsden does get a certain look in 'is eyes when they rest on the lady. But you two are gettin' way ahead of things 'ere. 'Is lordship ain't said nothin' about gettin' married."

The girls' faces grew gloomily, both realizing that Binx was right. Then Lady Rosalind smiled, "I just had a thought. If your sister is going to be a governess, why not be mine? Papa fired the one Grandmama had employed so I shall need a new one. Then you might come and live with us, too. I shall ask him after dinner tonight."

Anthea was in alt. "I am certain that Karis would much rather work for your father than some unknown lady."

Binx grinned at the pair as they dance around together arm-in-arm. "There can't be no 'arm in askin'."

Knowing she must go, Anthea requested that her friend send word as to the outcome of the meeting, then she took her leave. It was a surprisingly lighthearted miss who encountered her older sister in the fading light in the woods. After receiving a stinging reprimand, Anthea begged Karis's forgiveness and asked to be allowed to offer her cousin and aunt an apology.

At first, Karis was suspicious of her sister's benevolent mood. She wondered what had occurred to leave the girl so changed. But the improvement was so fortuitous, she was unwilling to question Anthea about the cause. Instead she took her straight to the rear parlor where the child willingly and prettily begged her aunt and cousin's pardon, even going so far as to volunteer to play the pianoforte for them after dinner.


"Papa, are you listening to me?" Lady Rosalind turned in her chair when her father failed to answer her question. She'd joined him in the library after he'd dined to ask him about Miss Lockhart.

"I am sorry, Rosebud. My mind was elsewhere." He'd been remembering the feel of Miss Lockhart's warm mouth. It was a thought that had played over and over in his mind since their encounter under the mistletoe. Telling himself he'd behaved like a rake, and no doubt given the lady a disgust of him, the marquis pushed the memory away. Bringing his gaze to focus on his daughter, he asked her to repeat the question.

"I asked if you intend on engaging a new governess for me?"

Marsden smiled and reached over, tousling his daughter's brown curls. "I would not have thought you so anxious to get back to your studies, little one."

"Well, as to that, I am not, but Anthea tells me her sister is to be sent away to be a governess and I thought . . . that we might engage her to be mine." Rosalind held her breath as she watched her father's reaction.

Marsden froze at his daughter's news. Miss Lockhart was being sent from Westwood to be a governess. So that was Miss Westwood's punishment. But he could give little thought to the conniving Dorinda, for he suddenly realized he might never see Miss Lockhart again.

"Papa, did you hear me? I want Miss Lockhart to be my governess and to live with us." Lady Rosalind eyed her father curiously. Whatever was causing him to behave in such a strange manner, as if he'd taken leave of his senses?

His daughter's words came to him through a haze of

emotions, and the marquis repeated her words in a daze. "You want the lady to live with us?"

The very thought of Karis Lockhart living under his roof caused an intense heat to flare deep within him. As if the heat burgeoned into a fire and suddenly burned through an obstructing wall, he knew he did want her with him, but not as some hired companion for his daughter. In that instant, he realized he loved Karis. He wanted her to be his wife.

But the memory of her unhappy face after he'd kissed her troubled him. She'd declared she wouldn't be returning to Whiteoaks. She'd rushed up the stairs never to return, then left the manor by the back stairs to avoid him. Very likely she never wanted to set eyes on him again, thinking him nothing more than one of those despicable gentleman who preyed on impoverished ladies without protection of father or brother. He'd ruined everything with one tantalizing kiss.

With that dark thought, he glanced up at the hopeful eyes of his daughter. "We cannot employ Miss Lockhart as your governess."

Rosalind sagged back in the chair, disappointment etched on her face. "But why, Papa?"

"Because, child, I fear I acted foolishly this afternoon, and she appears set against me. I doubt she will ever visit Whiteoaks again." Marsden sighed when he thought about the dinner he'd agreed to attend the next evening. Perhaps he could apologize, if he got a chance. But the lady would likely make some excuse to remain in her room to avoid meeting him again.

Lady Rosalind had no clue what her father was referring to but she remembered Miss Lockhart had appeared very flushed when she came to the nursery to take Anthea home. Obviously the lady and her father had argued. It was clearly up to her and Anthea to get them together so they might apologize. She wanted Karis and Anthea to live with them and she wouldn't allow a misunderstanding to end her dreams. She stared into the fire for several minutes, then smiled up at her father. "Don't be sad, Papa. I am certain that everything will turn out just as it should."

Marsden made the effort to smile at his daughter. "Ah, it would be nice to again possess the optimism of youth. Now off to bed with you, my Rosebud."

After his daughter exited, the marquis's thoughts centered on Karis Lockhart. He loved her, could she ever return his feelings? He suddenly felt as insecure as a young fellow new to Town. He drew comfort from the memory of her response to his kiss. Hope swelled in his chest. Knowing nothing would be resolved until he again came face-to-face with Karis, he retired to his bed determined he would find some way to offer the lady his heart.

The following morning he awoke to his daughter's distraught cries. The kittens had gone missing during the night and his Rosebud was heartbroken.

After a thorough search of the house revealed nothing, Lady Rosalind couldn't be consoled. Binx announced there was only one thing to do—summon the Lockhart sisters.

Karis sat in front of the nursery fire, a copy of Scott's *Lady of the Lake* open on her lap. Her aunt had ordered her to keep Anthea out of the way after the child had accidently knocked over a vase of hot house flowers during the bustle of activity surrounding the arrangements for the dinner that evening. Since Dorinda was in her room trying to decide which gown to wear, the sisters had the morning to themselves.

Anthea held Mrs. Damon, stroking her orange fur and whispering in the cat's ear as she gazed out the window. But Karis was too distracted to give much thought to the child's strangely secretive mood.

Karis pretended to read, but in truth, her thoughts kept straying to Lord Marsden and his kiss. The memory of his lips on hers left her feeling breathless. Her cheeks warmed when she realized how much she wished to have him take her in his arms again, even knowing he'd been merely offering her a Christmas embrace. Her heart skipped a beat when she remembered he would be in this very house tonight. Would she be able to keep her feelings hidden from him?

The nursery door opened and Mary entered. "Miss Lockhart, there's a message for you from Whiteoaks." The maid handed her the folded white vellum.

With trembling fingers, Karis read the brief note. The marquis begged her to come to the manor at once. Disaster had struck and the kittens were missing. He hoped she and Anthea might help him by bringing the kitten's mother. He'd signed the note with only the letter M.

Karis's heart hammered at the thought of seeing the marquis again. Could she behave as if the kiss had never happened? She must, for she would not leave him to handle such a crisis alone. She knew how distressed he would be over his daughter's unhappiness.

"Anthea, we must go to Whiteoaks at once. Bring Mrs. Damon for the kittens are lost."

Anthea didn't argue or ask any questions, which Karis, were she not so preoccupied, would have found strange. They quickly donned their wraps and hurried through the woods, bringing the protesting feline. Karis tried to keep her thoughts centered on Lady Rosalind and the lost kittens. This was no time for her foolish fancies about the child's father.

Within a short time they were being ushered into the Whiteoaks nursery by Mrs. Shelby. Binx and Lady Rosalind were seated near the fire as the child cried rather noisily into a handkerchief. Lord Marsden stood beside the window, a thoughtful expression on his handsome face.

Karis's heart lurched. She thought him devastatingly handsome in a blue morning coat and gray buckskins. He came to them, a look of gratitude in his gray eyes.

"Thank you for coming so promptly, Miss Lockhart. As you can see we are at sixes and sevens here this morning."

Anthea took Mrs. Damon to Lady Rosalind, and the child's cries ceased as she took the large mother cat from her friend, cradling it lovingly in her arms. The two girls fell to whispering and eyeing the conversing pair covertly.

Karis concentrated on the matter at hand, attempting to ignore the marquis's powerful presence beside her. "How do you think the kittens escaped the nursery, my lord?"

"That is the mystery of this strange occurrence."

"No doubt someone accidentally left a door open."

The marquis's gaze rested thoughtfully on his daughter. "Yes, no doubt someone did."

Anthea rose, coming to her sister's side. "Perhaps you should search the stables. You know how Mrs. Damon loves to look for mice in the hay. Very likely her offspring have the same instinct for the hunt."

Karis was about to protest that the kittens could not have gotten that far away as well as being too small to be mousing when the marquis interrupted.

"We have looked everywhere else. We may as well search the stables. Miss Anthea, you stay with my daughter and I shall accompany your sister."

Karis allowed the gentleman to lead her from the nursery, trying to ignore his enticing smell of sandalwood. Neither spoke while they made their way to the stables. Karis kept her eyes turned toward the ground, but she felt his lordship's gaze on her.

As they entered the building, she heard the muffled chatter of the grooms in the tack room at the rear of the stable. Finally she brought her gaze up to meet Lord

Marsden's compelling countenance. "I don't think it likely that the kittens could have come this far from the house."

The marquis grinned down at her. "Oh, I think it very likely they are here. No doubt helped on their long journey."

"Helped?" Karis could barely say the word as she stared into his twinkling eyes. She thought him in a surprisingly cheerful mood considering Lady Rosalind's anguish over her missing pets.

"Yes, helped by my daughter or—" Marsden stopped as the sounds of meowing emanated from behind a nearby pile of hay. He smiled and gestured for Karis to go before him. "As I suspected."

They circled the fresh hay, discovering a large picnic basket with the lid securely fastened. Karis hurried forward and lifting the container, released the latch. "They are all here, but why would Lady Rosalind do such a thing."

"I believe this was a ploy to get you to Whiteoaks. She thinks I can be tricked into hiring you as a governess. But she is sadly mistaken."

Karis's heart plummeted. The kiss in the Great Hall had made him think her an improper companion for his child. Who would hire a wanton as their child's governess?

Before she could order her dark thoughts, the marquis stepped forward as if he would take the basket, but instead he locked his hands over hers. The newly released kittens began to climb out and up her sleeve, but Karis paid scant attention as she gazed at the marquis's face so close to hers. There was such a burning look of intensity in his eyes, that she stood as if turned to stone even though inside she was melting like a snowflake on a warm hearth.

In a husky voice, the marquis said, "I don't want you as a governess, my love. I want you as my wife."

Karis stood speechless, uncertain her knees would hold her. The marquis loved her. By now all seven kittens had made good their escape from the basket, three climbing on her and four moving up the marquis's arms to his shoulder, hanging on with their sharp little claws, but neither took notice as their gazes locked.

They were jarred from their ardent absorption with one another when a daring black kitten tried to climb onto Karis's gray poke bonnet, causing the pair to laugh. Marsden plucked the adventurous felines from his lady love, then from himself and put them back in the basket, closing the lid. "Say that you would never be so cruel as to leave me alone with my mischief making daughter *and* a rambunctious litter of kittens. I love you, Karis. Will you do me the honor of becoming my wife?"

Karis couldn't believe her good fortune. He loved her. "I would not be so cruel as to abandon you, my lord, for I adore the kittens, I adore your daughter and most of all I adore you. I will marry you."

Taking the handle of the basket, the marquis removed it from between them, then encircled the lady's waist with his free arm and drew her to him, kissing her properly and deeply.

Releasing his love, the marquis smiled. "I had no idea when I brought my daughter to Warwichshire that I would have such a perfect Christmas."

As the kittens began loudly meowing to be released from the basket, Karis laughed. "I think this will be a 'purr-fect Christmas' for all concerned."

The marquis lovingly drew her back to him. "Purr-fect, indeed." Then his lips captured hers.

The now affianced couple were so lost in their embrace that neither noted two young ladies peeking around the stable door. After exchanging a startled glance, Lady Rosalind whispered, "Do you think it proper for Papa to be kissing my new governess?"

Anthea snorted. "Don't be silly. He would not kiss her so if he asked her to be your governess. You can be certain he asked her to marry him."

The marquis's daughter beamed her delight. "Then we shall be like sisters."

Satisfied with the results of their efforts, they turned and made their way back to the house arm-in-arm. Lady Rosalind said, "We are very good matchmakers, are we not?"

"Yes, indeed." A glint of amusement was in Anthea's hazel eyes. "Shall we try our luck again?"

"Who did you have in mind?"

Anthea ran the list of single females of her acquaintance through her mind and thought of her cousin Dorinda. She dismissed the lady at once, thinking she wouldn't wish that perfidious vixen on anyone. Besides, the girl would be in a rage when she learned of Karis's good fortune and not likely to be in the mood for romance. At last she suggested, "What say you to a match between Binx and Toby."

"Toby! I was thinking Binx and Jock a superior match."

"The coachman? Too old. Besides, Toby is very handsome."

The two young girls made their way back to the warmth of the nursery good naturedly arguing about their next victims, content with the knowledge that Christmas would be very merry at Whiteoaks.

# The Rose And Shadow
## Jenna Jones

# Chapter One

December, 1805

Topping the rise, Captain Derrick Palmer drew his gelding to a halt, then peered down into the scoop of the broad, familiar valley spreading out before him all the way to the distant scarf of storm clouds draped against the horizon. Absently, he shoved aside the flap of his navy blue Penniston cloak and rubbed at his healing wound. Reminiscences tickled just behind his clear blue eyes; uncomfortably, he shifted in his saddle, easing the stretch of puckered flesh along his outer thigh.

"Is this the place, then, Captain?" asked a young lad, gaining the crest on his own mount moments after his master.

"It is, Mr. Rawlins," the captain replied, shifting his gaze toward the small cluster of cottages far below settled like a pleasant musing between the swell of Langley Hill and the ice-crusted banks of the Isbourne. "Winchcombe lies there against those bluffs," he completed, leaning forward to stroke Spritsail's neck, quieting the great horse's curvetting.

"A pretty place by the look of it," the boy assessed, his smile warm, but travel-tired. "In which of the cottages were you born, sir?"

"I was not born in the village," the captain responded. Angling slightly, he pointed with his whip toward a three storey rectangle of golden Cotswold stone planted like a winter crop within an expanse of land criss-crossed by low, dry slate walls. "My home was there. My father was the squire."

"You were a second son," the young man concluded.

"No, the first-born," the captain corrected. "However, I sold the estate when I knew I would never return to Winchcombe."

A snow bunting chipped in a nearby beech; several moments slipped away on a lazy tack in the air current.

"And his lordship, the lieutenant, sir?" the lad at last continued, wisely sensing that a change of subject was called for.

"The viscount spent his childhood at Ash Park," the captain replied, again twisting in his saddle to indicate a long drive leading north out of the village toward the base of the bluffs, then disappearing into a thick, bare-branched copse. "From here, one can only see a portion of the house's roof. Do you see it, Mr. Rawlins? It lies beyond that rising of rock."

"I see it, sir. Is it there where we shall find the lady?"

Again the captain shifted uneasily in his saddle. "Unlikely," he more softly replied after releasing a lengthy exhalation. "I expect that we shall find the viscountess there . . ." he said, next swinging his crop toward a huge rambling pile situated high above the town at the end of a wide drive bordered by neatly clipped yews, its own yellow stone muted by the surrounding bluff's coldly cast shadows, "in Clarendon Manor."

Immediately he cast his gaze back upon the town. Memories surged again and were summarily dealt with. Far below, thin columns of smoke rose stiff and unmoving above each steeply pitched slate roof, apostrophes accentuating the afternoon's listless chill.

At last the captain again stirred. "Come along, lad," he softly ordered. "We'd best hurry if we're to bespeak a private room."

Clenching his jaw, he again touched his crop to Spritsail's shoulder, starting the gelding forward once more toward Winchcombe.


It was midafternoon when the two arrived at the Rose and Shadow, a tiny lichen-covered inn tucked almost beneath the Vineyard Street bridge where it crossed the Isbourne, adjacent to the spot where the townsfolk had, for as far back as anyone could remember, always dunked the town scolds. Above, rows of heavy slate tiles squeezed up a handful of white framed dormers from the steep slant of the roof. Neat bay windows, bedecked for the Christmas season with yew garlands, rowan berries, and brass-clutched candles of bright crimson, bulged into the inn yard to capture the feeble winter sun.

As the captain and Mr. Rawlins dismounted, several boys materialized to take command of their horses and lead them off to the stables. At the same time, a portly man burst from within sporting a generous smock, a spotless apron, and a wide smile of welcome.

"Well, well . . . good day to ye, sirs!" the man exclaimed, carelessly wading through the motley swarm of kittens that had instantly collected at his appearance, throwing his arms wide.

Tucking his bicorn under his arm, the captain turned and fastened his gaze upon the innkeeper. Then, taking only the twentieth part of a moment to study the approaching man, his features quickly eased into an unexpected smile.

"And to you, Mr. Bates," he at last responded, dipping into a slight bow.

The sudden comprehension that the stranger in his yard knew his name washed the starch from the innkeeper's jowls. Pausing, he blinked owlishly.

"Why, 'pon my soul, if it isn't Mr. Palmer!" he finally cried in recognition, at once starting forward with his hand extended, scattering an assortment of noses and soft paws.

"*Captain* Palmer now, sir," the other replied, limping, too, to close the distance between them.

"Why, y'don't say! Captain, is it?" Mr. Bates repeated, pumping his arm while exuberantly pounding upon the captain's shoulder.

"Aye, sir, in His Majesty's Navy," Mr. Rawlins proudly supplied, his steps to his captain's side inspiring a complaining chorus of mews.

"Is that right, now?" Mr. Bates dutifully queried. Unashamedly, then, he glanced down toward the captain's leg. "And taken with a wound, too, unless I miss my guess. By the saints, lad!" he suddenly exclaimed, his black eyes growing huge between their pillowed lids. "Were ye with Nelson, then? . . . at Trafalgar?"

"I was," the captain replied, nodding only once, "nearly two months past. I commanded the *Triumph,* a third rate of seventy-four guns out of Portsmouth."

"And lived to tell of it. Ah, lad," the innkeeper sighed, this time throwing his arm about the captain in sympathy, "those in that battle earned the whole country's regard. But to lose Lord Nelson . . . so noble a man. Such a sadness for England. Yet now, here ye are, aren't ye? Your duty done, now one of Winchcombe's own has come home."

"Actually, no, Mr. Bates," the captain responded, stiffening slightly, his smile slowly deserting his chiseled countenance, "my home is in Portsmouth now. I fear my sole reason in returning to Winchcombe is to do my duty as senior officer to Viscount Berkeley.''

"Your duty?'' the innkeeper repeated. "Was he aboard your ship when he took his wound, then?''

"He was. When he joined the Navy he asked that he might serve under me.''

"As he would, of course,'' Mr. Bates nodded. "As he always did even when the two of you were no bigger than two warts on the widow's nose. You always in the lead in your running here and about . . . his lordship always following. And that Miss Claire! Why, I recollect a time . . .''

". . . Far too long ago to waste thought upon, I am certain,'' the captain interrupted, "especially as my aide and I need your assistance in securing a room for the duration of our stay, as well as hot water and a stout meal.''

"Say no more, lad, you shall have it,'' the innkeeper replied. "What else might I do for ye?''

"You might find me ink and parchment to write upon,'' the captain told him. "As soon as possible, I must write to the viscountess.''

"Your duty, lad?'' the innkeeper asked.

"Yes. I am here to extend His Majesty's condolences and to tell the viscountess what I can of her husband's last days.''

"A sad duty . . . a sad duty to be sure,'' Mr. Bates murmured, slowly shaking his head. "I don't envy ye the doing of it. Poor little lass. Well, come inside, then,'' he directed, brightening a bit, again throwing an arm about the captain and turning him toward the door. "Whether your stay be brief or not, you are still from Winchcombe. You shall have my finest room, I vow, as well as the rarest slice of beef and, to ease your wound, my best comfrey poultice.''

Tired, hungry, and much pleased with the innkeeper's kindness, the captain motioned for Mr. Rawlins to bring their sea bags, then accompanied Mr. Bates into the tap room. His mind on creature comforts, he did not even notice the tiny gray kitten perched atop one of his immaculately polished black boots, its little needle-claws securely imbedded in leather, happily riding, still playing with that boot's tassel as he began to haltingly ascend the stairs.

A short time later, after hot water had been delivered to the pleasantly appointed quarters the innkeeper had let to him, the captain crossed to the room's oak-manteled hearth and eased himself into the fire-warmth held captive by an ancient settle. Making himself comfortable, he then bent down with the intention of removing his boots while Mr. Rawlins laid out a fresh shirt. Instead, he suddenly began to chuckle.

"Well, what have we here?" he laughed softly, discovering the gray kitten, unhooking each tiny claw one by one—having to repeat the process for several of them—then carrying the intruder up to where the two of them could—eye to slanted, sleepily blinking eye—study one another.

"It appears to be a kitten, sir," Mr. Rawlins grinned, laying out clean stockings.

"Not a bit of it," the captain countered, his eyes gleaming with pleasure, his fingers gentle against the animal's fragile ribs. "This, Mr. Rawlins, is a stowaway."

The kitten offered her opinion of the comment by yawning widely, intently focusing, then batting at the captain's eyebrow.

Adroitly, the captain ducked the infant's deadly swipe. "Such impudence for one so small and completely at my mercy," he tsked, placing the rag-mannered creature upon his lap. "And what is this?" he next asked when his stroking fingers touched an object foreign to the kitten's soft, cloud-gray fur. One puff of air answered the question. A circlet of bright green mistletoe had been woven about the kitten's tiny neck in a festive holiday collar. The discovery evoked yet another smile. "So someone has bedecked you for the Christmas season as well, have they? And quite fetching you are, too, I might add. However, I shall have to withhold any further compliments until another time," he continued, rising with the kitten in his arms, crossing to the door and opening it, then setting the happily purring creature down on the floor. "*Some* of us have duties to perform, after all. Run along, then, little stowaway," he commanded, nudging the kitten out into the hall. "Far be it from me to delay your spreading of Christmas cheer. Go on, now," he again urged, beginning to close the door. "Think of the mice who are waiting for you to give chase," he added, nudging the kitten once again before steadily narrowing the aperture. "Think of the tidbits awaiting you in the kitchen. Think of that nice warm spot before the fire."

"Think of the captain of the *Triumph* conversing with a kitten," Mr. Rawlins added with a grin, reaching out to take Captain Palmer's braided cutaway.

"Think of a midshipmen of the *Triumph* living the next year in the crow's nest," the captain countered.

Satisfied that he had made his point, he quickly divested himself of the remainder of his clothes, then submitted to the chuckling Mr. Rawlins's execution of his toilette.


Less than an hour later, Captain Palmer placed quill, ink and a sheet of costly parchment upon the room's antique writing desk, then seated himself before it. After trimming the quill's tip, he dipped it into the ink and began to fill the page with his communication to the viscountess.

My Lady,

By now you are sadly acquainted with the tragedy of your husband's death. As his captain, and as a man present at the time of his misfortune, I have traveled to Winchcombe to extend to you the king's own condolences, as well as to tell you what you might wish to know of the viscount's last hours. To that end, I am writing to request an audience to be scheduled, of course, at your convenience.

I have taken a room at the Rose and Shadow and shall remain there until I hear from you. I await word of your pleasure.

Sincere regards,
Captain Derrick Palmer
His Majesty's Ship *Triumph*

Enclosing the note within another parchment, the captain next addressed the outer sheet to Claire, Lady Berkeley, Claredon Manor, sealed it, then gave the letter to Mr. Rawlins.

"If you hurry, you should make it back to the inn before supper," he commented, again easing himself down onto the settle, once more absently rubbing his thigh.

"Is there a need for such haste, sir?" Mr. Rawlins questioned, hesitating. "I am sensible of how difficult this duty promises to be for you, and we have traveled far. Surely a few days' rest would not be amiss."

The captain shook his head. "Not two months past I sailed my ship straight into a firing line of French frigates, only to turn about and do so again and again. I can face one woman, Mr. Rawlins."

"Are you certain of that, sir?" the young boy asked again.

"Yes, deuce take it," the captain growled, casting the youth a dark scowl for his impertinence, "I am!"

Yet long after the lad had left, the captain still saw Claire Masterson's eyes in the small hearth's undulant fire.

# *Chapter Two*

"I find this aspect particularly pleasing," stated Neville Benchley, Earl of Clayton, standing before one of the windows of the parlor located to the rear of Clarendon Manor, gesturing with his quizzing glass toward the formal gardens just beyond the manor's wide, earthen terrace. "So much more *organized* than those untidy designs of Capability Brown, don't y'know."

"Oh, I quite agree," supplied his host, puffing puckers into his snug, dove gray waistcoat. "Wouldn't have the disheveled things, I vow. Wouldn't have 'em."

"Ah, but you take too much credit, do you not, Fillmore?" the earl chided, his pinched gaze sliding toward the solar's interior. "I am persuaded that such an elegant design must only have sprung from a delicate, sensitive mind. Am I mistaken, sir?" he asked, mincing on black slippered feet to stand uncomfortably close to the woman seated upon a Grecian style chair positioned to take advantage of a rectangle of weak sunlight illuminating a section of the room's patterned Aubusson. "Surely your garden owes its perfection to your daughter's fine hand?'' he elaborated, his gaze counting the small bumps aligned along her slim, white neck before sweeping down to pry into her bodice's shadows.

"Why . . .'' began the baron, his mind quickly recounting the hours he had spent pouring over the details of the garden's planning, "it does indeed, and you have the right of it, by God. How very astute of you, my lord. Is it not astute of his lordship, Claire?'' he asked, joining his house guest within the wan sun-wash.

Her head bowed in concentration, Viscountess Berkeley wove another tiny loop of lace along the edge of a square of fine lawn.

"Claire?'' her father repeated.

"What? . . .'' she said, suddenly looking up, her pale blue eyes huge, incongruous amid a wealth of lustrous black curls. "Oh . . . did you say something, Papa?''

Instantly, Fillmore's shrub-like brows collapsed into a frown. "Not only I,'' he began low in his throat, "but Clayton . . . our guest, if you recall.'' His point made, he then gathered himself. "My dear Claire,'' he added much more lightly, smiling between the other two, "you shall have our guest believing that you do not care for his company.''

"Then I have indeed been remiss, have I not?'' Claire responded, setting aside her small shuttle and spools. "Please accept my apology, sir,'' she added, quickly rising and hurrying toward the bell pull. "Would you care for tea? I confess I have been so absorbed in my needlework, I am persuaded it must be well past time for it.''

"I should welcome whatever might be poured by your hand,'' the earl murmured, doggedly following, again startling Claire by his sudden nearness, by his penetrating perusal; drawing her fingers to within improper fractions of his moist mouth.

"Indeed," the viscountess breathed, tugging herself free, "and if I offered you arsenic, sir?"

"Claire!" her father exclaimed.

Clayton, however, merely chuckled. "Then, my lady, I would die a happy man."

Drawing her lips into a thin line, Claire shifted again to supervise the entrance of the Clarendon butler, Dawes, and his placement of the refreshment tray.

"There has been too much death already," she at last murmured, seating herself before the tray and lifting the *Sèvres* pot to fill the first of the set's delicate porcelain cups.

"Ah, yes, you are referring to your husband, of course," the earl sympathized. "Poor, dear lady," he pronounced, flourishing a handkerchief about his nose and eyes before taking the chair directly across from her. "So much to bear for one so young . . . so very, very lovely."

"Nonsense," the baron intruded, landing on the seat beside Claire with such force that tea spilled onto the lemon tarts. "Never does to dwell on life's little unhappinesses, don't y'know. Best thing in the world is to move ahead, I vow, and so I have taught my daughter. Not one soul saw me languishing about after my wife's demise, I assure you. By the same token, neither shall you find Claire to be a woman who long cherishes her sentiments, sir. Why, I misdoubt it has been weeks since a tear last stained her pillow."

The cup Claire had been balancing suddenly clattered into its saucer.

Slowly her wide gaze swung to her father's. "How well you know me, Papa," she enunciated distinctly. Afterward, carefully replacing her saucer upon the tray, she glanced toward the butler. "You may go now, Dawes."

The butler bowed. "Very good, my lady," he intoned. Before he turned to go, however, he withdrew a paper from his black cutaway. "Might I add, my lady, that this letter addressed to your ladyship was just delivered moments ago. The messenger awaits without for your response."

"Thank you, Dawes," the viscountess replied, taking it from him.

"What is it, my dear? . . ." the baron asked, peering over the rims of his *pince-nez*, leaning over her hands, "something concerning our Christmas ball?"

Deftly, Claire covered the communication with her serviette. "I rather think not, Papa. Those plans are well in hand. Most likely it is a communication from Mrs. Beckworth concerning our efforts to restore Sudeley Castle," she replied, next smoothly rising to her feet. "No doubt some problem has arisen concerning the fair we are sponsoring soon to raise funds for it," she continued, gliding toward the door. "If you will excuse me for a moment, gentlemen, I shall take care of the matter."

"Well . . . if you must . . ." her father called toward her retreating back.

"Now, Fillmore," the earl soothed, patting the baron's hand, "we must let the ladies have their little charities. You will make haste to return, will you not, my dear? . . . my dear?"

Happily, the lady's response was clipped off by the closing of the parlor's solid oak door.


Once safely inside her room, Claire withdrew the letter from her pocket, quickly read the inscription, then, puzzled because she did not recognize the handwriting of its author, read it once again. Her curiosity piqued, she next turned the packet over in her hands. And then her brows joined. What could the letter mean? she wondered, rubbing her thumb back and forth over the small red disk. The circle of wax bore the British Navy's seal. Finally, deciding that she was a twiddlepoop to stand there wonder-

ing when she could be looking inside, she broke the seal
and removed the letter, then quickly scanned it.

Someone had come to the village on behalf of the Navy
to tell her what he could of Philip's death, she shortly
learned. A thoughtful gesture, she allowed, though hardly
necessary. She was far too sensible of how it had happened
... how it had actually happened. He had not died of
wounds taken at Trafalgar. No, her husband had really
died of regret, of guilt over what he had conspired with
her father to accomplish, of what he had caused.

Yet still, the officer had come all this way and wished to
see her. Therefore, she would of course grant him permission. After all, she really had no other choice. Quickly
Claire crossed to her rosewood escritoire and seated herself
before it, then withdrew parchment, quill, and an ink bottle
from the drawer beneath. However, dipping the quill into
the inkwell, she paused.

Where was it he wrote he was staying? she thought to
herself. Ah, yes, the Rose and Shadow, she saw at a glance
while aligning the paper to the angle of her hand.

And to whom is my response to be addressed? she next
wondered, again looking.

At the instant the viscountess saw the signature, tears
welled, spilled, freely flowed over her fire-blushed cheeks.


*Derrick.*

Here, in Winchcombe.

Weakened, trembling, Claire slowly leaned back against
her chair.

*Derrick,* she repeated, a sudden wave of warmth washing
over her at the simple intimacy of allowing herself, after
five long years, to merely think the beloved word. *Derrick.*
Just to picture him again, Claire all but whispered ...
his face, his hands; to once again recall his voice's deep,
rumbling sound. *Derrick. You've come back.*

Slowly, the viscountess's face dropped into the cup of her palms.

And remembrances came . . . of how it had been in the last week before he had left . . . of his wrenching devastation when she had told him she could not marry him . . . of her father's demands and Philip's complicity. Within days he had been gone and her heart with him. She had never thought to see him again.

Yet he had come. Not by choice, she quickly qualified, at last withdrawing a handkerchief from her sleeve to capture a rolling tear. No, never by choice. She was sensible enough of his pride to know that nothing would have forced him to return short of his strong sense of duty—and it *was* duty that had brought him back to the village. She had no doubt of that. He would not actually be wishing to see her, therefore, she reasoned, and suddenly her features wrenched. Not wishing to? He would despise the very concept, she admitted, her eyes releasing a new hot freshet. Still, his duty demanded that he had to, did it not? she reconsidered, again blotting her lids. As a result, he would have to converse with her. And that meant that there was yet a chance . . .

But was there? She had devastated him with her refusal five years ago. She knew that of a certainty because it had devastated her as well. Would he even allow her, therefore, to utter more than just the obligatory word of appreciation for his duly performed duty before he once more fled from her? She had to believe that he would . . . that somehow he had not lost every remnant of what he had once felt, that he would not seek to punish her, that somehow he would not, this time, reject *her* instead.

But she would have to be very careful; there was no question of that. Her father still was obsessed of his ambitions. If she had ever misdoubted that, she had only to look around her. She had no illusions concerning what he, not two months after her husband's death, was even now abetting on behalf of the earl. No hint of Derrick's presence could come under his notice, therefore, or she was certain her father would find yet another way to put a period to all her desires. She would have to be discreet, she acknowledged; careful not to meet with him where word of it might enter the wrong ears.

That meant that Clarendon Manor was out of the question, of course. The servants were her father's and would report any of her actions, she considered, absently brushing her quill back and forth over the underside of her chin; likewise, for the same reason she could not invite Derrick to her own home at Ash Park. Nor, given her father's influence in the community, could she really trust in the discretion of her friends. Therefore, only one alternative remained to her, she concluded: to meet at his quarters. She would write and ask him to reserve a private parlor at the Rose and Shadow for the morrow. No matter if the propriety of her decision was questionable, she vowed, straightening her spine; no matter that she put herself at risk. She would not let this final chance escape her. No, if Captain Derrick Palmer could not safely come to her, she determined, she would quite simply go to him.

That decided, her response was quickly penned.

"Well, now, there ye are," Mr. Bates exclaimed when the captain entered the bustle of the tap room a short time later. "Rested up a bit, are ye?" he asked, fitting a glass beneath the spigot protruding from one of the nearby casks and draining a bumper. "How's that leg?"

"Better, thanks to that foul-smelling poultice, I am loathe to admit," the captain replied with a smile, easing himself into one of the room's well-used chairs.

"My mother's recipe," the innkeeper laughed, setting the glass of dark beer down on the table adjacent to the captain's chair. "Drink up, lads," he then said to the room at large. "Next one's on the house in honor of the captain here who made it through Trafalgar."

"Here, here!" cried several, looking up from their game of hazard near the casks.

"To the captain!" toasted one, lifting high his glass.

"To Lord Nelson, God bless 'im!"

"You old pinchpenny!" shouted out another. "Only *one* round, Mr. Bates?"

While the laughter ricocheted about the room, unexpectedly, the tiny gray kitten jumped up onto the captain's lap.

"Back again, are you?" Derrick commented, two fingers ruffling the fur between the kitten's ears, his soft question passing unnoticed beneath the shuffled progress of the tap room's patrons toward Mr. Bates' ale casks.

In response, the kitten cleansed a paw, then, her frail form vibrating, circled and settled within the cup of one pantaloon's crease.

Not long after, one of the stooped elders absorbing the heat from the huge hearth wheezed, "What was it like, boy?"

The captain glanced upward; across the tap room, attention focused upon him. Conversation faded into an expectant hush.

Slowly, for comfort's sake and so as not to disturb the sleeping kitten, the captain raised his wounded leg and settled it upon an adjacent chair. "Do you know, sirs," he began in his deep, warm timbre, "that for the last two years before his death, Lord Nelson never once set foot upon land?"

"By the saints," Mr. Bates murmured for all of them after a lengthy pause.

"Imagine it, gentlemen," the captain continued. "For two years he alone carried the weight of England. He, as well as Napoleon, knew all too well that the Royal Navy was all that stood between the French and England's complete destruction. All it would take would be one mistake on his part . . . one miscalculation . . . one error in his evaluation of intelligence, and we would all be sitting here sipping glasses of watered-down bordeaux instead of bumpers of this fine English stout. Yet his lordship shouldered the burden. For two years, gentlemen, he hemmed the French fleet in, sailing, always sailing, to cover each of the fleet's escape routes."

"But they did escape, did they not, sir?" a younger man asked, coming to sit beside him, the disturbance rousing the kitten just enough to start her paws alternately pushing into the captain's taut abdomen.

"Yes, early in this very year," Derrick responded. "Napoleon and his admiral, Villeneuve, devised a set of feints designed to deceive Lord Nelson and permit their escape. You see, Napoleon knew that in order for him to defeat England, he had to gain control of the Channel, and he could not manage that without his fleet."

"But our Navy was there," one of the gamblers offered.

"The very reason why Napoleon next devised a way to draw them off," the captain told them. "It was his and Villeneuve's idea for the French fleet to first break free of Nelson's guard through deception, then, once free, to sail across the Atlantic—drawing off our fleet from its protection of the island—and, after joining up with their allies, the Spanish, to double back again and take control of the Channel, assuring the ability of French troops to cross into England from Boulogne."

"Bastards!" someone spat out from near the fire.

"Yet it was a brilliant plan," the captain admitted. "It's only flaw, aside from the condition of the French ships, was the fact that it did not take into account Lord Nelson, an even more brilliant man."

"Here, here!" several reprised.

"Tell us what he did, lad, tell us what he did!"

"Somehow, out of dozens of conflicting reports, the

admiral was able to piece together what the French planned. Following his instincts, he pursued the French all the way to the West Indies, resupplied—when his adversaries did so only inadequately—then followed them back across the Atlantic again. Our British ships successfully turned them from the Channel, as you no doubt know. Nelson then pursued Villeneuve to Cadiz."

"Is that when he devised his trick?" a young lad asked from the dark corner he had chosen to tease a broom straw in front of several rapt cats.

"So you know about that, do you?" the captain responded with a broad smile, giving the gray kitten a stroke and a soft pat. "Well, lad, it is indeed. And the deuce of a trick it was, too. Damme, if the admiral didn't surprise us all with it!"

"What did he do?" several of his listeners asked.

Softly, the captain chuckled. "I am persuaded you all must know that in the usual course of sea battles, both sides position themselves side-by-side in long lines, then blast away into each others' broadsides. In his brilliance, however, the admiral abandoned this tactic."

"He sailed *into* the French instead!" the youth burst out.

"That he did, lad," the captain grinned, tracing the pattern with his hand. "First he formed his ships into two divisions. Then he signaled us all from the *Victory*, 'England expects every man will do his duty.' That done, he next bid us to mark our adversaries and fall off the wind. When we had all done so and turned, he boldly sent us straight into them."

For several moments, the only sound heard in the tap room was the loud ticking of the mantel clock.

And then the entire room burst into cheers.

At last, Mr. Bates quieted. "Tell us of the admiral, lad," he requested above the remnant enthusiasm of the others.

"He was shot from the mast-head of the *Redoubtable* in

the early afternoon," the captain told them on a quiet sigh. "His spine was shattered. He was carried below decks while the battle was still raging. Several hours later, his fleet's victory was reported to him. Upon hearing of it, he died of his wound."

"And you, sir?" asked the youth, folding his legs beneath his lap of kittens. "How were you wounded?"

"That is an impertinence, Thomas," Mr. Bates scolded.

Yet the captain did not take offense. "I was hit during the explosion of one of Mr. Shrapnel's shells on board the *Triumph.*"

"Shrapnel's! But he's one of ours, is he not!" one of the gamblers cried.

"Yes, and a favorite of Wellington," the captain smiled before shaking his head. "I have no idea how the French fleet laid hands on the shells. I can only guess that some of the ordnance must have been smuggled into their hands by French agents. At any rate, a great many good men were killed that day because of them."

"The viscount," Mr. Bates concluded, bringing the captain another foam-topped glass.

"Yes," he nodded, lowering his gaze. "He threw himself in front of me when we heard the round's incoming whine, taking the full force of the explosion." Suddenly the captain looked up. "Let it be known to all of you . . . to every man here . . . to every citizen of Winchcombe, gentlemen. It is because of the viscount's heroism that I still draw breath."

"To the viscount, then, lads," Mr. Bates charged them, standing to attention, holding his glass high.

"To the viscount," the assembly repeated, standing, too; poignantly giving one of their own fallen the honor he had selflessly earned.

As they were settling again, Mr. Rawlins slipped through the door to the tap room, then pressed the viscountess's reply into his master's hands.

# Chapter Three

During the night, a change in the wind brought a touch of warmth to the Isbourne valley, chasing the tawny owls from their nests to hunt for voles, blowing away the midnight sky's ragged collection of blue-tinged clouds. By midmorning of the following day, the inn yard had been ground into a muddy mire. Snow sagged along the length of the bay windows' festive garlands; icicles leaked from between the roof's ancient slates. And in one of the Rose and Shadow's private parlors, Captain Palmer, adjusting the fit of his coat for the thousandth time, paced.

What was he to say to her? he wondered, pausing long enough to take up his glass of porter from a small table at the room's center and toss down a quick swig. Deuce take it, what does a man say to the woman who betrayed his trust after five long years? More to the point, why should he even care what he said? And yet it could not be denied that he did.

Because the woman was Claire, of course. Because, once, he had settled his dreams on her. Because, once, very long ago, she had been his own heart. Yet even that would not signify, he allowed, turning his head, fingering aside the stab of his collar point. The difficulty lay in the fact that, after five years, she still was.

Then, suddenly, as if he had conjured her, she was there, poised within the entrance, her eyes huge, expectant, above her shapely nose; her lips parted. And she was lovely, he quickly evaluated, chewing on his inner cheek. Every bit as lovely as the last time he had seen her; every bit of it, deuce take it.

"Hello, Derrick," Claire whispered, starting forward, her slowly formed smile tentative above the snug fit of her mourning coat, dark curls he had once caressed wildly defiant beneath her black velvet hat.

At the sound of her voice, old pain knifed through the captain's heart. He stiffened, narrowed his gaze; aside his wound, a fist tightly clenched. In that moment, he wished to be anywhere other than the Rose and Shadow Inn. After five long years, she was again standing before him, looking at him in that same way she had always done, with that same tilt of her head. Perspiration beaded on his forehead; trickled down his ribs.

He, too, started forward. Unlike the viscountess, however, the captain was bent upon making for his ship.

Yet at the exact moment his boot inched forward, the gray kitten suddenly leaped straight down from the wooden chandelier above him onto his gold braided epaulet.

The captain rebounded high into the air.

Startled as well, enchanted by the surprise, Claire began to laugh.

"Well, I have met your midshipman, Derrick," she at last declared, her voice warm with mirth, "but what is this one's rank?" she completed, reaching out to carefully disengage what seemed to be hundreds of tiny claws from the braid, then drawing the rumbling creature away to cuddle it close to her black woolen bodice.

"Stowaway," the captain responded gruffly while he brushed composure back into his uniform, his lips, too, quirking into a half-grin in spite of his determination for it not to happen, his brows losing their downward slant.

Once more the viscountess's smile blazed. "And what is this?" she again inquired, fingering the makeshift collar.

"Mistletoe, my lady," Derrick replied, giving the kitten a stroke with his large finger. "I imagine Mr. Bates is responsible for that."

"I see. And . . . who is responsible for your calling me 'my lady?'" she asked softly, looking up at him, capturing his gaze.

"I should think you are, madam . . . by your own choice," Derrick replied, sobering instantly, turning his back to escape her regard, easing his return to his porter glass.

"I had no choice," Claire countered softly, following, "and so I would have told you if you had not run from me that day."

Slowly, the captain replaced his glass and turned to face her. "What do you mean?"

"Did it never once occur to you that there might be a reason for my unexpected refusal?" she whispered, her lids coloring faintly with emotion. "My father forbade me to accept you."

Pensive for a moment, the captain then shook his head. "The woman I knew five years ago would have defied him," he bit out, again turning away.

"And so I did," Claire insisted, "but . . ."

"But what, madam? . . ." the captain interrupted, twisting toward her again, his cobalt gaze connecting with hers like a whiplash, "but the baron threatened to cut you off without a penny? You knew I could support you. Why did you not come to me?"

"Papa made no threats, Derrick, only statements. And I tried to come to you, but you had gone to the sheep auction in Chipping Camden," she explained.

"Then why did you not go to Philip, tell him of your father's *statements,* and ask for his help?" he asked, his eyes still snapping.

"I did!" Claire cried, freeing one arm from its support of the kitten to stretch it out imploringly toward him. "I did go to him. But what I did not realize . . ." she breathed, clutching the tiny creature's softness again while she struggled to speak, "was that he . . ."

". . . Yes, madam?" the captain asked, still coldly, yet with a wary nudge.

"What I did not realize was that Philip was in league with my father . . . that he had been all along," she finally responded, tucking the kitten even more tightly beneath her chin before she sank into one of the table's rude, windsor chairs.

After a few moments, the captain rested a row of knuckles upon the table. "I think you had better explain," he commanded, memory flashing behind his eyes . . . of the three of them as children growing up together . . . of the viscount saving his life.

"Derrick, Papa would not allow our marriage because of his desire that his descendants should be titled," she told him softly. "Moreover, never once did he indicate that to me, nor the fact that from the time Philip was in short coats, for that sole reason he had been selected by Papa to become his son-in-law. I also did not know that Papa, years before my come-out, had not only told Philip of his desires, but actually betrothed me to him. When I went to Philip that day, he . . . he . . ."

"He what, madam?" Derrick asked softly, rigidly. Then, more firmly he demanded, "What did Philip do?"

"He told me what Papa had done . . . that he was my betrothed," she whispered, her blue eyes flooding, leaking onto her flushed cheeks. "H-He said that he had the right . . ."

"Devil take it, madam! . . ." Derrick at last cried, seizing her shoulders and dragging her to her feet, "what happened?"

"He . . . forced . . ."

Instantly, Claire was crushed against rows of golden braid.

"My God! . . ." Derrick breathed, drawing her even closer, protectively curving himself about her slight frame.

"Derrick . . ." Claire returned, feeling that at last she had come home, her lips brushing the captain's neck, tasting it, even as she spoke.

Imprisoned between them, the kitten complained loudly, then, altogether rag-manneredly, began to twist and squirm.

"Do you see why I could not tell you of it?" Claire asked some moments later after the two had seated themselves at the table, taken a dish of tea, and the kitten had once more been cuddled into complacency within the folds of the viscountess's black bombazine.

"Because, had I known, I would have killed him."

Claire followed this pronouncement with a soft smile. "No, because I was in disgrace, Derrick."

"There is no disgrace in what could not be prevented!" the captain exploded, shooting from his chair.

"Yet I was false to you," Claire quietly confessed. "Can you forgive me?" she ventured softly, looking up at him. "Can you ever understand?"

"Yes . . . of course. Of course I can," the captain stated more firmly as, dropping once again into his chair, he realized that, indeed, he already had. "Yet at the same time, I simply cannot credit it. As you, I have known Philip since we were in leading strings. How could he have done such a monstrous thing? More, knowing what was between us . . . what he had done to you . . . why did he still ask to serve under me?"

"Guilt," Claire told him softly. "Regret of his betrayal of our friendship. From the beginning, it consumed him. After we were married, he was never . . . that is, we never . . ."

Drawing in a deep breath, the captain stiffened. "Devil a bit," he murmured, his gaze growing dark with understanding. "So that is why he took the Shrapnel."

"What?" the viscountess asked, blinking away some of the moisture riding her lids.

"That is what I came to tell you," Derrick told her, enfolding one of her hands. "Philip was fatally wounded because he threw himself between me and one of the Shrapnel's the French were using against us. If he had not, of the two of us, I would have been the one to die, madam. As it was, I took only a leg wound."

"Oh, Derrick, he was trying to set things right, was he not?" Claire breathed.

"It seems so."

"And has he?"

Slowly the captain stood and crossed to the window. "It has been five years, my lady," he said roughly, bracing a hand against the white painted frame.

"Yes," the viscountess whispered, gently stroking the sleeping kitten, feeling her hopes fade.

Hearing the dejection in her voice, the captain surreptitiously studied Claire out of the corner of his eye. Her head was bowed; her shoulders had shoved folds into the bodice of her expertly fitted pelisse.

And his heart paused.

"Of course, I do have a week or two before I have to return to my ship . . ." he finally commented.

Startled, Claire glanced up at him.

". . . Therefore, there is really no compelling reason why I must be quickly away. Too, I have considered the possibility that the country air might be beneficial to my injury, not to mention Mr. Bates' comfrey poultices."

"Shall you stay then?" Claire whispered, her breath all but ceasing, persuaded that in the next few moments her heart was going to pound its way out of her chest.

Still staring out at the inn yard, the captain nodded and pursed his lips. "I believe I shall, for the nonce, at any rate. And . . . if we should happen to meet . . ." he added, setting the suggestion adrift against the window's ice-rimmed panes of wavy crown glass.

Catching hold of it, her spirits rising, Claire's mind flew into action, quickly cataloguing how she might make such a thing come about without attracting the village's notice.

". . . Then it should probably be at Hailes," she suddenly, decisively, completed. "I often go to the ruins during Christmastide."

"Do you?" the captain queried, turning back toward the room. "As it happens, so did I in years past. And often with an *al fresco* meal."

Claire released a light, lovely laugh. "I cannot say that I have ever picnicked in December," she chuckled.

"Pity. Only consider the advantages, madam," the captain grinned. "It is true that one may have to thaw one's sliced beef between one's hands, but the wine is nicely chilled."

"I can certainly see that the idea has vast appeal," Claire again laughed. "Perhaps we shall see one another then," she added, rising and placing the kitten, still curled, upon the warmth lingering on her seat. "Good day, Derrick," she offered, extending her hand, "and thank you for what you have told me."

"Good day, my lady," he responded, making his leg.

Near the door, the viscountess paused.

"Claire," he quickly corrected, yielding to the authority of her tipped head.

# Chapter Four

"Where the devil is she?" Clayton demanded the following morning, throwing open the door and, with one foot carefully aligned in front of the other, striding into the manor's study.

Startled by the interruption, the baron looked up from his ledger. "That will be all for now, Dawes," he said, glancing next toward the tall butler standing at his elbow.

"Very good, sir," Dawes replied, bowing himself unobtrusively away from his master's presence.

"I have looked everywhere," complained the earl, fading onto a scroll-armed sofa placed near the fire. "I wish her company while I take my morning gallop."

"Growing eager, are you?" Fillmore smiled, wiping his quill. "Well, patience, my lord, patience. I assure you the wait shall be worth it. No doubt Claire is about one of her 'little charities' as you call them . . . or perhaps the preparations for our ball. Christmas Eve is only three days away, don't y' know."

"Well I know it," Clayton groused. "It was to be the

evening you announced our betrothal, if you recall. And yet the lady seems no closer to accepting my suit than when I first arrived. You said she would be willing, Fillmore.''

"And so she shall be, sir," replied the baron, swinging his abdomen away from the edge of his desk before rising and pouring them both a cup of Armagnac-braced nog, "if not in the next several days, certainly on the evening of the ball."

"How can you be so certain?" the earl questioned, accepting the refreshment, peering at the baron through his quizzing glass.

"Why, because I shall see to it," Fillmore replied, again seating himself at his desk, "or rather you shall. Cease your megrims, sir," he admonished, again taking up his quill. "I know what to do to assure Claire's compliance should it become necessary."

"And it will work?" the earl asked, dabbing a perfumed handkerchief at the meandering of perspiration wilting the points of his collar.

"It will, my lord. You may rely upon it."

Dismissing the matter, the baron bent his graying head and once more returned to his ledger.

"I did no such thing, sir," Claire denied with a laugh, one arm laced through the captain's, the other carefully holding the skirt of her black kerseymere riding habit out of the collected snow while the two wandered among the graceful, ruined arches of Hailes, an eight-hundred-year-old abbey. "I did not put frogs in your tutor's bed. Goodness, I only had seven years in my dish at the time! Such behavior would have been the outside of enough," she insisted, an unseasonably balmy breeze lifting several charming curls from their constant caress of her slim neck.

"Well, I certainly did not do it," the captain vowed after a time of watching the dance, tossing his walking stick up to catch it again with his hand, "though I paid the price for the deed. Old Algood broke a cane over my back that day."

"Which you likely deserved for some other infraction that had gone unpunished," Claire ventured, brushing a bit of snow off one of the loose stones still receiving support in spite of the abbey's crumbling.

"Must have been Philip, then."

"For shame, Derrick, blaming a man who cannot come to his own defense," Claire chided. "Besides, Philip detested frogs."

"Then how did the two get there?" the captain asked, rubbing at his wound, coming to a halt within a series of arches that had once been the abbey's main sanctuary.

"We shall probably never know," Claire proclaimed, looking admiringly at the remains of the floor's heraldic tiles. "And, for your information, sir, there were not two frogs, but three."

The captain's brows soared.

"Claire . . ." he growled just before his brows' beetle.

Grinning widely, the viscountess quickly sidestepped his implied temper.

"Oh, Derrick," she next divertingly exclaimed, her pale blue eyes sparkling with happiness as she twirled about on the snow and threw her arms wide, "did I not tell you that this is the best of seasons to visit here? Listen! Can you not even now hear beautiful Christmas masses being sung by ancient choirs?"

The captain listened.

"My apologies, madam, but all I hear is the crack of Algood's cane," he said after a short time, again beginning to limp in her direction.

"Pish tosh," Claire scolded, once more scooting out of reach. "Do you know about this place, sir?" she asked, again looking about. "It was built by Henry the Third's brother, Richard, Earl of Cornwall, in praise of his having survived a shipwreck. Once, Richard's son, Edmund, presented the abbey with a phial of blood he claimed was Christ's."

"Which it was not, of course," the captain assumed.

"Unhappily. Shall we sit down for awhile?" she suggested sympathetically, again noting his labored step. "I am persuaded that your wound is troubling you a bit, is it not?"

"A short rest would not be amiss," the captain allowed with a nod, taking her elbow, then directing her toward a sheltered corner of the ruin decorated with portions of faded medieval artwork. "How would this do? We shall ask Mr. Rawlins to bring the basket along and spread a blanket for us."

"Excellent," Claire replied with a smile even as the captain turned and motioned for the midshipman, who had been following at a discreet distance.

Several moments later, comfortably seated, the captain reached over and opened the small withy basket lid. Inside, the gray kitten lay curled fast asleep atop a scattering of Rose and Shadow serviettes.

"Lud . . . Stowaway!" the captain murmured within his half-smile, carefully lifting the little one onto his warm lap. "This is getting to be beyond anything."

"She's darling, isn't she?" Claire noted, glancing up at him with a wide smile, giving the top of the kitten's ear a flick which then sent it into a spasmodic twitch. "Or is it a she?"

"Aren't all of them?" Derrick replied, returning to her a quick grin. "What I cannot fathom is how she got in there," he commented, fingering aside the mistletoe collar and scratching beneath her chin. "I saw them pack this basket myself."

"In exactly the same way those frogs got into Mr. Algood's bed," Claire offered in reply, turning aside to unpack the basket, her eyes impish above the quirk of her lips, "if I were to guess."

The captain's bark of laughter awakened the little mite. By way of an apology, he gave her his knuckle to lick.

At last, his chuckles dissipating, he looked at Claire. "You are incorrigible, you know," he murmured, all his pleasure in the day, in her company, gleaming in his eyes, "and always have been."

"I know," Claire answered remorsefully before returning a mischievous smile.

Enthralled by the sight of her, the captain's levity slowly died.

"You are also beautiful ..." he told her softly, suddenly—the declaration coming out of nowhere; his whole body tensing, quieting, all at the same time.

Claire's smile gentled with surprise. Caught by the fierceness of his gaze, she stared at him ... until he moved, beginning to lean toward her gradually, languidly. Suddenly, his lips were but inches from hers.

"Am I?" she breathed.

The captain nodded. ". . . And you are mine," he whispered, slowly, so slowly closing the distance between their hearts.

At that moment, however, the kitten repaid the captain's inattention by pausing in its cleansing of his knuckle to drive home several of its tiny feline swords.

"Ouch!" the captain exclaimed, just as suddenly jerking back to his place.

"Derrick, don't you dare!" Claire cried with a laugh, neatly parrying his ire.

Reluctantly, the captain subsided. "Devil a bit! Do you recall that phial of blood you said Sir Edmund tried to fob off on Hailes?" he asked, carefully inspecting his punctures, rubbing at the wounds.

"Yes, Derrick," she replied, now quite busily opening glass jars and oiled papers, wisely masking her mirth.

"Well go find it, if you please," he commanded. "Here is more to add to it."

"You are being ridiculous, you know. Eat this instead," Claire suggested, diverting him with a laden plate.

Mollified but still grumbling, the captain took her offering, then bit into a breast of grouse.

Contentedly sitting beside him, Claire filled her own plate and observed him with furtive glances—the way his lashes sparkled, the movement of his muscles as he chewed—her smile soft in the ancient shadows of the afternoon. He had said she belonged to him, she secretly smiled.

It had not been a mistake, had it? she suddenly fretted. He *had* said she belonged to him, had he not? Or had he?

No, she had heard him herself. He *had* said the words, she more moderately decided.

Still she had to be careful, she immediately reprised. Her father was a powerful man in the valley no matter his lowness of rank; she could not risk his intelligence of the captain's return. Therefore, she would make no further arrangements to see him until after the hectic pace of the yuletide season had passed . . . well, at least until after the Christmas ball. She knew all too well what could happen. By no means could she yet let down her guard.

Lost in her thoughts, she did not see the kitten's head, ruffle-furred, pop up past the rim of the captain's plate. For that reason, too, she also did not notice the sudden swivel of its tiny countenance in her direction; more, she was never sensible of the very old knowledge that lived in its steady gaze.

"Oh, excellent, Dawes!" Claire pronounced later that afternoon in the Clarendon Manor ball room. "That will make the grandest of yule logs for the Christmas ball. Do have the men lay it beside the hearth, will you? At the moment, Bess needs your help stringing the garlands.''

"Very good, my lady," Dawes replied, directing the several straining footmen to proceed forward.

"Tizzy," Claire next directed one of the busy maids, "you may leave off your polishing for the moment. Come help me arrange these flowers."

"As you wish, milady," Tizzy replied, hurrying to do her mistress's bidding. "And shall you wish to use this to lay the tables?" she asked after she had joined her, fingering several bolts of shimmering cloth.

"No," Claire responded, running a fingernail over the fabric's richness as well, "this shot silk shall be draped in various places about the room. I want it to look as if an ice storm has occurred inside."

"Which is the reason, of course, milady," Tizzy giggled, "why you wished for such a big yule log."

"There you are, my dear," Clayton suddenly called from the doorway, interrupting—completely fizzling, if the truth be known—Claire's light laugh over Tizzy's jest.

At the earl's entrance, Claire drew in a fortifying breath. "My lord," she intoned, dipping into a curtsey.

"Here now," he added upon reaching her, seizing, then raising her up by her hands, "surely there can no longer be any need for that between us, can there? . . . given the closeness that has grown between us over the past six weeks?"

"You are too kind, sir," Claire responded, firmly dragging her fingers from his grasp. "Goodness, can it truly be six weeks since you came to visit us? Why, how remiss of us to delay you here for so long! Your estates must be positively foundering," she assessed, taking up the bolt of shot silk into her arms, then holding it like an impenetrable barrier against her breast. "I vow, my lord, as much as we may rejoice in your company, I am persuaded that once

Twelfth Night has come we cannot in good conscience ask you to remain longer in Winchcombe.''

"Claire!" her father cried sharply, pausing in the doorway to present his admonition.

"Yes, Papa?" Claire instantly responded, spinning about.

"Shall you now have Clayton thinking that he is not welcome?" he blustered, reaching her side, his face unnaturally mottled between his thick, wiry sideburns. "And put down that cloth."

"Nonsense," Claire replied to both suggestions, moving away with the bolt. "Besides, my opinion does not signify, does it? . . . since my presence at the Manor is only due to my promise to aid you in the preparations for the yuletide festivities, and his lordship is *your* guest? And I cannot put the cloth down, Papa. I have only this day in which to complete these decorations."

"One day? Whyever? . . ." the baron sputtered, throwing up his hands.

". . . Because I must be at the Sudeley Castle Fair on the morrow," Claire interjected, giving the bolt to one of the nearby footmen, unrolling a portion, then envisioning how it might look as a backdrop for the champagne fountain. "The following day, of course, is the Lord's, and must rightly be spent at Sunday service. Now if you will excuse me, gentlemen . . ." she finished, again beginning to instruct the servants.

"I shall talk to her," Fillmore assured the earl *sotto voce,* a pent-up breath gushing from his broad nose.

"It will do no good, I tell you," Clayton complained, flourishing a handkerchief over his pale, thin lips. "Look at her! She hates me! Fillmore, you promised!"

"I did, indeed, my lord . . . and, I assure you, I will fulfill my oath," the baron comforted, firmly ushering his guest toward the door. "Only give me my few moments, sir. Wait for me in the drawing room. All will be well."

After the earl had disappeared, Fillmore turned back

toward his daughter. "Claire," he pronounced stonily, "I wish to speak with you. In my study." Then, pivoting once again, he exited the room.

Rewrapping the bolt of silk, Claire laid it upon an adjacent buhl table and slowly followed her father into the hall.

The baron was already standing at his desk when Claire arrived.

"Be seated," he instructed when she appeared in the entrance, "and kindly close the door."

"Of course, Papa," she said, doing his bidding before crossing to the scroll-armed sofa, sitting down upon it, then adjusting her shawl. "What did you wish to speak to me about?"

"Your duty to our line," he informed her, lowering his corpulence, too, into the sigh of his desk's leather chair.

"Odd," Claire remarked, fanning herself. "I seem to recall having this conversation before."

"Hardly to your detriment," her father stated. "Owing to me, you are now a viscountess."

"Lacking a viscount," Claire countered. "Also owing to you. Very good, Papa."

Across the desk, Fillmore's flesh again mottled. "Watch your tongue!"

"I am only speaking the truth," Claire told him levelly. "It is true that because of your schemes, Philip and I were forced to marry. But it is also true that because of what you condoned, we had no issue; more, we never would have."

"Only because Philip was weak and could not abandon a meaningless childhood friendship with a commoner to his own good! . . ." the baron insisted, pounding upon his desk, "because you, Claire, were too damnably strong!"

"And still am, Papa," Claire stated softly, rising. "Do

not think that I am insensible of what you plan. I will not marry the earl.''

''His offer is forthcoming,'' her father told her flatly, rounding his desk and taking hold of the handle of the door. ''You will accept it.''

''I will not.''

''You will,'' the baron countered ominously, ''if you know what is good for you.''

''I am no longer a child!'' Claire cried. ''This time I shall not let you force me. I swear it!''

Yet long after her father had left her, Claire was convulsed with chills.

# Chapter Five

"And where be ye off to this fine day, sir?" Mr. Bates called from the tap room the following morning upon seeing the captain descend the stairs.

"To Clarendon Manor," the captain replied with a slow smile, stepping into the heavy pungency of onions, tobacco, and roasting mutton hinting of the mid-day meal. "I am persuaded that it is past time I paid my respects to Lord Fillmore."

"Indeed . . . oh, but you shan't find him there, I fear," the innkeeper informed him, leaning his rush broom against one of the half-timbers, then wading toward him through a gauntlet of kittens intent upon shredding his hose.

"No?" the captain replied, watching the kittens with amusement, absently glancing about for Stowaway.

"I think not, sir. I'd wager the whole household shall be at the Sudeley Castle fair," Mr. Bates told him, bustling to a stop at his side. "There'd be his lordship . . ." he elaborated, counting upon his fingers, "that Earl of Clayton what's been his houseguest for . . . how many weeks has it been? Well, the whole lot of 'em, I vow.''

"And her ladyship?" the captain asked.

"Oh, Miss Claire for certain. Why, her ladyship's at the head of it, ye ken."

"Is she?"

"Thought up the whole scheme for financing the restoration," Mr. Bates proudly smiled.

"Then I misdoubt I shall be paying my respects instead with my pocket," the captain concluded with a rueful chuckle, firming his bicorn upon his Bedford crop while he started for the door.

"That ye will, sir," the innkeeper agreed. "Take care now."

"I shall, Mr. Bates," the captain replied, turning to wave goodbye beside Mr. Rawlins, who had been awaiting his appearance with Spritsail.

Nearby, however, seizing the advantage given it by its prey's inattention, the gray kitten leaped out from the shadow of the horse trough, raced forward, then, springing, tightly fastened all four paws about the captain's leg.

"Ho, little nubbin!" the captain cried when the kitten's rear paws began to furiously pedal against his unmentionables and ten tiny foreclaws bit into his knee. "Where have you been?" he asked, bending down and lifting the still-boxing creature into his embrace. "Have you tired of mice and decided to go after bigger game?"

Suddenly ceasing its struggles to stare raptly up at the captain, the kitten slowly stretched out a paw and placed it aside his cheek.

Chuckling softly, the captain sighed, "Very well, I yield. You have bested me, little one. *Touché.*"

Moments later, he swung gracefully into Spritsail's saddle, galloped out of the inn yard, then spurred the gelding onto the Vineyard Street bridge crossing the Isbourne. Contentedly riding the captain's epaulet, the kitten elevated its nose and flared its nostrils; a seeking, an homage to the clear, winter breeze.

Less than an hour later, the castle appeared in the distance at the top of a slight rise in the rolling terrain. Halting momentarily, the captain studied the familiar crenelated outline of the Portmare Tower to the right of the castle's arched entrance, a tower named for the French admiral whom Sudeley's fifteenth century owner had once imprisoned there, then continued on to the large rope paddock which had been constructed not far from the castle's western curtain wall.

Dismounting, he gave Spritsail over to the care of a young lad happily earning extra pennies in the service, then struck off toward the fair's neatly aligned collection of brightly striped tents and wooden booths. The twentieth part of a moment later, he was enveloped by the milling crowd.

Disdainful of the whole of it, the kitten, still perched like royalty upon his shoulder, occasionally cleaned needful portions of the captain's jaw.

"I tell you it is too early for the Mummers," complained the baron, standing with Claire and Clayton close to the lichen-mottled stone of the tower. "Shouldn't see them until Boxing Day."

"And so you shall, Papa," Claire countered, busily organizing a gathering of young girls into a circle for a clipping dance. "It was very kind in them to agree to perform their play for us twice this year, don't you think?"

"I am persuaded that once again you are being far too modest, my dear," Clayton broke in with a sweet smile. "Not a man in this village would refuse to change his ways were it to be required of him by you."

"How very kind in you, my lord," Claire politely responded, signaling for the girls to take each other's hands, "and how patient for you to await me so steadfastly. And with so much else occurring all about that is far more entertaining . . ."

"Nothing could be more entertaining than your company," Clayton magnanimously interjected.

". . . And so much food . . ."

"Hmm, yes . . ." Clayton commented, absently rubbing his abdomen as he began to scan the grounds. "It does smell simply divine. But where have you put it, my dear?"

"At the end of your nose should you choose to follow it," Claire muttered softly while she started the dance moving, "and should snuff not have rendered the path obscured."

"Claire . . ." the baron warned close beside her in a growl, all the while clapping to the rhythm of several accompanying flutes.

"You have only to follow the row of weavers' booths, sir," she quickly, and more loudly, amended, taking a moment from her own clapping to point off to her left. "Not far from the paddock you shall find stalls selling hot chestnuts, puddings, portions of our double Gloucester cheese, meat pies . . . and even a deer roasting on a spit."

"Capital!" Clayton exclaimed, twirling his quizzing glass. "What say we all be off, then?"

"Certainly go if you like," Claire told him. "I, however, must clear a place for the Mummers' performance in this sad crush, find someone to list the entrants in the horse race, and judge the women's chattering contest."

"Seems it shall have to be just the two of us, then, I suppose," the baron concluded, starting toward the booths.

"On the contrary, Papa," Claire called. "If you recall you agreed this year to judge the local ales."

Pulled up short, her father placed a pudgy finger aside

his chin. "So I did," he murmured. "Well, Clayton, you shall just have to accompany me instead."

"Perhaps a bit later, Fillmore," the earl returned, continuing on toward the paddock. "Did I hear you correctly, my dear? You did say roasted venison?" he called back just before he disappeared.

"Claire . . ." the baron began.

". . . The ale stalls are near the start of the race course, Papa," she quickly inserted.

Above a sharpened gaze, one of the baron's brows rose. "If I did not know better, my dear," he at last responded, "I might think you were trying to rid yourself of Clayton and me. But, of course, you are an intelligent woman . . ." he added, stroking a finger along her jaw, "certainly intelligent enough to realize that you never shall."

Watching her father's retreat, Claire stood for a few moments stilling her heart before she scurried away to gather wool sacks for the day's upcoming race.


The captain was just rounding a booth selling bottles of Day and Sons' Universal Medicine Chest for Disorders of Farm Animals when he spied Claire, amid loud applause and shouts of laughter, presenting a bladder of snuff to a round-faced dairy maid who had just proved that she could rattle on and on the longest. Pausing, he watched her enjoying the maid's pleasure in her dubious accomplishment, laughing just as brightly as the others, even bending once to embrace the ruddy-faced woman's neck.

He, too, smiled as he again started forward; in that moment, he was very glad he had overcome his forebodings and returned to the village of Winchcombe.

"Good morning," he greeting upon arriving at her side, his grin wide enough to allow entrance to an entire venison haunch.

Hearing his voice, Claire spun about. "Derrick!" she

gasped in dismay. "What in heaven's name are you doing here?"

Taken aback, the captain's brows soared. "Giving Stowaway an outing," he responded, reaching up to chuck the kitten under the chin. "To my mind, the grinding task of eliminating all those vermin at the Rose and Shadow has the poor thing looking a bit ... how shall I say it? ... gray."

In spite of her concern, Claire laughed. "Gray, indeed," she chided with a half-smile, taking the purring kitten into her arms. "I suppose next you shall tell me there is a worrisome leanness to her whiskers. Derrick, how did you know about this fair?" she again pursued, nervously glancing beyond his broad form.

"Claire, there are handbills for this event everywhere," Derrick replied, "not to mention the fact that I room with Mr. Bates, who a generation ago would have made a formidable town crier. As it happens, he told me about it when he learned that I was on my way to the manor to pay my respects to your father. He was certain it would be a wasted trip as you would all be here. Where is the baron, by the way?"

"Oh, somewhere about, I imagine," Claire quickly responded just before suddenly seizing his arm. "Actually, Derrick, I am quite relieved that you have come," she stated, frantically searching for somewhere to secrete him before he was seen.

"Are you?" he asked, his countenance brightening again with a lop-sided smile.

"Oh, yes. I have no one to organize the sled races, you see," she quickly improvised. "Would you help me?"

"Of course. However, I think it only proper first to speak with ..."

"Believe me, sir," Claire claimed, tugging him toward a gradual slope leading away from an adjacent booth occupied by a seller of the famous Whitney blankets, "whatever you have to say to my father can wait until later. For now, however . . ."

". . . Oh, Claire!" suddenly cried a portly woman bearing down upon them from the stalls of the ironmongers.

Applying a quick mental clamp to her frustration, Claire halted. "Yes, Mrs. Beckworth?" she pleasantly returned.

"My dear, I simply do not know what to tell them," the woman bemoaned upon reaching them, flourishing her handkerchief.

"Who?"

"The Mummers!" the woman exclaimed.

"What about them?" Claire stated. "They should already be performing."

"But that is just it, you see," Mrs. Beckworth responded. "They could not begin without their headdresses, and someone, it seems, has stolen them."

"Good heavens!" Claire exclaimed. "Have you set some of the townsfolk to looking for them?"

"Why, no," the woman told her, placing a finger upon her chin. "I never thought of that. Claire, my dear, you always have such good ideas."

For the twentieth part of a moment only, Claire closed her eyes.

"I fear I shall have to attend to this," she then apologized to the captain.

"Of course, you do. As a matter of fact, we shall both go," Derrick told her, this time taking her arm.

"No!" Claire immediately countered, remembering that the ale tasting was taking place in the vicinity of the Mummer's ground. "That is . . . you must certainly stay here and begin the sledding. Look there . . ." she gestured, "the children already await their contest. Do remain and see to it, will you, Derrick?" she coaxed, starting again toward the castle. "And promise me you shan't go anywhere else until I return for you. I shall be back in a trice."

Abandoned, the captain called out, "Claire, you still have Stowaway."

"Oh, dear, so I do," she returned distractedly, holding up the scrabbling kitten though not slowing her progress a whit. "Never mind, however. I shall take good care of her," she pronounced. "Shan't I, little one?" she continued with a smile, receiving a lick upon her nose. "Why, after I locate the Mummers' headdresses, I have in mind to buy you a fortifying micemeat pie. Of course, perhaps you would prefer a rat pudding boiled in milk."

The sled races, as one might have guessed, ended as soon as they began. Therefore, soon finding himself left to deal with his own restlessness, and in spite of the viscountess's admonition, the captain again began to wander about, after a time deciding that as long as Claire had not yet returned to claim him, he might as well stop by the paddock to judge how the young lad was caring for Spritsail.

Striding quickly to the roped-off area, he whistled softly. The gelding nickered in response, then trotted over for the carrot he knew his master always produced from his pocket.

"So the bay is yours, is he?" a tenor voice queried just to the captain's left.

A glance revealed a gentleman dressed in yellow nankeen inexpressibles and a bottle green cutaway rocking on his Wellingtons, studying the gelding.

"He is," Derrick replied, turning back to offer his treat.

"Looks to be a prime goer," Clayton evaluated, dropping his quizzing glass back onto his Waterfall before taking another bite of the pudding he had been holding behind his back within another thin slice of meat.

"He gets me where I need to go," Derrick stated, listening to the carrot's crunch, watching a dragonfly tip-toe over a fence post.

"Indeed. I am Clayton, by the way," the earl told him, extending a grease-soiled glove.

"Captain Palmer, my lord," Derrick completed, taking the offered hand and bending into a brief bow.

"Palmer, eh? Well, Captain Palmer, you seem to be the owner of perhaps the only horse here today that might possibly beat mine. Do you intend to race him?"

"No, my lord."

"Pity," the earl said around the chewing of his sausage. "No spirit in him, eh? Not like my Alabaster over there," he compared, pointing toward a prancing white gelding trying even as they watched to nip one of the handlers. "Well, it is as it should be, I suppose," he concluded with the glint of challenge in his gaze. "Bit of an embarrassment for you to be bested by me, what? . . . you being an officer in his majesty's Navy—a hero, I misdoubt—and me, merely one of the idle nobility."

"You may pass your life as you choose, my lord," Derrick told him after giving him another brief glance. "It is of no concern to me."

Tossing aside the rest of his pudding, the earl suddenly closed the distance between them and seized the captain's arm. "Come now, man," he cajoled. "Should you win, I shall make it worth your while."

Again the captain looked at him.

Moments later the two men were digging in their spurs to the explosion of the race's starting pistol.

At the same time that the sound was reverberating against the castle's curtain wall, the viscountess, having located the Mummers' headdresses and now hurrying to return to the sledding slope, found herself most vexingly waylaid yet again by the mayor's plea for help in his duties,

a request every villager within hearing distance knew was
nothing more than a wish to have an important personage
in attendance when his firstborn swept everyone else's sons
from the field in the woolsack race. No matter what the
reason, however, unable to escape, Claire tucked the kitten
inside her reticule, then, sighing with resignation, began
distributing heavy burlap bags.

It was as she was thus engaged that she suddenly spied
her father stumbling from the adjacent ale booths and
heading more or less straight for the horse track.

"Papa, where are you going?" she cried, quickly fobbing
her duty off on an unsuspecting bystander, then hurrying
to catch up.

"T' the race," the baron told her, pausing to wipe perspiration from his flushed face.

"The race? Which race?" Claire asked in a delaying
tactic, all the while dragging upon his elbow as she furiously
tried to imagine how far apart each who should be avoiding
the other might now be spaced.

"Th' horse race, of course," her father declared, starting
forward again. " 'S the only reason I came, don't y'know."

"Ah," Claire replied, rapidly considering that Clayton
*must* still be at the food stalls . . . Derrick at the slope . . .
happily, neither no where near the race course. "Very well,
Papa," she finally allowed, giving a relieved nod, "enjoy
the event."

"So good of you to give me your p'mission," the baron
commented with a slight, swaying bow.

"Goodness knows you have earned it," his daughter
evaluated, judging the color of his nose. "However, you
do know that it has already begun, do you not? I heard
the starting gun several minutes past."

"Catch th' finish of it, then," the baron pronounced,
once more weaving away.

Suddenly Claire's fingers flew to her lips. "Papa, perhaps
you had better wait for me," she exclaimed when her

father stumbled again and altogether flattened a yeoman farmer. "I shall only be a moment, after all," she added, smiling a rueful apology toward the man, then helping them both to their feet. "I have only to begin the woolsack race. Wait, Papa! Oh, Papa, do wait!"

Instantly comprehending that waiting was the last of her father's intentions, Claire quickly spun about, called out to the woolsack racers to make ready, then, after far too short a pause to be fair, dropped her handkerchief. The twentieth part of a moment later, the meadow looked for all the world as if the gate had just been opened on a pen which for the winter had been keeping the year's new spring lambs from a crop of bright green grass.

Coincidentally, at exactly the same time, too, the first of the contestants in the horse race galloped out from under the cover of the distant trees and began pounding toward the finish.

Again a roar went up. Responding to it, Claire whirled about just in time to see Clayton's Alabaster emerge from the beech copse to thunder after . . . good heavens, Derrick's gelding! And as if that bit of intelligence were not shocking enough, immediately after, she spied her father wobble into the thinning crowd, which was even then beginning to amass near the prize booth, to a position just adjacent to her where he could not help seeing who was in the lead even if he were sightless.

"Papa!" she gasped, pressing panicky fingers to her lips. "Good heavens, *now* what am I to do?"

In answer to her plea, the tiny gray kitten poked its head into the sunshine, leaped from her reticule, then sprang into the passing burlap bag of one of the energetically hopping woolsack race contestants.

At last the clamor quieted.

"Oh, Papa, are you all right?" Claire asked after the

mayor's son, unsure what evil had invaded his woolsack, had jumped, twisted, and squirmed so far off course that he had battered his way through the horse race onlookers straight onto the beleaguered baron. "Papa?"

"My apologies, milady!" the horrified young man offered for the hundredth time since he had scrambled out of the bedeviled sack. "I swear to you that I meant no harm, but . . . suddenly something was in there with me!"

"I know, James. See?" Claire replied, pointing to the peeking emergence of the kitten's head from beneath the burlap's lip. "There is your culprit. Yet the apology is rightfully mine. I am afraid the kitten was in my care when she took her notion to jump into your woolsack."

"Still, milady," the youth worried, "I have injured his lordship. He has not yet come around. Please allow me to do something to help."

The suggestion gave the viscountess pause.

This was the answer, she realized, the perfect solution to the whole bumblebroth. It would take several moments for the awarding of the horse race's first and second prizes, would it not? . . . ample time for her to spirit her father away to the manor none the wiser concerning Derrick's presence. And as for Clayton, what did it matter that the two had met? He had no way of knowing that she and Derrick had once loved one another . . . la, still did, she was convinced. All that remained, then, was to remove her father . . . that, of course, and the overwhelming task of insuring that Clayton never afterward mentioned to his host the name of the man he had raced!

"Very well," Claire at last smiled, "you may help me carry him home, if you will. Do you have a wagon?"

"Close by, milady," the youth nodded, instantly rising. "I shall fetch it."

"Excellent," Claire replied, cushioning her father's head. "Oh, and James? I shouldn't worry too much about his lordship's injuries if I were you. I strongly suspect they are due less to your collision than to the fact that my father rather enjoyed judging this year's casks.''

The youth softly smiled. ''Very good, milady,'' he then responded, taking his leave with a bow.

At the offer of a cushion from one of the villagers, Claire gratefully gave her father's head over to a more comfortable situation and arose, afterward glancing about for Stowaway.

''Where has she got off to now?'' she wondered.

Yet, mysteriously, even after a second search the kitten seemed to have simply vanished.


Not long after Claire and her father had left, just as the captain was pocketing his prize money and the vowels he had gained from Clayton near the finish line, the gray kitten again climbed up to perch upon one of his glossy Wellingtons.

''Stowaway!'' he exclaimed, glancing down at the sensation of extra weight. ''I thought you were with Claire. Where is she?'' he asked, hoisting the kitten up onto his shoulder again, then scanning about.

There was no answer of course. Yet the kitten gave what comfort it could by rubbing its tiny head against the firm flesh of the captain's cheek.

# *Chapter Six*

Sandwiched between her father and the earl, Claire entered their pew the following Sunday morning pleased with her success. It had taken a bit of doing, of course, and several deft changes of subject, but she had so far managed to keep hidden Derrick's presence from her father's household and, therefore, to extend the time he might remain in the village—time he wouldn't need, she admitted, if the nodcock would only hasten to drop the handkerchief and sweep her off to Portsmouth.

Yet she knew she must give him the necessary time. For five years he had thought her beneath contempt. For as long as necessary, therefore, she would have to continue to block and parry, delaying the confrontation that surely would occur as soon as her father learned of him. Assuming, of course, he wished to remain in Winchcombe for just a little longer, she fretted, lost in thought ... assuming that in spite of everything he was again coming to love her.

Then, suddenly, even as the thought tingled over her spine, the daydream spoke.

"Good morning!"

Starting, Fillmore and Clayton squared their shoulders and slowly turned.

As might be imagined, Claire more quickly spun about.

It was true, she thought with a wide-eyed blink. It had not been a flight of fancy. He *was* sitting on the pew directly behind her . . . dear heavens! in full sight of her father . . . adjusting his dark blue cutaway tails after laying his bicorn beside him on the polished mahogany.

Aghast, each for his own reason, the three stared at the captain, looking for all the world like three of the imps carved just behind them upon the choir screen.

The captain returned their regard with a pleasant smile.

"Derrick!" Claire finally gasped, clinging with gloved hands to the pew's high, straight back. "Whatever are you doing here?"

"Why do you seem to constantly ask me that? . . ." he countered with a grin, "and to disappear. Yesterday you seemed to go up in smoke. Which reminds me . . ." he added, pointing ahead, "doesn't that imp fashioned just above the font resemble Stowaway?"

"Derrick!" Claire pleaded softly, her pale blue eyes growing huge.

"In a moment, Claire. First I must greet your father. Good morning, sir," the captain offered, fully prepared for the reaction he was engendering, afterward murmuring toward Clayton, "my lord."

"Palmer!" the baron at last managed to wheeze, looking altogether apoplectic. "You!"

"I say, do you know one another?" the earl companionably asked, dropping his quizzing glass. "Captain Palmer's gelding is the one who bested Alabaster, don't y' know."

"No, I did not know," Fillmore growled, slowly swiveling his gaze toward his daughter. "Undoubtedly I alone out of the whole town. Obviously you are not newly arrived . . . *Captain* Palmer, is it?"

The captain nodded. "I have been here several days," he said, sensible of Claire's anxious expression and the wan hue to her otherwise rosy cheeks. "I came as the viscount's senior officer to tell Claire what I could of Philip's end."

"And have you done so?" the baron inquired stonily.

Still smiling, Derrick did not allow himself a glance toward Claire. "I have," he stated, his voice as steady as his gaze.

"Obviously, then, you are not seeing one another for the first time," the baron concluded.

His jaw clenched once; then, oddly, he smiled.

"Nor should it be the last," he suddenly, astoundingly, declared.

"Capital!" the earl interjected.

Claire turned to stare at her father. "Papa?" she breathed.

"Now, Claire, my dear, it is not often that a hero returns to our midst, after all," Fillmore justified. "No, my boy, you must by all means be feted. I have it!" he exclaimed with a soft pop of two fingers encased within his glove. "You shall be the guest of honor at our Christmas ball. You would not mind, would you, Clayton? Surely you agree that the captain must not be allowed to leave us without giving us the opportunity to laud his contribution to the war."

"I would not mind in the least," Clayton stated generously. "I should deem it a pleasure to step aside."

"Then consider it done," the baron pronounced.

At last Claire found her tongue. "Papa, I am persuaded that Derrick . . ."

". . . Now, my dear, you must cease being such a Cassandra," the baron scolded. "Captain, we shall expect you on the morrow."

"I shall be delighted, sir," Derrick responded, a bit nonplussed.

Just then the choir began its entrance, filing one by one into the ancient loft as it filled the vaulted stone with soaring echoes of *The Holly and the Ivy*. Along with the rest of the congregation, the three again faced forward and settled.

It was a long time into the vicar's Christmas message, however, before Claire gave up trying to anticipate what had so precipitately popped into her father's cunning mind.

Christmas Eve floated into Winchcombe on soft, wet snow flurries that quickly coated bare branches, steep slate, and yellow stone. The villagers retreated to their roasting geese and expectant offspring. From every cottage, soft yule firelight spilled in warm, golden wedges upon the trickling cobblestones.

Far above the village in the manor house, however, the viscountess spent the day overseeing a myriad of last minute details: the perfect placement of the china and silver upon pure white damask in the supper room, the attachment of pencils to the dance cards, the arrangements of candles, greenery, oranges and nuts on each of the first floor tables, the distribution of the servants' gifts. And in the ball room, shimmering under its swathing of silvery shot silk, the taking of a cup of wassail with everyone belonging to the household, followed by the traditional lighting of the huge yule log.

With the setting of the sun, Claire realized that she was exhausted, not so much from the ball preparations, she knew, but more from concern over what her father might truly be thinking. Had he had a change of heart as it seemed? . . . seen and regretted the misery he had caused? Or was it all a ruse? And if it were, then what was he planning? . . . more, why had he and Clayton been holed up in his study the better part of the afternoon?

Too tired and anxious to think of the matter further, Claire ordered tea to be sent to her chamber, then ascended the stairs for a bit of quiet and a short nap. And she needed it, she realized, reaching her door. All too soon she would know the answers to her questions; all to soon her maid would come again to force her to her fate followed by a footman with the copper hip bath.

"What do you mean they once had an understanding?" Clayton cried out, bearing down with all ten knuckles upon Fillmore's desk.

"I-It was nothing, I assure you," the baron pleaded, drops of perspiration forming in the large pores peppering his forehead. "They were but children, my lord. It was a flirtation of the moment."

"I think you had better explain," the earl suggested, disgustedly dropping his quizzing glass to mince toward the fireplace.

Seeing that he had no other choice, the baron sank back into his chair with a sigh. "Before Claire married the viscount, she had already betrothed herself to Palmer."

"Then you are telling me, sir, that the woman you are intent upon fobbing off on me is a jilt," Clayton concluded, moving next to a small adjacent table and pouring himself a snifter of Armagnac.

"No!" the baron exclaimed, rising suddenly to his feet. "Anything but, my lord. I never gave my permission to the foolishness in the first place! Why would I when a title was at stake?"

"Why, indeed," the earl commented, staring hard at the other man, a wrinkle of vexation crossing his brow. "I conclude, then, that Claire agreeably gave the captain his *congé.*"

The baron's hesitation was noticeable.

"Well?"

Haltingly moving to pour himself a glass, the baron then produced a handkerchief to dab at his forehead.

"My daughter is loyal, sir," he finally said. "A quality you shall come to appreciate, I misdoubt."

"She did not dismiss him," the earl concluded, still steadily boring into him.

The baron dashed down his brandy, sloshing a bit onto his chin. "I-I admit that in the end, I had no choice but to force her to it."

"How?"

Twice, the baron swallowed. "On the day I informed her that she would not gain my permission to marry Palmer but had been betrothed by me to the viscount instead, I knew Palmer would not be in the village."

"And? . . ."

"The three of them had been friends all their lives," Fillmore explained, again dabbing at his layered flesh. "I knew that if she were denied her desire and Palmer were not available, she would run to the viscount."

"And did she?" Clayton asked, slowly pouring them both more brandy.

"She did."

"What happened then?"

"It was all arranged," the baron stated, throwing back another dash. "And he *was* her betrothed, after all . . . the same as married in most books."

Several moments crawled.

"Good God!" the earl finally breathed, sinking down onto the scroll-arm sofa. "No wonder she resists me! And now with Captain Palmer back . . ."

"It means nothing, my lord," the baron reassured. "Never forget that now *you*, sir, are her betrothed."

"Meaning what? . . ." the earl cried, flying to his feet, "that you expect me to claim my bride in the same fashion?"

"I had counted it an option . . ." the baron left dangling into the room's quiet. "Unless, of course, you do not wish . . ."

"I do not!" Clayton spat.

"Very well, my lord," the baron soothed. "No need to take offense. Besides, that method caused more problems than it solved. So be it, then. We shall revert to my second plan."

"Your second plan?" Clayton queried beneath an arched brow. "And what might that be, sir? Am I to kidnap her?"

"Of course not," the baron replied dismissively. "In truth, you are to do nothing. I shall do the doing."

"Fillmore," Clayton responded warily, "you had best tell me what is it you are suggesting."

"It is simple, really," the baron smiled. "I shall tell the truth to the captain."

"And that will get rid of him?"

"I have no doubt of it," Fillmore replied. "In fact, my lord, once he knows how matters stand between you and Claire, I doubt we shall ever see the man again."

The captain still had not arrived by half past eight o'clock that evening when the viscountess finished greeting the last of her guests and signaled her father to disband the reception line. The house was dressed to perfection; fires crackled in every hearth, brass gleamed, bright red tapers in their arrangements filled the rooms with welcoming candlelight.

Yet worry over his whereabouts ate at a hollow place within Claire's outer peace.

In fact, never before had she felt so disquieted. It was more than just the embarrassment of being required by her father to attend such a prominent social occasion only two months into her mourning; more, too, she knew, than the awkwardness of having only the hem of a simple black mourning gown to throw over her arm at such a festive event. In truth, what was unsettling her the most was her concern that her father might have already seen to the accomplishment of whatever he had planned for the captain.

That he had a plan, of course, was not even in question. She knew all too well the demeanor her father had been wearing since their return from the Christmas service the previous morning, and she had seen the furtive glances that had passed between him and the earl on numerous occasions. But had the scheme already come to pass? she wondered, biting upon her lower lip. Was it even then too late? And if not, how was she to stop what was coming? Claire could not imagine. She only knew that she must.

Suddenly, however, the orchestra struck up the introduction to a piece by Mozart and Clayton, bowing before her, extended his glove. Responding with a low curtsey, Claire politely took his arm and followed him into the brightly lit ball room. Moments later, the two joined hands for the evening's opening minuet, as duty demanded of her as hostess, and him as highest ranking guest.

Had she but looked in the direction of the doorway only a few moments later, however, she would have seen the captain's entrance.

Resplendent in his Naval uniform, the captain stood stiffly ill-at-ease for a moment, then, at last catching sight of Claire dancing with the earl, smiled and relaxed. She was beautiful, he thought, watching the candlelight play upon her dark curls as she performed the dance's intricate steps. And just the same, he realized . . . an imp moved to mischief and bursts of fire; intelligent . . . a woman of bright spirit gentled by a merciful heart.

And he loved her.

More, better still, she loved him, he was convinced.

Even after five years of misunderstanding, the miracle of Christmastide for them was that nothing had really changed. They were still in love. It was as simple as that. Simple, too, what he planned tonight to do about it. He would ask her to dance, and then once again tell her how he felt. And she would accept it, devil take it! . . . because if she did not, until Claire Masterson again agreed to become his wife, he vowed, no power on earth would budge him from the deuced house.

"Ah, Captain, good evening," the baron offered, his sudden greeting shattering the fervency of Derrick's thoughts.

Turning quickly toward him, the captain bowed. "Good evening, sir," he responded, straightening with a smile. "My apologies for my tardiness. The snow is falling a bit more heavily now."

"Think no more of it," the baron generously dismissed. "Ah, I see you have spied Claire and Clayton," he continued with a gesture in the dance floor's direction. "They make a splendid couple, do they not?"

"They are both skilled," the captain agreed.

"Skilled, eh? More than that, I should say," Fillmore chuckled. " 'In tune with one another might be more to the point. But that is as it should be, considering . . .'"

"Considering? . . ." questioned the captain after a time, still enjoying the sight of Claire's sweetly flushed face.

Again the baron chuckled. "Deuce take it, I really should not speak of it yet, but I am quite beside myself, and you being Claire's childhood friend . . ."

". . . Is there something you wish to tell me, sir?" Derrick finally asked, growing a bit vexed.

"Indeed there is, my boy," Fillmore said conspiratorially. "Well those two should look suited to each other's company, I vow." Suddenly, he signaled Dawes to approach with the champagne. "Here now, let us drink to the evening, shall we?" he suggested, handing the captain a glass, then leaning further forward and placing a gloved hand upon his sleeve. "Tonight is a momentous occasion for them, don't y'know," he told him, taking another glass for himself. "It was agreed to weeks ago, of course, but on this very special night, my boy . . . and let us drink to it, shall we? . . ." he added, tipping his flute, "I shall have the joy of announcing their betrothal."

With a swiftness that nearly felled him, all sound ceased, buried beneath a steady pounding threatening to explode the captain's skull.

"Well, my boy," the baron's voice broke through hollowly, "raise your glass. What do you think?"

"My congratulations," Derrick managed to say before the whole of his world crashed down about his feet.


She did not love him, the captain repeated again and again, numbly wandering about the card and supper rooms. Dear God, he had misinterpreted everything! Yet at Hailes . . . no, it was he who had moved to kiss her, not the other way around; more, upon the other occasions they had met, she had been wary at his appearance. He had been persuaded that she was merely still troubled by her father. A far simpler conclusion, however, was that she was discomfited because he had appeared uninvited at an occasion in which she was in Clayton's escort.

What was he to do, therefore?

Run, his impulse screamed. Run anywhere. As far and as fast as you can.

Yet for propriety's sake, as well as the wish for an avoidance of questions, he knew he could not. And there was Claire, of course. She would not understand his leaving so precipitously, and without even a word. After all, in none of his misunderstanding was she in any way at fault.

So he would see her one last time, he concluded. God help him, he would need to; he had no strength to fight the impulse. He would dance with her, therefore, just as he had planned. He would look into her beautiful eyes

. . . see one last smile . . . before he left forever, he would hold her one last time in his arms.

That decided, the captain battened down his courage, then steadfastly strode toward the hurt.

# *Chapter Seven*

"Derrick!" Claire exclaimed, turning away from Clayton at seeing his approach, her face instantly blossoming with joy and relief. "You have come at last," she said, gliding forward, stretching out both her hands. "I have been . . . concerned."

"Have you?" the captain replied, squeezing her fingertips. "Then I must offer my apologies," he said softly, his warm regard piercing into hers. "I would not ever knowingly cause you distress. I hope you know that."

The odd intensity of his response alarmed the viscountess, giving her pause. "Of course, I do," she at last responded, her smile marred somewhat by a new wedge of worry between her brows. "Derrick, has something happened?" she asked. "You must tell me if it has."

"No, nothing," he replied with a gentle smile. "Nothing has happened." And then he dropped her hands and politely bowed. "Except that I have developed the most pressing desire to escort you onto the dance floor," he told her, rising again.

"What, *you?*" Claire laughed, opening up her fan.

"Remarkable, is it not?" the captain grinned. "Of course, until this leg has healed I shall not be the most adept of partners, but . . . shall we?" he asked, extending his elbow. "Or shall I require Clayton's permission first?"

"Certainly not," Claire scolded with a smile, taking his arm.

"Good. I should dislike that chore," Derrick pronounced, leading her away to an empty place within a forming quadrille square. "And have a care for my toes, if you please," he warned much more softly as the music began.

"For *your* toes!" Claire giggled as he enfolded her hand.

"Certainly," the captain responded in a whisper the other dancers could not hear. "After all, I am the one skilled at negotiating a heaving deck."

"And how does that signify?"

"It means that I have balance, my dear," the captain expounded.

"A necessity for you, of course," Claire agreed just as *sotto voce*, moving forward with him toward the opposite couple. "Yet I have developed my own skills over the years," she told him.

"Such as? . . ." he asked, his eyes gleaming with expectancy.

"You may easily negotiate a heaving deck, sir," she responded, "but, if you recall, I am the one skilled at catching frogs."

"Point taken," he softly allowed, then grinning at each other like perfect bedlamites, the two circled the other couple and retreated back to their original place.

"Shall we walk for a moment?" the captain suggested at the quadrille's conclusion.

"I should like that," Claire answered, once more taking

his arm, "unless it would be more comfortable for your leg to sit awhile."

"Actually, walking is good," Derrick replied, slowly drifting with her past the supper room, "and, truly, my wound is almost completely healed. I recommend Mr. Bates' poultices," he added. "One can hardly bear to be in the same room with them, but they do powerfully draw."

"Do they?" Claire commented with a chuckle.

"Yes . . ." Derrick affirmed. And then he ran his fingers across his Bedford crop. "Deuce take it, Claire, the last thing I wish to discuss is poultices," he announced.

"What then?" she asked with an easy smile, pausing within a quiet corner beside a potted palm.

For long moments, the captain stared searchingly into Claire's pale blue eyes. Then, ". . . Nothing," he finally replied. "I would rather simply look at you," he softly murmured, his stare again intensifying.

"You would?" Claire breathed, her smile softening beneath her coloring cheeks.

"I rather like that pastime," he whispered. "And being with you," he next told her, slowly stretching out his hand toward her face. "And touching you."

On the heels of that wholly improper admission, suddenly, he shook himself. "Forgive me," he requested flatly, stiffening as he dropped his arm to his side again and stepped back. "I misspoke."

"Never, Derrick!" Claire countered, nonplussed, reaching out to touch his sleeve. "Is it possible that you could still not know that you could never . . . !"

". . . Beg pardon, my lady," Dawes suddenly interrupted.

Quickly gathering herself, Claire turned. "Yes, Dawes?"

"Cook is in a pet, my lady," he told her in his practiced monotone.

"Why is that?" Claire asked, smoothing her vexation.

"Millicent has dropped the trays of lemon tarts," Dawes

informed her. "Unless you come straightaway, my lady, I fear she shall soon draw blood."

"Good heavens! Very well, I shall come," Claire conceded. "But, Derrick, please wait here until I return. We must finish this conversation."

Yet when the viscountess again entered the ball room some moments later, she did not even need to search for him to know that the captain had gone.

"What have you done?" she demanded of her father after she had tracked him down in the card room.

Pausing in the collection of his winnings, the baron glanced in her direction. "One thing I have not done is create a scene," he told her awfully, slipping several coins into a leather bag and then slowly rising.

"Papa . . ."

". . . If you are experiencing some difficulty, Claire, at least have the courtesy to accompany me to my study before you discuss it," he scolded, excusing himself from the next deal of the cards, then preceding her the short distance down the hall to the mahogany paneled room. "Now, what seems to be the trouble?" he asked, offering her the scroll-armed sofa, then seating himself behind his desk.

"The trouble?" she queried sharply, refusing the offer with a slash of her hand. "I am persuaded that you know very well what is troubling me. What have you said to Derrick?"

"The captain?" Fillmore asked innocently.

"Yes, the captain," Claire affirmed. "He has left the ball. Why?"

"I have no idea."

"Papa!" Claire cried in vexation, afterward, muscle by muscle, calming herself. When she again felt in control, she softly, evenly completed, "I shall not marry Clayton."

"You will."

"And what do you intend to do to bring that about?" she even more tautly asked, leaning down upon his desk. "Have me defiled again?"

"I shall not have to," the baron responded mirthlessly. "You will marry Clayton because Captain Palmer shall not even have you now."

With that intelligence rebounding inside her skull, Claire stiffened and blanched. "What have you done, Papa? What have you said to him?" she breathed, her gaze huge with apprehension.

"What I had to," her father stated flatly. "As I did before, I told him that you and Clayton were already betrothed."

Aghast, Claire only just caught the buckle of her knees. *"Papa! . . ."*

"Resign yourself to it, my dear," he counseled. "Your future resides with Clayton. Besides, by this time, I misdoubt the captain has already left."

"No," Claire whispered, her fingertips rising to her lips. "He cannot have . . ." Then, quite suddenly, she drew herself up into a ramrod posture.

"No!" she stated, staring ahead toward a distant point. "It has been less than a quarter hour since I was called to the kitchen. He cannot have left yet."

The twentieth part of a moment later, she had already gathered her skirts and fled.

"Claire!" she heard her father exclaim as he, too, tore open the study door. "He is gone, I tell you. Deuce take it, I shall not let you abandon all I have gained for you! Claire, come back here!"

"We belong together, Papa . . . and he has not left me," she called back to him. "I know it. Life would not be so unjust," she proclaimed, rounding the corner and apprehending Dawes.

"My lady?" the staid servant said, peering down at her after she had rushed up to him and seized him by the arm.

"Dawes, you must help me," Claire whispered. "Oh, will you? It means everything!"

"Of course, my lady," he readily replied.

"My father will not like it," she warned him.

"Then we shall not tell him, my lady," the elder suggested.

Suddenly washed with hope, Claire smiled. "I shall need a carriage, Dawes, as quickly as possible," she informed him, running immediately afterward to seize one of her guests' pelisses from the small store room where they had been hung. "Any one of those still remaining in the drive will do. Just something to get me quickly into the village."

"Very good, my lady," Dawes stated, following. "To the Rose and Shadow?"

"Yes," Claire told him, pausing only long enough to allow him to open the manor's entrance door. "And a driver!" she added as an afterthought, dashing out into the snow. "I shall need a driver, Dawes."

"On the contrary, my lady," he said, leading her toward the carriage of one of the later arrivals still standing near the end of the circular drive, "you have one."

"Thank you, Dawes," Claire grinned.

Only moments later, the carriage was racing down the rutted road in a headlong dash toward the inn.

Before they had even left the manor grounds, however, the baron had stormed out of his study to pursue his wayward daughter, only to collide quite smartly with the approaching earl.

"Fillmore, whatever? . . ." Clayton gasped in vexation as he recovered, brushing order back into his blue velvet evening clothes.

"Never mind that now," the baron urged, starting forward again, dragging the earl along. "We must stop her. She has gone to him."

"What!" the earl cried, balking.

"You must believe me, my lord," Fillmore coaxed, again pulling Clayton along in his wake, "there is no time for explanations. If Claire finds the captain at the inn, she will run away with him."

"Good God!" Clayton exclaimed as the two donned hats and cloaks. "But how shall we arrive in time?" he asked, glancing about as he exited the house. "There is no sign of her in the drive."

"Leave that to me," the baron told him, striding toward the stables. "A carriage leaving from the manor must take a circuitous lane down the bluff. We, however, shall take horses over a far shorter path through the trees. We shall intercept her."

"Make certain of it, Fillmore," the earl commanded.

"Never fear, my lord, she is already in our grasp," he told him, sending a stable boy scurrying off for mounts.

It was already the dawn of Christmas morning when the carriage Dawes had pilfered rattled through the slumbrous village of Winchcombe and up to the Rose and Shadow. Happily for Claire, the inn's bay windows were not dark, but still glowed with a festive warmth, though she could see that there were no patrons in the tap room, those worthy souls undoubtedly having left long ago to spend the holiday evening with their loved ones. But at least Mr. Bates must still be about to respond to her summons. Therefore, immediately upon Dawes' jumping down from the driver's seat and opening the smoothly veneered door, Claire eagerly stepped down onto the incrusted snow and started forward.

"Wait but a moment while I knock, my lady," he properly warned.

"Thank you, but . . . no, Dawes," Claire told him, stopping his progress with a hand upon his forearm. "You must let me see to my own needs now. I am persuaded that you must return to the manor immediately. If you do, there is the chance that you might arrive back quickly enough to resume your duties without Papa even knowing that you have been gone. I am certain you would agree that it would not be to your benefit for him to know that you have helped me."

"Indeed not, my lady," Dawes confirmed with a nod. "Yet it is not proper . . ."

". . . None of this is proper," Claire interrupted, her smile fading a bit, "nor is what Papa plans. But I must do what I must, and so must you. Please go now, Dawes," she pleaded, "so that I shan't have to worry about you as well."

After a moment's hesitation, the butler nodded. "Very well, my lady."

Moments later Claire watched the borrowed carriage bounce back out onto the road.

Then, suddenly . . . "Very touching, my dear," sounded from just around the inn's dark corner.

Too late, Claire spun about.

"Papa!" she cried, even then starting to run.

Yet in moments her father and Clayton were upon her, seizing her arms behind her back, muffling her cries of alarm.

"What do we do now?" Clayton rasped when they had for the most part subdued her, rebounding from a kick in the shin, recapturing a slippery arm. "We shall never get her up on horseback at this rate."

"We shan't have to," Fillmore replied. "Follow me around to the back . . . quietly, man!" he hissed when a slit between the earl's fingers allowed the escape of a small, indignant shriek. "As I recall, there is an outer door in the rear leading down into the inn's storage rooms. All we need to do is hold her there until we make sure the captain has gone. Once that has happened, there will be no point in her resisting further."

Decisively, the earl nodded. "Take her legs, then," he ordered.

Complying, the baron swept Claire's thrashing appendages up into his arms and together the two transported her, twisting and arching, down an ancient set of steps leading into the inn's cold, musty ale cellar.

"Shall you be wanting a clean shirt, sir?" Mr. Rawlins asked, separating one from the several he was packing into the captain's sea bag.

"No, the one I am wearing will do," Derrick replied, gathering his toiletries from the wash stand and carrying them toward the bed.

"So would some sort of explanation," the lad cheekily muttered.

The captain shot him a chiding glance. "It is enough for you to know that my business here is concluded," he told him. "It is merely time to leave."

"In the middle of the night?" Mr. Rawlins questioned, wrapping the captain's shaving brush and razor within a worn strop. "On Christmas Eve?"

"Yes, deuce take it!" the captain exclaimed. "Now get on with it, if you please."

Yet, even as he spoke, soft insistent scratching noises suddenly intruded from the hall.

"What now?" the captain muttered, striding over to yank upon the door's rope handle.

As soon as the opening was wide enough, the little gray kitten scooted into the chamber, tumbled forward, then once more climbed up on one boot's pristine polish.

"Stowaway," Derrick murmured, his vexation dissipating ahead of his smile. "What are you doing here at this hour?" he asked, bending to his accustomed task of hoisting the tiny creature up to his broad shoulder.

This time, however, when his hands drew near, the kitten bit deeply into one of the captain's fingers.

"What the deuce? . . ." the captain exclaimed, instantly recoiling, rubbing at the wound.

In answer, the kitten jumped down from his boot with a tiny cry and, after pausing to peer back at the captain with its gray, almond eyes, padded once again toward the door.

"What is it you want, little one?" the captain asked again, then, glancing toward Mr. Rawlins, he inquired, "What do you make of this?"

"Could she be hungry, sir?" the lad responded.

"Hard to imagine considering she lives at an inn," the captain replied with a frown, running fingers through his hair when the kitten meowed again. "Yet she does have a good deal of competition," he allowed. "Very well, Mr. Rawlins, carry on with our packing. I shall go down to the kitchen to see if I can muster up a dish of cream. Come along, then, Stowaway," he ordered, starting forward, along the way bending again to scoop the kitten up and away from the figure eights it was purringly rubbing around and between his legs.

The kitten would have none of it, however. No sooner had the captain stooped than it yowled again and skittered away from his hands. Once again it halted just out of reach to stare unblinkingly up at him. Then, turning, it dashed away once more on silent paws.

Again the captain straightened and shook his head. "Very well, then," he conceded, "as that seems to be your preference, *you* lead the way if you like. Set sail, little one," he directed, pointing out the door after casting a puzzled smile back toward Mr. Rawlins.

Yet after they had descended to the inn's ground floor, the gray kitten did not turn toward the kitchen as the captain had expected. Instead, and most oddly, it immediately dashed toward the narrow stairs leading down into the dark, silent ale cellar.

"Release me this instant, sir!" Claire cried after the earl had eased his hand's tight clamp over her mouth and her slippers had again touched down upon the dirt floor of a small room off the main cellar containing the best of Mr. Bates' bottles of claret.

"Be silent, Claire," her father commanded, seizing her and marching her toward the room's small table.

"I shall not," Claire vowed as Clayton struck a lucifer and touched it to the table's stunted candle. "I am of age, Papa," she cried, ignoring the light shaping itself into a feeble globe. "You have no right to force your will upon me."

"Yet I shall always have an obligation to see that you do not do something foolish, daughter," the baron patiently replied. "My lord," he next suggested, "perhaps if you might find a bit of rope? . . ."

". . . Rope!" Claire exclaimed.

"Of course," the earl responded, searching only two shadowed corners before discovering a thick coil.

"Foolish or not, Papa, what I do shall be *my* choice," Claire insisted, beginning again to wriggle.

"Not in this, my dear," her father argued, once more tightening his grip. "Not when it comes to my progeny," he vowed, forcing Claire down onto one of the table's unmatched wooden chairs, tugging her arms behind its slats, then signaling Clayton to come forward.

"Papa, stop this instant!" Claire again cried, wrenching her arms against the restraint.

"And certainly not when it comes to that upstart, *Captain* Palmer!" the baron added, ignoring her altogether.

"This is idiocy, Papa!" Claire stated hotly as Clayton gained her side, her voice choked with tears. "What makes you think that I would not follow him to Portsmouth at my first opportunity? I love him, Papa," she sobbed. "Do you not understand that? I love him! I always have."

". . . As I have always loved you, Claire," the captain suddenly, softly, interjected from the chamber's entrance.

"Derrick!" Claire gasped, her gaze slewing toward him, tears of overwhelming joy, of relief, splashing down upon her plain, black bodice.

"Steady on, my love," he commanded gently, stepping into the ring of light, the kitten adding its mew of reassurance from his shoulder. "I am here now. As for you, release her," he next directed the two men still staring at him goggle-eyed. "Claire is coming with me."

Suddenly, the earl's pinched features wrenched. "Fillmore, you promised!" he cried, at last finding the will to move, as well as his voice. "You shan't have her!" he then hissed, starting toward the captain. "I vow it. He promised her to me!" In the next moment, quite unexpectedly, he swung the coil of rope he had been holding in a wide arc and slammed it down directly atop the the captain's wounded thigh.

Instantly, Derrick dropped to his knees.

Acting quickly, the baron seized the advantage. Tugging Claire to her feet and shoving her against the chamber's plastered wall, he then took her empty chair into his hands, raised it above his head, and advanced toward the stunned captain, his muscles tensing, prepared for the time they would bring it crashing down upon his head.

"Derrick!" Claire cried when she realized what was about to happen.

Immediately, the captain pivoted about and lifted his arm in defence.

The chair wavered.

*"Papa!"*

The scream was just the diversion the tiny gray kitten needed to spring from the captain's shoulder, then bury all ten of its little needle-claws into the flesh of the baron's face.

"Egad!" he cried spinning about, dropping the chair to clutch at the incubus who had attached itself to his cheeks; then, maddened by pain, flinging the tiny creature off somewhere amid the claret racks. "What evil is this?" he gasped, staring at his hands as he turned toward them again, his face striped with the blood oozing from ten tiny cuts.

"Stowaway!" Claire breathed, rushing toward the wine racks.

"Claire, no!" Derrick sharply commanded, at last gaining his feet again, then swiftly drawing his sword. "Come here to me, love," he finished more softly, holding out his hand.

"But, Derrick, the kitten must be badly hurt," Claire argued, hesitating.

"And we shall take care of her," the captain replied, his sword still raised, his gaze cutting a steady path between the earl and the baron. "But first I must see you safely by my side. Come here, Claire."

With no further hesitation, Claire carefully skirted the other two men, then moved willingly into Derrick's embrace.

"As for the two of you," he next said, swinging the tip of his sword back and forth, "I am persuaded that you shall immediately wish to return to your guests."

"Never, you low-born scoundrel!" Fillmore growled.

"What under heaven is going on here?" Mr. Bates suddenly queried from the dark shadows near the chamber door.

"From the look of it, either a family reunion or a kidnapping, Mr. Bates, wouldn't you agree?" the captain responded. "The question is, which shall the *ton* believe, sir?" he asked the baron. "I wonder."

Still hotly glaring, the baron subsided, recognizing his defeat.

"Do you intend to say nothing?" the earl cried.

"No."

"Fillmore, you promised!"

"Quiet, Clayton!"

"Mr. Bates," the captain asked politely, "will you show the gentlemen out?"

"Of course," the innkeeper replied beneath a somewhat stupefied look.

"Claire . . ." the baron began.

". . . Goodbye, Papa," she said with a soft smile, wrapping her arms about Derrick's waist. "Someday I hope you will understand that I am where I belong now . . . where I have always belonged."

"I shall take good care of her, sir," the captain reassured.

Slowly the baron nodded, then started for the door.

"And you intend doing nothing? Six weeks!" the earl muttered as he followed. "Do you realize that, Fillmore? I have wasted six weeks!"

"Claire, you will marry me, will you not?" Derrick asked when the two of them were at last alone.

"Yes," she replied, smiling up into his eyes.

"I am not a wealthy man," he warned her. "Not yet, at any rate. But you shall never want, my love, I promise."

"I accept your promise. And, as to your wealth, that I already know," Claire laughed. "Now will you kiss me, please?"

"Claire, I am attempting to prepare you for future hardship," he groused, "yet all you want is to be kissed."

"Yes!"

"Imp," the captain chuckled, and in the next moment, his warm mouth covered Claire's hesitant, hovering breath.

"The deuce," he murmured much later, when all Claire's sensibilities had been reduced to tomato aspic.

"That horrid, was it?" she sighed, collapsing against his chest.

"Mmm, hardly that," he laughingly replied. "Habit forming, more like. No, what I am bemoaning is that fact that I have no token for you to seal this pledge we have made between us. Deuce take it, Claire, I do not even have a present for you for Christmas!"

"Yes, you do," Claire countered, looking up at him with a radiant smile and patting his chest. "You can give me the one thing that did the most to bring about our happy ending."

"Which is? . . ."

"Stowaway, of course."

Suddenly, both sobered.

"Stowaway!" they cried, slapping hands to their cheeks.

"Lud, how could we forget the little one?" Derrick cried, quickly releasing Claire and striding over to the claret racks.

"Oh, yes, poor dear!" Claire agreed, taking up the candle. "Over here, Derrick. I believe she fell somewhere in this area."

Quickly they began to search, stooping down to peer and run their hands beneath each aging structure, turning over each dusty bottle from top to bottom, inspecting each gap. Yet more than half an hour later, there was still no sign of the kitten.

"What could have happened to her?" Claire asked, finally dusting off her thoroughly soiled hands.

"To whom, my lady?" Mr. Rawlins asked, strolling into the room lazily chewing a bite from the sweet bun in his hand.

"To Stowaway," Claire told him. "She saved the captain from being knocked unconscious by my father during their struggle."

"She did? Knocked unconscious, eh?" Mr. Rawlins repeated with a grin.

"There were extenuating circumstances," the captain growled, casting him a cursory glance.

"When she attacked him, my father threw the kitten against these racks," the viscountess continued to explain, "yet we cannot find her now."

"Perhaps the kitten managed to crawl from the room," Mr. Rawlins offered, taking another bite.

Immediately, the captain shook his head. "We would have seen it," he stated.

"Yet it must have, mustn't it, sir? . . ." he asked, "since the kitten obviously is not here?"

Faced with that bit of logic, the three next began to search the remainder of the building. Moreover, upon receiving direction from the captain on toward morning to hire a traveling chaise for Claire's comfort in their return to Portsmouth, Mr. Rawlins even searched the yard.

Yet still, much to their disappointment, the tiny gray kitten was never seen again.

The sun was still an orange ball hanging low over the horizon when distant church bells began to ring across the Isbourne valley heralding Christmas morning. In the inn yard of the Rose and Shadow, the hired traveling chaise pulled to a halt before the captain's party. Waiting with Claire on his arm, the captain stifled a yawn and squeezed her hand. A glance told him that her eyes, too, were dark with fatigue. It was understandable, however. Given the circumstances of the previous evening, not since Clayton and the baron had left the night before had any of them managed to rest.

"My thanks, Mr. Bates," the captain offered when the horses had settled and he had handed Claire up into the carriage.

"My thanks, too, lad . . . for your patronage," the inn-keeper replied, shaking the captain's hand. "It was good to see you again."

"And you," Derrick stated sincerely. Slowly, then, he cast his gaze about the inn yard, searching one last time for the kitten, impressing memories upon his mind. "I shall never forget you, sir, nor the Rose and Shadow."

"Nor shall we ever forget Stowaway," Claire added, her lovely face framed by the carriage window. "Nor, too, Mr. Bates, your help with the earl and my father."

"Oh, think nothing of it," Mr. Bates dismissed, again rubbing his chin. "Glad to be of what service I can. But what a trial for you, Miss Claire! . . ." he added, "what with his lordship holding you down in my cellar, and all! I must say, it is curious, is it not? . . . how history repeats itself?"

"What do you mean?" Derrick asked.

"Oh, do you not know the tale, then?" the innkeeper asked. "I thought surely having grown up in the valley . . ."

"I imagine I was busy with other pursuits at the time," Derrick said with a smile. "What tale is connected with your inn?"

"Why, a lovely, romantic tale to be sure," Mr. Bates replied, leaning against his broom. "By coincidence, it is also the story of how the Rose and Shadow got its name."

"Is it?"

"Oh, aye, and an old one it is, too," he told them. "In fact, the tale harks back hundreds of years to Cromwell's time."

"To the Civil War!" Claire murmured.

"Indeed, milady," the innkeeper affirmed. "The war between the Royalists and Cromwell's Roundheads. A hard time . . . a hard time. If you recall, your ancestors lived in the manor even then."

"And were hard-pressed to do what so many of the nobility tried . . ." Claire interjected, "to save their estates by appearing to be loyal to each side."

"They must have been successful," Derrick commented. "The Fillmores still hold the manor."

"Aye," Mr. Bates agreed, "just as they did then when the daughter of the manor was a lovely young maiden named Rose."

"Yes, of course!" Claire exclaimed. "There is a portrait of Rose Fillmore hanging in the manor gallery."

"But I'll wager *not* one of the young man she fell in love with, milady," Mr. Bates said. "He was a fine young Roundhead officer."

"Oh, dear," Claire commented, sobering a bit, glancing again at Derrick as she began to see where the story was heading.

"Aye," Mr. Bates nodded, " 'tis true. You see, the Roundheads held this inn for their headquarters during a part of the war. The story goes that one day Rose and her officer met at Hailes . . ."

". . . Hailes?" Claire questioned, glancing much more pointedly toward the captain.

"Aye," Mr. Bates sighed with a smile. "Quite a romantic place, that, I misdoubt you will agree," he added with a wink. "Well, it was love for Rose and her officer right away. As you might suspect, after that, the two met in secret again and again. After a time, as young people will, they began to make plans, even knowing that the officer would not be acceptable to the family because he lacked position or wealth. Still, in this very inn yard, on the day before Christmas Eve, the young officer asked Rose to be his bride."

"Did she agree?" Claire asked, a slight frown marring her brow.

"Oh, yes, milady," Mr. Bates stated with a smile, "wholeheartedly. And the officer was, as you might imagine, overjoyed. Yet, poor lad, he had no gift to give her to plight their troth."

"No gift?" Claire whispered, her gaze locking with the

captain's this time, remembering their own words in the small cellar chamber the night before, wide-eyed at the uncanny parallel. "What did he do?"

The innkeeper softly chuckled. "Why, he selected one of the kittens that were always scampering about the stables to give her . . ." he replied, "a pretty gray one it was. Then he gave it to her as his pledge," Mr. Bates smiled. "He said it was because the kitten was the color of her eyes."

"He gave her a kitten," Derrick repeated, reaching over to take Claire's hand.

"A gray one, like Stowaway," Claire added.

"That she was," Mr. Bates, laughed. "A clever name, Stowaway," he next remarked. "Be she your kitten, milady?"

"Why, no, she is one of yours, Mr. Bates," Claire told him.

"Mine? Indeed. Can't say as I remember a gray one about the place . . ." he pondered. "Well, of a certainty, with so many running here and there, one or the other of them'd be easy to overlook. Be that as it may, however, Rose was afraid of the questions her new pet might inspire, so she left the kitten with her officer for safekeeping until the time they had planned for their elopement."

"When was that?" Claire asked, already certain she knew.

"The night of the manor's Christmas Eve ball, milady," the innkeeper responded, "just like what happened to you. On that very night the officer took the little gray kitten from Rose and put her atop his shoulder. To their surprise, the kitten climbed right into his shoulder pack and made herself at home. Watching the little one blend into the darkness of the bag," the innkeeper sighed, leaning more heavily upon his broom, "gave Rose the idea to name her Shadow."

"Rose . . . and Shadow," Claire softly repeated. "Indeed a romantic story," she added, staring into Derrick's eyes.

"Ah, but not what happened next," Mr. Bates disagreed.

"Oh?" Derrick asked.

"Aye," Mr. Bates told him. "On the evening of the ball, you see, Rose discovered that she had been betrayed."

"How?" Claire breathed.

"Her own handmaid told her father of her elopement," the innkeeper responded. "More, Rose learned that in his anger over what the officer intended, her father had given over trying to remain at peace and had gathered a force of Royalists to attack the Roundheads billeted at the inn and drive them from his lands. Even worse, milady, Rose learned that the Royalists had been instructed not to let her officer escape with his life."

"And so she ran to warn him, did she not?" Claire concluded, knowing that it was true.

"That she did, milady," Mr. Bates nodded firmly, "that she did . . . only to again be betrayed. Her father, too, rode for the inn, seized her as she arrived, then, just as *your* father did, carried her down into the very chamber where you, yourself, were detained."

Claire's pale blue gaze was wide now, frightened; fixed hard upon . . . within . . . Derrick's.

At last the captain spoke. "Go on, Mr. Bates."

"Well now, captain, sir," the innkeeper said hesitantly, sensing the tension that was building near the carriage, "perhaps here is where I should end the telling. From now on the story do get a bit peculiar . . ."

"Please, Mr. Bates, we should like to hear it," Claire insisted, still clinging to Derrick's hand.

"Very well, milady," the innkeeper finally nodded, "if you be certain, I shall tell you what I know of the story. I b'ain't be saying myself whether or not it be true, mind you. You must decide for yourselves if you wish to believe it."

"We understand, Mr. Bates," Derrick stated. "What happened after Rose was taken down into the cellar?"

"Well, at that very same time," the innkeeper all but whispered, "the story goes that up in the officer's room, the little kitten began to set up an awful clamor. Hearing it, the officer opened his pack to see what was the matter."

"What happened?" the captain asked.

"Why, she jumped out of the bag like a Fury," Mr. Bates told them. "Not only that, but the very second her little paws touched upon the floor she set off at a run that led the officer straight down to that belowstairs chamber."

"Derrick!" Claire breathed.

Unnoticed by the innkeeper, the captain squeezed her fingers. "Go on, sir," he urged.

"Well, you can imagine the baron's surprise," Mr. Bates continued, "and his anger at being discovered. Because of it, what did his lordship do then but draw his pistol to slay the upstart officer!"

"And did he?" Claire asked, her voice a thin thread.

"Ah, no, milady," Mr. Bates told them, "for, you see, as if that tiny kitten knew ahead of time what was going to happen, she sprang at the baron's face, dug in her tiny claws, and sent him staggering backward into the lantern sitting on the table."

"What happened next?"

"The lantern crashed to the floor, milady," Mr. Bates responded. "Within moments, the whole of the inn was afire."

"And the kitten?" the viscountess softly inquired.

"Sadly, milady, the story goes that she took the pistol ball square in her tiny heart."

"No," Claire breathed, her eyes misting with tears.

"What happened then?" Derrick quickly asked, handing Claire his handkerchief.

"Well, the inn burned to the ground for one thing," Mr. Bates softly told them. "When it was rebuilt, the proprietors renamed it the Rose and Shadow ... in memory, don't 'know."

"But what of the people in the basement room?" Derrick asked, his own voice husky.

"As to that, only one body was found . . ." the proprietor responded, his lordship's. Of the two lovers, nothing was evermore heard."

"Was the kitten recovered?" Claire whispered.

"Oh, no, milady," Mr. Bates dismissed. "There would be nothing left of one so small, don't y'know. It *was* odd, though."

"What was?"

"Well, the story has it that on the night the young officer and Rose were to elope—Christmas Eve it would be—the young man had woven a garland of mistletoe about the kitten's neck as a celebration of the season and his pledge to Rose."

"Mistletoe?" Claire repeated, her eyes growing even more huge.

"Aye, mistletoe," Mr. Bates affirmed with a nod of his head, "the symbol of everlasting life to the ancient Druids, don't y' know. But more . . . that same garland was said to have been found amid the charred remains of the old inn."

"Why is that necessarily odd?" Derrick asked.

"Why, just think about it for a moment, lad. An inn is filled to the brim with spirits. When one catches fire, it burns fast and wicked hot. By the morning . . . Christmas morning . . . nothing would have been left standing of the inn, I can tell you. Yet the mistletoe collar was found. And of even greater wonder, it bore not a sign of scorch," he told him, his voice a soft hush.

"How can you be certain?" Derrick asked.

"Can't, of course," Mr. Bates said with a shrug. "Yet them what found it said that the little garland just lay there in the midst of all that blackened ruin as green as the spring mountains. Odd, is it not? . . ." he said, slowly shaking his head, "going through a fire that destroyed the kitten, yet coming out as fresh as the moment it had been picked?"

It was several moments later before the captain could speak.

"So for you, then, it has become a tradition," he at last surmised.

"What, lad?" the proprietor asked.

"Weaving Christmas mistletoe garlands about the necks of your kittens," he explained.

"Why, no, lad. Whatever gave you that idea?"

"Mr. Bates, do you mean that you do *not* place those same mistletoe garlands upon your kittens as a remembrance?" Claire broke in.

"Goodness, no," the innkeeper laughed, straightening from his broom. "Mistletoe garlands for my kittens? Only look about you, milady," he suggested, helping Derrick into the carriage. "I run a busy posting house here. Now when would I have the time for such nonsense? Ah, but I be delaying you with my foolish tales," he said, stepping back. "Well, goodbye, lad, and good luck to ye. Goodbye, milady. Safe journey."

"Goodbye, Mr. Bates."

Moments later, the chaise started across the Vineyard Street bridge to take the captain and his betrothed south once more toward Portsmouth. It was a long way down the road, however, before Claire finally broke the silence.

"Do you believe in ghosts, Derrick?" she hesitantly asked.

"No . . . of course not," he finally murmured. "Of course not," he could not help repeating, wrapping his arms comfortingly about his beloved.

*The Magnifikitten*

*Judith A. Lansdowne*

# *Chapter One*

Lady Annabelle sat, quite stiff and straight, in the corner of the pew at the very rear of the chapel of St. Martin's-in-the-Fields, her head bowed, her eyes closed, her kidskin-gloved hands writhing in her lap. She wished to hold them motionless, but she could not. They twisted and fluttered and shook of their own accord and would not be stilled. Behind her in the vestibule Joseph, one of her brother's footmen, sighed and rested his broad shoulders against the cold wall. Outside, the sunshine which had foretold a glorious winter's day when Lady Annabelle had left her brother's town house was fast disappearing behind ominous clouds. She would be forced to leave soon. The team could not be kept standing much longer in such uncertain weather and John Coachman would be anxious to get them home. But she could not leave yet. She had to be absolutely certain that God had heard her prayers and that He truly understood the seriousness of the matter.

Not one tear stained Lady Annabelle's pretty pink cheeks or lingered upon the dark fringe of her lashes as she murmured The Lord's Prayer. She was far beyond tears now. She had been beyond them for almost two months. Tears, she had discovered, were not of the least use in the matter. But prayer, she was quite certain, would bring the exact assistance she needed. And she did so need assistance, because she and Devon and Georgianna had done all they could think to do and it had not been enough. Not nearly enough.

Nibbling upon her lower lip and closing her eyes as tightly as she could, Lady Annabelle abandoned The Lord's Prayer in favor of a more personal and direct explanation of what she required, because God had to understand and He had to help her. Harry's entire future depended upon it.

J. Tildon Dillsworthy pulled the collar of his greatcoat up around his ears and tugged his hat lower over his brow. Damnation but it was cold and growing colder every moment. Thank goodness he was almost there. Another fifteen minutes or so and he would be safe and warm before the fire in Green Street. Then the weather might do its worst. With an involuntary shiver, he switched his horse's reins to his left hand and tucked his right hand deep into his coat pocket.

Above him the clouds that had gathered rapidly parted for a moment allowing a bit of sunlight to strike the tiny tower of St. Martin's-in-the-Fields and glint down into his eyes. Almost there, he thought thankfully, and set his mount at the tiny wall that surrounded the chapel's grave-yard thinking to gain St. Martin's Lane without taking the more roundabout course. But as the gelding landed upon the opposite side, a kitten leaped into the air directly beneath Figment's nose. The gelding whinnied, jolted aside, reared, then bucked, and then tossed a thoroughly astonished Dillsworthy to the ground where he cracked

his head upon the gravestone of one Horace Watley,
Father, Sadly Missed.

The gentleman's curly-brimmed beaver hat skittered
across the graveyard in company with a rainbow of fallen
leaves. Figment fumed and fidgeted for a moment more,
then came to a standstill. And as Dillsworthy rolled over,
groaning, the kitten approached him cautiously from
behind a gravestone and, discovering that the man paid
her not the least attention, scurried into the pocket of his
greatcoat.

For the longest time Dillsworthy's mind wobbled and
spun and he could not quite grasp what had happened.
"Devil it," he mumbled at last, putting a hand to his brow
and feeling a lump rising there. When he brought the
hand down the fingers of his glove were tinged with blood.
"Devil it," he muttered again. "Tossed." Unsteadily, his
stomach lurching at the movement and his head
throbbing, Dillsworthy took hold of the gravestone above
him and tugged himself to his knees. He sighed and gained
his feet. Then, seizing hold of Figment's saddle to steady
himself, he peered about him, saw the chancel door and
with a shiver made his way to it and pushed it open. Shakily
he clutched the door frame with both hands as behind him
the wind intensified, rattling tree branches and cracking a
limb. The sun flared again for a moment and silhouetted
his tall, lean figure in the entranceway.

Lady Annabelle's wonderfully wide blue eyes opened at
the sudden rush and wail of the wind into the chapel. Her
perfectly delectable lips formed into an astounded little O
at the sight of Dillsworthy. Behind her, Joseph straightened
perceptibly and stood away from the wall.

"Oh!" gasped Lady Annabelle, one hand fluttering near
her breast. "Oh, my goodness!"

Dillsworthy turned his head at the sound of her voice
and glimpsed a tiny figure in the shadows of the nave, a
figure that looked remarkably like a young lady. And then

quite inexplicably the floor of the chapel began to undu-
late and rose toward him in a most unorthodox fashion.

"How marvelous," Lady Annabelle breathed, rising and
making her way hurriedly up the aisle and into the chancel
where Dillsworthy had crumbled. "Thank You! Oh, thank
You!" she whispered glancing soulfully upward at the
chapel ceiling. "I did never expect such an instantaneous
answer. Truly I did not!" Thoroughly agog, Annabelle
knelt down beside Dillsworthy and studied him. "Joseph,"
she called after a long moment as she smoothed Dillsworthy's hair back from his brow and discovered the lump
and the blood. "Come quickly. I need you."

Even stretched his length unconscious upon a cold stone
floor with a bit of blood trickling down his brow, J. Tildon
Dillsworthy was not impressive. That fact startled Lady
Annabelle quite as much as his injury and caused her to
nibble at her lower lip. She had been hoping, she admitted
to herself as Joseph hastily provided her with a handkerchief, for someone a bit more awe-inspiring. But perhaps
because it was so very close to Christmas and all, perhaps
the most magnificent of them were already taken.

"Do ye know this gent, my lady?" asked Joseph, kneeling
down beside her as she dabbed at the blood on Dillsworthy's brow. " 'Pears as he's had a accident, it does."

"Yes, it does appear that way, but perhaps that is how
it is intended to appear, do you think?"

"Think what, my lady?" asked the footman, taking Dillsworthy's measure in one long glance. "Hit his head on
somethin' I reckon."

"Do you think so? Well, but, of course! That provides
the perfect excuse to take him home with us, does it not?
Yes, I see now. That is exactly what was intended and it
will make everything so much more uncomplicated."

"Home with us, my lady?"

"Indeed," Lady Annabelle declared, satisfied with her
quick deduction that Joseph was not intended to know the

wonderful truth of the matter. "We cannot allow him just to lie here, Joseph, all alone and helpless. Quickly, fetch John Coachman to help you carry him to the coach."

"I reckon I kin carry the bloke easy enough, my lady," muttered Joseph. "But there be a horse peering in at us through that door. His horse I'm guessin'. I reckon the gentleman were on his way to somewhere in perticuler and come acropper somehows."

"Indeed. Well, you had best go fetch the horse and tie it behind our coach, Joseph, and then return and help me with him. And close the door behind you, do. The wind is most chilly."

"Yes, my lady." Uneasy at leaving his charge alone in the presence of a strange gentleman, Joseph nevertheless gave a respectful nod and took himself off to capture the gent's horse. "Be back in the shake of a cat's tail," he mumbled to himself. "Bloke can't be causin' my lady no trouble in so short a time. Not senseless like he be, he can't."

"There, he is gone now," Annabelle whispered to the inert Dillsworthy as Joseph shut the door behind him. "Oh, you cannot imagine how happy I am to see you."

"Mrrrow," came the most unexpected reply, and the kitten scrambled from the pocket of Dillsworthy's greatcoat and clambered most ungracefully up onto Dillsworthy's stomach. "Mrrrow," it repeated, settling upon its haunches and fixing Lady Annabelle with a most curious stare.

Lady Annabelle smiled. She had not smiled in a goodly number of days and the mere feel of her lips quivering upward at the corners sent a thrill to her heart. "Everything is going to be all right now, is it not, kitty? Well, of course it is. I can feel it in my very bones."

"Mrrrpfff," the kitten responded encouragingly and then pounced upon one of the brass buttons on Dillsworthy's greatcoat and attempted to tug it from its anchor. This made Lady Annabelle laugh. At first the sound shocked her and she ceased at once, but as the kitten persisted in its silliness, she allowed herself to laugh again and found that she had sorely missed the sound of her own laughter.

J. Tildon Dillsworthy groaned and put a hand to his brow. His head ached and there was the oddest sensation in the region of his stomach and he was quite certain he had heard the trill of a woman's laughter. His brown eyes blinked open and shut and then open again. "Who? What? Where?" he stuttered out in a soft, hesitant voice.

"You are in St. Martin's-in-the-Fields," replied Annabelle quietly, the smile still upon her face and the laughter not yet absent from her eyes. "In London. London is in England, you know. Oh, welcome, welcome, welcome!"

"Huh?" asked Dillsworthy, struggling to sit and sending the kitten scrambling to the floor.

"I am overwhelmed. Truly I am. And to see you arrive in such a fashion! It was most dramatic to be sure. And so clever of you to appear injured. Joseph has not the least idea that you are anything but a gentleman fallen from his horse. You are not quite as large as I expected."

"Huh?" Dillsworthy was not quite certain he was conscious. The young lady gazing hopefully into his eyes was easily the most delightful vision he had ever seen. The hood of her cape had slipped back to reveal a general hubbub of dark curls encircling a lovely face that boasted wide blue eyes and the most perfect lips, plump and luscious and utterly desirable.

"And I did imagine that you would look more fervent and that your shoulders would be—well—broader," she continued incomprehensibly. "Oh, oh, do forgive me. I should not have said such a thing. You are perfect just as you are I am sure. And I am so very pleased that you are here. And honored, too. And I shall be thankful to you forever for rescuing my Harry."

Dillsworthy rubbed at his eyes with both fists but when

he took them away, she was still there, beaming joyously at him. "Who are you?" he asked at last, noting that a kitten appeared to be climbing up into his lap but choosing to ignore that vision in favor of the vision of the lovely lady.

"I am Lady Annabelle," announced the vision. "I am Harry's fiancée. Do you have a name?"

"Well, of course I have a name," murmured Dillsworthy, shaking his head in an attempt to clear the fog from his brain.

"What is it?"

"Dillsworthy."

"Dillsworthy? How very odd. I thought that you would be called something like Raphael or Gabriel."

Dillsworthy was certain he had broken an entire stack of plates in his cupboard. He could not for a moment grasp the significance of this lady's conversation. Raphael? "Well, tarnation," he sighed, making a grab for the kitten that was just then digging its tiny claws into his greatcoat in an attempt to scale him as though he were a fortress. "You are the creature sent Figment to rearing I'll wager."

"Mrrrrow," responded the kitten happily, dangling from Dillsworthy's hand and batting enthusiastically at his nose.

"Does this creature belong to you, my lady?"

"To me? My goodness, no. It is yours."

"Mine?"

"Do you not remember bringing it with you, Dillsworthy? It was in your pocket."

"In my—?"

"Mrrr-pfst-pfff," declared the kitten for all the world as though it were quite aware of the conversation. "Mrrr-pfff."

"Well, I have no idea how it got into my pocket. Perhaps it belongs to the parson, eh?"

"Oh, no. The Reverend Mr. Wilde detests cats. He will

not have them anywhere around. Why if he saw it here, he would have it drowned straight off. No, I am quite certain it is yours. Perhaps He sent it without telling you."

"He who?" asked Dillsworthy, thoroughly befuddled.

"Well, I'll be, uh, dashed. It has one yellow eye and one green eye."

"Oh yes, I noticed that at once," replied Annabelle. "And it is every color possible for a kitten to be. I have never seen a kitten to equal it. That is why I am positive He must have sent it with you. Though I cannot imagine why. Harry has never expressed any particular fondness for felines."

With a vague sense of otherworldliness, Dillsworthy allowed Joseph and John Coachman to tuck him neatly into the Earl of Lackenshire's coach with a fur rug about his knees. "You are related to the Earl of Lackenshire, Lady Annabelle?" he asked, ignoring the kitten which was attempting to scramble back into the pocket of his great-coat.

"He is my brother. And he will be most pleased to make your acquaintance, I am sure. And he will give you the very nicest of his guest chambers and—"

Dillsworthy blinked. "Guest chambers?"

"Well, yes. You must live somewhere, Dillsworthy. Harry will not have you, you see. Harry will not have anyone except Georgianna, and he is not in the least pleasant to her. But she will not abandon him no matter how brusque he has become because he is her only brother and she loves him dearly."

"But—"

"You are not to worry, Dillsworthy. My brother has gobs of room. And once I explain to him that you have come to rescue Harry, he will welcome you with open arms."

"But he does not need to welcome me with open arms,"

managed Dillsworthy, choosing for the moment to ignore the thoroughly incomprehensible reference to rescuing someone named Harry. "I am already in possession of a town house."

"You are?" Lady Annabelle's pretty blue eyes widened considerably. "Oh, my, how efficient! And you have only just arrived! Where is it, your town house? Do you know?"

Dillsworthy fished the kitten out of his coat pocket and set it back upon the banquette beside him. It occurred to him that perhaps it was Lackenshire's sister who had lost her mind and that he, himself, was perfectly normal. "The house is in Green Street," he murmured, staring at the kitten which had discovered that the fur rug was just the thing to roll about on. "Number seven Green Street."

"Why that is Sir Alfred Edgerton's residence!" cried Lady Annabelle. "Oh, what a fortunate choice! You will be immediately next door to Harry! I ought to have known."

"You ought?"

"Oh, yes, because God knows absolutely everything and so He certainly would know where would be the best place for you to reside. Is it not wonderful, Dillsworthy, how He takes charge of everything if only one asks Him to do so?"

"Y-yes," stuttered Dillsworthy. "Exactly so." She *was* mad. He was sore and his head ached and there was now a kitten with one yellow eye and one green eye scampering up on to his shoulder, but he was not the person in this coach whose wits had gone abegging. And what a sad thing, too, because she was such a lovely, vivacious young woman. But she was definitely mad.

Dillsworthy glanced out the coach window, noted that they were pulling to a halt before a magnificent house in Leicester Square, and wondered what would be best to do. Ought he to escort Lady Annabelle into her home and request a brief audience with her brother to inform him of his sister's tragedy or ought he to simply part from her at the door and go on to Green Street? "Does your brother know about—about—the trouble with Harry?" he asked quietly. "Ought I to step inside for a moment, do you think, and speak with him privately?"

"Oh yes, I wish you will," nodded Lady Annabelle. "Harry and Dev were schoolboys together and Devon is quite as concerned about him as I am. Well, perhaps not quite as concerned, because Devon is not engaged to marry Harry, you know. But he is most worried. He says that Harry is determined to ruin his entire life and that I shall not marry him unless he comes to his senses. It would be so kind in you to reassure Dev that everything is going to be all right. And he will be utterly thrilled to meet you. I am positive that Dev has never before met a genuine angel!"

A genuine angel? Dillsworthy was so startled at her words that he jumped up and hit his head on the top of the coach and sent the kitten tumbling to the floor.

"You are not accustomed to coaches in heaven, I expect," smiled Lady Annabelle sweetly. "One cannot actually stand straight up in them."

"Mrrrr-pffft-pfffle," sputtered the kitten in exasperation, shaking its head and then taking a hearty swipe at Dillsworthy's boot. "Mrrrrow-pffft-pfffle!"

# *Chapter Two*

Miss Georgianna Roth stared gloomily down at the pages of Mrs. Winchester's latest novel and sighed. Apparently not even the redoubtable Mrs. Winchester could divert her from thoughts of Harry this afternoon. Dash it all, but she would like to push her brother up against his bedroom wall and pummel him until he came to his senses. She loved him and Belle loved him and Lord Lackenshire and all of his friends loved him as well. Why could Harry not believe that? Why did he persist in setting aside their every attempt to include him back in their lives? Georgianna's gaze drifted from the volume in her lap to the snow blowing against the windows. The threatening weather of yesterday had become a full-fledged storm and London was being wrapped in pristine white for a while at least. Soon enough it would become a gray, damp sludge. But for the moment it was a welcome and a cheering sight. In a fortnight it would be Christmas.

Pine boughs and holly and sprigs of mistletoe decorated the house in Green Street. Bright red and gold ribands climbed its balustrades and twined up its newel post. In every room reminders of the season glistened and glowed. In every room, except in Harry's rooms. Georgianna sighed at the thought. Christmastide had always been Harry's favorite time of the year. Yet now, not only would Harry not allow himself the joy of sharing the holiday with his friends, but he would not so much as acknowledge that Christmas was upon them. Despite all of Georgianna's efforts, Harry continued to hide behind the enormous wall he had erected around himself, dismal and restrained and reclusive. Why, he had barely spoken a word to her this morning, merely acknowledging her greeting with a nod and then closing his chamber door practically in her face. And he had not dressed today either. Evidently no matter what she did or said, Harry intended to spend the remainder of his days in a pair of old breeches, a collarless cambric shirt and his robe, unshaven and never touching a comb to his hair.

Oh, Harry, she thought in despair, why can no one reach you? With a tiny sigh she set her volume upon the cricket table and wandered to the windows, drawing the lace curtains aside to stare dejectedly down into the street. "If it were not for Belle and Lord Lackenshire I should go perfectly mad," she murmured to herself. "I am beginning to feel like a recluse myself."

All of Society had gone to the country for the holidays. Even their Uncle Nevil, Lord Rothingham, had given up on Harry for the nonce and departed for Willow's End. Every house in Green Street was locked up tight except for their own and Sir Alfred Edgerton's. Georgianna peered down at the stoop of the house next door. "I wonder who has opened up the Edgerton's house. I expect Sir Alfred has rented it out for the winter. Though why anyone would choose to winter in London of their own free will, I cannot imagine."

* * *

Tyre had selected a handsome forest green morning coat from the armoire and, deftly avoiding the kitten which was sitting at Mr. Dillsworthy's feet batting contentedly at the tassels on Mr. Dillsworthy's Hessians, he helped his gentleman to shrug into it. "Mrs. Duggan has filled the landau with any number of boxes, Mr. Dilly," he murmured. "And Oscar has bought us a hayer's wagon and we have packed it as full as it can hold of the wood and the apples. And it is still snowing."

"It is? To any great degree?"

"Considerable, Mr. Dilly. You must be certain to wear your hat and your gloves and your muffler."

"Yes, I will. Maggie, do cease that nonsense," Dillsworthy added, picking the kitten up and tossing her onto his bed. "I cannot walk with you always under my feet. What, Tyre? Why are you staring at me with such apprehension?"

"It is not apprehension, Mr. Dilly."

"No?"

"It is merely that I have been pondering."

"Uh-oh," grinned Dillsworthy, the grin transforming his very ordinary face into a visage of boyish charm. "And over what have you been pondering, Tyre?"

"I have been pondering over the lady you spoke of last evening, Mr. Dilly—the one who thought you were an angel."

"Yes?" Dillsworthy stared down his perfectly straight nose directly into Tyre's eyes.

"Well, perhaps she is not mad, Mr. Dilly."

"Not mad? A young lady who believes me to be an angel is not mad, Tyre?"

"Mrrrr-ow?" queried the kitten sitting on the bed, one green eye and one yellow eye fastened upon Dillsworthy's tassels.

Tyre lowered his eyes to fasten his gaze upon Mr. Dillsworthy's tassels as well. He truly ought not to have begun this conversation. Still, at breakfast the entire staff had discussed Mr. Dilly's recent adventure and they had all agreed—from the butler, Teal, right down to Flower, the little clock maid—that if ever an angel had been sent into their own lives, that angel had been Mr. Dilly. And perhaps the young lady had every right to name him an angel as well.

"It is like this, Mr. Dilly," Tyre murmured. "The young lady was in a church and she was quite likely praying for—for—heavenly aid, so to speak."

"Yes?" Dillsworthy cocked an eyebrow.

"Mrrrrrr?" queried the kitten hunkering down upon the feather ticking.

"And she quite likely had closed her eyes—in prayer, you know—and when she opened them she saw—"

"A man who had fallen off his horse and hit his head upon a gravestone."

"Yes, but she thought she saw an angel, Mr. Dilly. Because she wished to see an angel, don't you see? And if you are determined to discuss the thing with her brother, well, I do not think that you ought to begin by labeling his sister a lunatic."

"You are correct there, Tyre. Lackenshire would most likely take offense if I were to begin by saying that. It is fortunate that he was not at home when the coach pulled to a stop, I think. I was so nonplussed that I might well have accused his sister of being short a sheet at the precise moment I saw his face."

"Mrrrow," agreed the kitten emphatically. "Mrrrow-pffttt!" And with the greatest of abandon she sprang from the bed, attacked Dillsworthy's boots and gave one of the tassles such a magnificent swat that she fell over backward from the force of the blow. She then righted herself and dodged between Tyre's legs and up on to the shaving stand, skidding across it and sending soap, razor, brush and towel bouncing to the carpeting.

"Devil!" exclaimed Dillsworthy, caught between a laugh and a growl. "I knew I ought not to have brought you home with me, you rascal. You are going to be an enormous amount of trouble. I have been attempting all this past year to learn to be more hard-hearted, Tyre, but apparently," he chuckled, with a significant glance at the kitten who was now dangling perilously from the table runner, "I have not yet got the hang of the thing."

"No, Mr. Dilly, you have not," Tyre agreed. "Nor are you likely to get the hang of it. You were not born to it, you know. Hard-heartedness."

"No," Dillsworthy chuckled, strolling across the carpet and kneeling down to free the kitten's claws from the table runner and set her firmly upon the floor. "There. You are rescued, you minx. I promise I will not call the lady a lunatic, Tyre. Is there something else on your mind?"

"It is only that—well, the young lady did say that—well, *are* you going to rescue her Harry, Mr. Dilly?"

"Tyre, I have not the vaguest idea who this Harry person is, or if he truly requires rescuing."

"If 'tis the gentleman next door like the lady said, he is Major Harry Roth, Mr. Dilly. Of the Light Brigade. Wounded at Oporto his butler, Mr. Parker, told our Mr. Teal."

"Major Harry Roth? Of the Light Brigade?"

"Indeed. And not once since we have opened up this house has that major poked his nose out of his door. No, and his Mr. Parker says that he'll not see visitors either. Mr. Parker has orders to turn away all of his friends. I should think that sounds like a gentleman who requires rescuing from something, Mr. Dilly."

"Most likely," nodded Dillsworthy. "But if all of his friends are turned away, Tyre, what makes you think that I shall gain entrance?"

"Well, because you do have a way about you, Mr. Dilly."

"Mrrrpuff," agreed the kitten, scampering across the carpet to sit at Dillsworthy's feet and stare adoringly up at him. "Mrrrpuff!"

"Oh!" Georgianna fairly jumped as something quite light scrambled into her lap and a most inquisitive face with one yellow eye and one green one peered up at her from beneath the pages of Mrs. Winchester's book. "Well, my goodness, wherever did you come from?"

"P-pardon, miss," panted Parker, coming to a breathless halt at the doorway and leaning, exhausted, against the frame. "He, she, it came scuttling through the front door and ran straight up the staircase. I attempted to c-capture it, miss, but it is a g-good deal faster than I am."

"But you are extremely fast though, Mr. Parker," declared a voice from the corridor which Georgianna did not at all recognize. "I was amazed to see it, myself. A veritable streak of lightning you are. Good day to you, Miss Roth," the voice added, as a tall, thin gentleman with a curly-brimmed beaver in hand and a bright red muffler wound around his throat peered past Parker into the room. "So, there you are, you scamp. Come here at once, Maggie."

"Mrrrow," replied the kitten, stomping upon Georgianna's blue woolen gown, making a nest for itself in her lap.

"No, do not mrrrow me. I am quite certain that Miss Roth has not sat down upon that settee simply to give you a comfortable place to nap. I am sorry, Miss Roth," continued the gentleman not for an instant giving Georgianna an opportunity to speak. "Your Mr. Parker did attempt to turn me away, you know, but then that little scoundrel scrambled out of my pocket and right in through your doorway. It was not in the least your butler's fault," he pronounced most righteously as he strolled toward her across the Turkish carpeting. "It was my fault. Every bit of it. I am Dillsworthy," he announced, coming to a halt before her and bowing. "I have taken up residence next door for the remainder of the winter. I thought merely to stop by and pay a courtesy call upon my neighbors."

"I am most pleased to make your acquaintance, Mr. Dillsworthy," Georgianna replied as soon as she was certain he was not going to keep right on speaking. "And—and Maggie's acquaintance as well. But I am afraid that my brother is indisposed and since I am without even the semblance of a chaperon at this time—"

"Of course, of course," murmured Dillsworthy, taking Mrs. Winchester's book from her hands and placing it upon the cricket table beside her and then lifting the kitten from her lap and cradling it in one arm. "Mr. Parker, however, could quite adequately be a chaperon if he were thus inclined, could you not, Mr. Parker?"

"Oh, ah, yes, sir," replied Parker, straightening.

"I thought so. You must simply take that chair there, opposite the hearth, Mr. Parker, and keep hold of this obnoxious kitten. There. Perfect. Now, Miss Roth, we have our chaperon," declared the gentleman, unwinding the muffler and setting it, his hat and gloves upon the nearest table. He then proceeded to doff his greatcoat and lay that across the back of a Louis XIV chair. And then he pulled a wing chair half-way across the room, until it faced Georgianna squarely, and he settled into it.

Georgianna stared at him aghast. Of all the presumptuous males she had ever met! And what was Parker thinking to sit there, cowed, stroking a kitten while this brazen stranger virtually rearranged her parlor? And why on earth did she herself not protest and send the man packing? Georgianna was just about to rise to her feet and point with spectacular authority toward the doorway, thus silently yet forcefully dismissing this upstart when he harrumphed rather oddly, swiped at the brown locks that had tumbled across his brow and began to speak again.

"I do realize, Miss Roth, that I am being impertinent, but I must have a word with you."

"How fortunate then that your kitten escaped into my residence, sir," Georgianna replied. "And how fortunate that you were not loath to follow it."

"Well, I could plainly see that I was not going to gain entrance unless *something* happened," Dillsworthy smiled ingenuously, "so I set the Magnificat scampering down my leg and into the house and the entire situation was solved!"

Dillsworthy's smile was so engaging that Georgianna, who knew perfectly well that she ought to give this gentleman the most scathing setdown, found it extremely difficult not to smile back at him. "I vow, Mr. Dillsworthy, you have gained entrance to this establishment under false pretenses and I ought to have you tossed out upon your ear."

"Yes, but I can see that you are fighting to keep a straight face, Miss Roth, and so I know that you will not."

"What was it you called your kitten?"

"The Magnificat."

"Mr. Dillsworthy, that is blasphemous!"

"No, is it? Why?"

"Because The Magnificat is one of the vesper prayers. You cannot name an animal after it."

"Oh. But I did not name her after the prayer especially. It is only that I found her in a church, you see, and she is certainly magnificent with all those colors of fur and one green eye and one yellow eye, and she is a cat, Miss Roth. Of course, she is not truly a cat as yet," mused Dillsworthy. "I expect I might call her The Magnifi*kitten*. Would that be more acceptable?"

Georgianna giggled. She had not giggled since Harry had returned in March and she was abruptly aware of how wonderful it felt to giggle. Her green eyes purely glowed with the enjoyment of it. "You are not from London, Mr. Dillsworthy?"

"No, no, from Kent actually but my Uncle Alfred has given me the use of his house for the remainder of the winter. Generally, everyone in Green Street travels to the country by the end of November and so the house is perfect for my—well, for me. I was greatly surprised, let me tell you, to discover that Rothingham House is occupied this winter. Are you related to the Earl of Rothingham, Miss Roth?"

"The earl is my uncle."

"I see. And Major Roth is your brother and he is also Lady Annabelle's fiance, is he not?"

"Indeed he is. How are you acquainted with Belle, Mr. Dillsworthy?"

"We have just recently met. Lady Annabelle is the reason I have come to visit you actually." The abrupt frown that encompassed Miss Roth's features gave Dillsworthy a moment's pause. "You are not fond of Lady Annabelle?" he asked.

"Well, of course I am fond of Belle. She is to become my sister-in-law. Why should you think—"

"Because you are quite suddenly frowning, Miss Roth."

Georgianna opened her mouth and closed it again without uttering a single word. She had no idea what words to utter. Most certainly she could not betray to a perfect stranger her deep distress over Harry's and Annabelle's future. No, she could not do that, though her concern for those two dear people had brought about the scowl.

"I am quite certain," mused Mr. Dillsworthy with the most curious expression upon his face, "that there is a much more subtle way to approach this thing, Miss Roth, but I cannot at present think of it."

"What *thing,* Mr. Dillsworthy?"

"Lady Annabelle is not completely lunatic, is she?"

"Belle?" Georgianna gasped in amazement. "Lunatic? Belle?"

"I gather you do not think so."

"Most certainly not!"

"No, well, there it is then. Tyre—he is my valet—Tyre did say that it might not be so, that Lady Annabelle might be perfectly sane. Yesterday I could not imagine that to be the case, but I was terribly groggy and most confused at the time."

"At what time, Mr. Dillsworthy?"

"In the church, Miss Roth, when Lady Annabelle was wiping the blood from my brow, and in her coach, too. I had not the least inkling what she was actually thinking. And then when she informed me of it, I was completely flabbergasted and did not once think to deny it. Because I thought she had gone 'round the bend, you know."

Georgianna stared at him in silence. In the church? Wiping the blood from his brow? In the coach? What on earth had Belle and this gentleman been doing together?

"Well, but that is neither here nor there now, because I have met you and I find I like you very much and so I have decided to do it," declared Dillsworthy, his kindly brown eyes flashing with what Georgianna could plainly discern was a confident determination.

"To do what, Mr. Dillsworthy? I am afraid I do not follow your line of thought."

"I have decided to accede to Lady Annabelle's wishes in the matter of your brother, Miss Roth."

"Belle's wishes? In the matter of my brother?"

"Indeed. I have definitely decided to rescue Harry. Only, you must explain to me just what I am to rescue him from."

# Chapter Three

Major Harry Roth glared at himself in the looking glass. Ordinarily he would have avoided coming near the thing, but just this once he wished to see exactly how he looked. He had not actually looked at himself since that first time in May when he had finally been permitted to leave his bed. He had not cared, since then, to look at himself again. With one glittering green eye he studied himself in the mirror and involuntarily he shuddered. He had lost an enormous amount of weight. The shoulders that had once been broad and muscular now appeared most horribly shrunken. And so did his arms and legs for that matter. And the series of scars that covered his right shoulder and meandered down his arm and across his hand all the way to the place where two of his fingers were missing, though the awful redness of them had lessened, were now beginning to stand out even more dreadfully because they were turning a dead white and puckering. But all of this, he told himself, he could accept. It would be a struggle to do so, to accept it, but he could.

It was his face he could not accept. That one lone eye which glittered so ruthlessly and forced bile to rise from the pit of his stomach. That one lone eye. It had taken him forever to adjust to looking at the world through one eye only. But now, now that one eye saw everything. And it saw everything much too clearly. Where the other eye had been, a black patch was adjusted mercifully over the empty socket. A series of scars erupted around it, some of them wandering up into his hairline and others down over his cheek. But these scars were smaller and less chilling than those covering his shoulder and arm and hand—smaller and less chilling, but ever-present for everyone to see. A man could cover his shoulder and his arm. A man could stick a hand with missing fingers into his pocket. But a man could not go out into the world hiding one entire side of his face.

Harry's heart stuttered and dropped. There was no hope then. It had been the oddest thing, but for a moment, when he had first awakened this morning, he had felt a fluttering of hope. That was why he had come to stand before the looking glass. Something had changed. Deep inside of him, he had gotten the oddest feeling that something had changed. But it had been a dream. Nothing had changed. He was no longer the handsome, vibrant young man who had ridden off to war and glory. No. He was some freakish semblance of a man whom everyone pitied and whom no one could gaze upon without disgust.

Well, and that was it then, was it not? His life was over. He would write to his uncle immediately and request permission to take up residence at Rothingham's estate in Hampshire. No one ever visited there. Aside from the income it provided, it was the least desirable of the Rothingham residences. Surely his uncle would allow him to remove to the place. He would set himself to study the newest innovations in agriculture and put them to good use, thus making his exile a profitable one on Rothingham's behalf. Yes. Certainly his uncle would agree to that.

And Belle? Harry could feel a grinding in the pit of his stomach at the mere thought of her. Poor Belle. Poor, dear, loyal, sweetest Belle. Well, but she should be overjoyed to be freed from an engagement to a veritable freak. And she would not be surprised at it. After all, he had been refusing to see her since first he had regained his senses and come to realize the dreadfulness of his wounds.

Though she still comes every day to sit with Georgie, he reminded himself, pulling on his breeches and shrugging into his shirt. *I cannot think why she does that. She knows I will not see her. I cannot bear to see her. Not like this. Not knowing she will smile bravely at me and be shrinking away inside at the thought of marrying such a monstrosity as I have become.*

In the parlor directly below his chambers Lady Annabelle had already come to call and now fairly quivered with excitement as she peered from the window. "Oh, Georgie, there he is! Come and see him, do!" she cried.

"Come and see whom, Belle?" asked Georgianna, setting aside the tea things, rising and crossing the room to stand beside her almost-sister-in-law.

"There, there at the reins of that wagon. That," she breathed, turning to Georgianna with the most serious and awe-filled expression upon her lovely face, "that is Dillsworthy!"

"Dillsworthy," Georgianna repeated, glancing from Belle to the scene on the street below and back again.

"Does he not look magnificent with that high beaver hat and that bright red muffler 'round his neck. I did think, you know, that he was rather—unprepossessing—

when first I saw him. But he is not. I can see now that he is not! He looks exactly as he ought, sitting so upon the box."

"Exactly as he ought?" Georgianna was fairly baffled and stared back down upon the scene outside. "Belle, you are not making the least bit of sense. How is it that you think Mr. Dillsworthy looks, dearest?"

"Like a warrior chieftan about to lead his troops into battle," sighed Belle. "Oh, I know now that I was wrong to think for one moment that the best of them had been taken and that God had been able to spare me only the merest left-over."

"Annabelle Lake, tell me this instant what you are speaking of," demanded Georgianna in a playful but determined tone. "Below us on the street I see a most ordinary gentleman bundled against the cold, seated upon a hayer's wagon of all things, with a plethora of servants bustling about. And that is all I see—no warrior chieftan, no troops and not the first sign of any sort of battle. No, and when we spoke yesterday, I found Mr. Dillsworthy to be quite outrageous, let me tell you."

"You—you spoke with Dillsworthy, Georgie?"

"Indeed. He gained entrance to this very parlor in the most scheming fashion yesterday afternoon. And he would not be dismissed. And he had the sheer audacity to make himself perfectly at home despite my wishes and to declare to me that he had conceived a notion to rescue Harry!"

"Oh! Oh! Oh, Georgie!" Belle spun from the window, engulfing Georgianna in a most energetic and enthusiastic hug while practically jumping up and down. "It is going to be a glorious Christmas after all! Harry is to be saved at once! Oh, I knew Dillsworthy would do it! I knew he would!"

Laughing, Georgianna struggled to disengage herself

from the exuberant Lady Annabelle. "Truly, Belle, you are acting a perfect ninny. It is no wonder Mr. Dillsworthy questioned your sanity."

"He did what?" asked Lady Annabelle, allowing herself to be led back to a chair before the hearth and provided with a steaming cup of bohea.

"He asked me straight out if you were a lunatic," grinned Georgianna, settling into a chair herself. "And I of course, not realizing how pixilated you have suddenly become, assured the gentleman that you were not. I vow," Georgianna added with a giggle, "I have not laughed in the longest time, and here I am giggling away for the second day in a row. There is something about this Mr. Dillsworthy."

"Indeed," nodded Lady Annabelle, her dark curls bouncing becomingly. "He is wonderful, Georgie. I knew from the moment he appeared how it would be. Dillsworthy is a perfect angel!"

"Well, I should not call him that, precisely," mused Georgianna. "Mr. Dillsworthy is a bit devilish, I think. Whatever is going on?" she added as a multitude of voices began to bellow in the street below.

Upstairs, Major Roth hurried to his window to discover what was producing such a row. "What the devil is going on," he muttered to himself. "Good god, that fool is backing up over the curbing! He'll take out Aunt Minnie's favorite rose bush next. Oh, Lord, he *is* going to take out Aunt Minnie's rose bush!" Without a moment's hesitation, Major Harry Roth fumbled with the lock and then threw open the sash. "Cease backing at once, you maniac!" he shouted with a deal of vehemence, attempting to be heard over the numerous other shouts from the members of Dillsworthy's staff who were rapidly exiting the vicinity of the hayer's wagon. "Send him forward, man! Send him forward!"

Below, in the front parlor, both Georgianna and Belle started at the sound of that voice. "It is Harry!" Annabelle cried, jumping up and rushing to the front window, followed immediately by Georgianna. "Whatever is he doing outside? What can he be shouting about?"

Georgianna could not imagine. Surely Harry had not left the premises. He had not left the confines of his chambers since March. But it did sound as though he were standing upon the front stoop.

"Where did you learn to drive, you lunatic? Loose the reins and send your horse forward!" Major Roth bellowed, leaning out from his window to such a degree that he was quite visible to everyone below. The deep, resonant voice that had more than once mustered troops upon a battlefield now roared into the frigid air as clearly and authoritatively as ever it had in combat. "No, do not keep tugging at him. He'll not stop with you tugging on the reins that way. You are making him back even farther! Oh, damnation!" brayed Harry, as the right rear wheel of the wagon crunched over his Aunt Minnie's favorite rose bush.

"Harry is leaning from his window, Georgie," announced Annabelle excitedly, as she herself bent almost backward through the hurriedly opened parlor window to gaze upward at that gentleman. "Oh, how wonderful to have a glimpse of him at last!"

"If you are not careful, it will be your final glimpse, Belle," chuckled Georgianna, grabbing her almost-sister-in-law around the waist as Annabelle perched precariously backward upon the sill. "You will fall in a moment and break your head wide open. What on earth is he raving about? Oh, great heavens," she added, catching sight of Dillsworthy's wagon below them. "Aunt Minnie's rose bush!"

Dillsworthy glanced over his shoulder and upward at the

two people in the windows above him. His eyes sparkled with joy. It was working already. With the merest twist of his wrist and a gentle easing of his fingers upon the reins he brought the heavily muscled bay to a halt and then with a tiny flick, sent the horse forward. The right rear wheel of the wagon lurched back over the rose bush whose brambles had caught in its spokes and tugged the bush completely out of the bit of ground it had occupied for the past ten years, dragging it across the flagway and into the street.

Georgianna gasped to see it.

In the second story window, Major Roth groaned and hung his head only to find himself staring down into Lady Annabelle's joy-filled eyes. His first inclination was to duck immediately back inside, but then he noted her most precarious position upon the sill. "Belle," he called down to her gruffly, "get back inside immediately. You will fall and kill yourself."

Most certainly they were not words of love, but they were the first words that her Harry had spoken directly to her in nine months and Annabelle's eyes glistened with happiness at the mere sound of them.

"Do not worry, Harry," Georgianna called, "I have got her 'round the waist."

"Yes, well, pull her back inside, do, Georgie."

"G-good afternoon, Harry," Annabelle stuttered through lips trembling with joy, refusing to be pulled back inside.

Major Harry Roth could not think what to do. His head told him to draw back into his room at once, to spare Belle the ghastly sight of him, but his heart cried out for him to stay where he was for just a moment more—just a moment more. "I—I—good afternoon, Belle."

"It is m-most p-pleasant to see you again," smiled Annabelle upward. "I—I have missed you, Harry."

"Y-yes, well, do let Georgie help you back inside, Belle. It is perfectly frigid out here and you will catch your death."

"B-but, Harry—"

"Lady Annabelle, do as the major says," called another voice. "You are like to freeze else. I say, Major Roth," Dillsworthy added as he watched Lady Annabelle drawn safely back within the parlor by Georgianna's unseen hands, "quite sorry about this." And Dillsworthy held the mangled remains of Aunt Minnie's rose bush sadly up for Major Roth's inspection. "I expect it will not do to replant the thing, eh?"

"Replant it? When it looks like that? And with the ground frozen and covered in snow besides? Who the devil are you, and what in blazes made you think you knew how to drive a wagon?"

"Name's Dillsworthy. I am Sir Alfred's nephew. From Kent."

"Do they not teach people to drive in Kent?" Major Roth growled.

"Apparently not," laughed Dillsworthy, his cheeks grown as red as his muffler from the cold. "My coachman is down with the grippe just when I need him most. But I shall endeavor to muddle through. I do apologize, however, for your bush. It will not happen again." And with a tip of his high-crowned beaver, Dillsworthy spun on his heel and strolled away.

Major Roth, with an exasperated sniff, drew back into his chamber and tugged his window tightly closed. Dillsworthy. Who the devil was this Dillsworthy? Sir Alfred had never mentioned any nephew named Dillsworthy. And why should the fellow show up now, in the dead of winter? Anyone with any sense would have remained in the country.

Major Roth, rubbing his hands together for warmth and moving toward the fire blazing on the grate, was not, however, terribly curious and would quite likely have dismissed all thoughts of the gentleman from his mind had it not abruptly occurred to him how quickly Annabelle had followed Dillsworthy's instructions. Had not he, himself, ordered Annabelle from the window sill? But she had not listened to him. No. But one word from this—this country squire—and she was gone back into the parlor as meek as a lamb. Why? Obviously they were known to each other. But Belle had never been to Kent that he knew of. No. Never once in her life. Had she met this Dillsworthy here in London, then? And what power did the man hold over her to make her accede to his wishes so promptly?

"Did you see?" Annabelle asked excitedly, once again taking a chair before the hearth in the front parlor. "Oh, Georgie, already dearest Harry is on his way back to us. Why, he actually opened his window and roared at Dillsworthy!"

Georgianna's emerald eyes met Annabelle's sapphire ones and they both grinned. "Do you mean to tell me that you think Mr. Dillsworthy *intended* to back that dreadful old wagon over Aunt Minnie's favorite rose bush?"

"Indeed. And it worked, too."

"Yes, you will get no argument from me there. He most definitely brought Harry out of his sulks for a moment or two. Not that I should enjoy to have Harry bellowing like that at me, mind you. But at least it is something. Until now, all he has done is sit and sulk and mutter mindlessly to himself."

"And—and he said good afternoon to me," added Annabelle in a most wistful tone. "And he ordered me to go inside. Oh, Georgie, he does still care for me. I knew he did, only it has been so very, very long since I have had the least sign of it."

* * *

J. Tildon Dillsworthy tossed what remained of Aunt Minnie's rose bush into his butler's hands and climbed back up onto the box of the wagon. "Do something with it, will you, Teal?"

"Indeed, Mr. Dilly," murmured that worthy, staring down at the brambles in his gloved hands. "What?"

"Burn it, I expect. But ask McDonough before you do. Mayhap he can take a cutting from it or something. At least a part of it may live on. Scotty, Jemmy, Madden, are you aboard?" he added, glancing over his shoulder to check that his stable boy, his fire boy and his head groom had gained places amongst the load of goods in the wagon. "Very well then. We are off for true this time. Tyre, climb up here beside me. We shall be late in returning, Teal, because we must stop at the coal yard in Bridge Street. Ah, there comes Oscar with the coach now."

A shining black traveling coach came rumbling up the street, the coachman waving as he passed the wagon. With considerable skill, Dillsworthy gave his horse the office to start and fell into line behind it. "I do hope the good major is no longer watching," he grinned, as he urged the bay into a trot.

"Not a sign of him, Mr. Dilly," Tyre replied. "I never saw such a sight as you backing over that bush. You looked the veriest whipster."

"Yes, and it did the trick. I knew we would get his attention once you all began to shout. And we were correct to wait until Lady Annabelle should be there before we did the thing too. It has been a while since he has laid eyes upon her I think. Did you see the look upon his face when he noticed her?"

"It is kind of you to help them, Mr. Dilly."

"Well, I cannot see why we should not, Tyre, if we can. After all, we are come to London to lend a hand where we can. And though titled ladies and majors of the Light Brigade are not generally in our line, well, it is no hardship for us to do what we can for them.''

"No hardship whatsoever," agreed Tyre as they turned into Green Park behind the coach and a light snow began to fall. "No hardship whatsoever, Mr. Dilly."

# *Chapter Four*

"Mr. Dillsworthy, I am most grateful to you for taking an interest in Harry," Georgianna began somewhat hesitantly the following morning as that gentleman appeared before her. "But it is most inappropriate for you to be visiting *me*."

"It is?" asked Dillsworthy, crossing the Turkish carpet to take up a position before the fireplace. "Devilish cold out," he murmured, lifting The Magnifikitten from the perch she had taken upon his shoulder and setting her upon the floor. "Why did you tell Mr. Parker to send me up then, if it is inappropriate?"

"Because I—because you—I wished to thank you for driving over Aunt Minnie's rose bush yesterday. Belle thinks that you did so purposefully to draw Harry out."

"Was it so very obvious then? And here I thought I had done the thing quite subtly."

"Oh, I am quite certain that Harry has no inkling that you planned the incident. Why, he mumbled about your lack of driving prowess for hours yesterday Arlesby said.

Arlesby is my brother's valet. He is the only one Harry does not immediately turn out of his chambers. Perhaps you might return, Mr. Dillsworthy, when Belle comes to visit. She comes practically every afternoon at two. And it would be quite acceptable for you to visit the two of us together for we will chaperone each other, you see."

"Your brother will not see Lady Annabelle when she calls?"

"He will not come down and though Belle would go up to him despite the impropriety, he refuses to open his door to her."

"What impropriety?"

"Mr. Dillsworthy, it is most unacceptable for a young lady to be visiting a gentleman in his bedchamber. Certainly even you realize that."

"Even if they are affianced? No, I did not realize. I am not quite up to snuff on all the rigamarole, Miss Roth."

"Mrrr-yow," agreed The Magnifikitten, settling upon her haunches and gazing adoringly up at Dillsworthy.

"Yes, mrrr-yow indeed. As if you *were* up to snuff on all the rules of Polite Society, you little twit. No," Dillsworthy added with the cock of an eyebrow, "do not even think it, Mags. We are paying a call and I will not have you acting the hoyden."

"Acting the hoyden, Mr. Dillsworthy?" Georgianna could feel the smile slipping onto her face. Really, it was the most amazing thing how often she had smiled in the past few days. "What is it you think she intends to do? She is behaving quite properly."

"Yes, but in a moment she will be after the tassels on my Hessians. I can see it in her eyes. And I did not bring her with me to be attacking my tassels in the middle of your parlor."

"Why did you bring her?"

"Because she is the most wonderful little creature and has the most amazing propensities."

It was Georgianna's turn to cock an eyebrow. "What on earth do you mean, Mr. Dillsworthy?"

"Well, I have every intention of making your brother's acquaintance this morning."

"I do not think that Harry will come down to you, Mr. Dillsworthy."

"Of course he will not. If he will not see his own fiancée, why should he make the effort to meet a perfect stranger? But that is why I have brought Mags."

"You think Harry will wish to see a kitten?" asked Georgianna, amazed. "Mr. Dillsworthy, Harry is not even excessively fond of dogs. A kitten will never lure him from his chambers."

"No, but that is where Maggie's propensities come in," Dillsworthy assured her knowingly. "You will see, Miss Roth. I shall make the major's acquaintance. Maggie will see that I do."


Major Roth was just tumbling out of bed when a quiet scratching sounded upon his bedchamber door. "Go away!" he bellowed. "I have just got up." The scratching, however, continued. Grumbling, Harry slipped into his robe. It would be Georgianna, of course. Had it been any one of the servants they would have ceased to plague him immediately he roared at them. "Well, what is it, Georgie, that is so very important that it cannot wait?" he mumbled, tugging the door inward. "I—" Harry swallowed the rest of the sentence and gazed, perplexed, up and down the corridor. Georgianna was not there. No one was there. With a sigh, he turned back into the room and slammed the door behind him. Now he was hearing things!

"There. In," whispered Dillsworthy, peeking neatly around the corner once the door had closed.

"Really, Mr. Dillsworthy," Georgianna murmured as she

huddled against the wall beside him, "I cannot think why I am allowing you to do this."

"Because you wish to rescue Harry just as much as does Lady Annabelle," Dillsworthy replied quietly, "and nothing you have attempted so far has done the job."

"Yes, but I do not even know you."

"Well, but you know that I am Sir Alfred's nephew and that I am at present living next door. What more is there to know? I am not proposing to marry you, Miss Roth, only to help your brother. And I cannot do it all at a distance. I must gain an audience with him. I expect this is the very best way."

"But how will you know when it is time?"

"I will know," nodded Dillsworthy confidently. "Believe me, I will know."

"Damnation!" roared Major Roth from behind his closed door. "Arlesby! Parker! Georgie!"

"Now, I believe, is the time," whispered Dillsworthy. "Hold the servants at bay, Miss Roth. I am depending upon you to give me time no matter how much ranting and raving he does." And with that Dillsworthy was around the corner, down the corridor and pushing open the door to Major Roth's bedchamber.

"Arlesby?" Roth growled as he turned toward the door. "Good god, what the devil are you doing here? Get out! Arlesby! Parker!"

"I heard you call and I knew this must be the place."

"What place? You do not belong in this chamber! You do not even belong in this house!"

"No, I expect I do not," shrugged Dillsworthy. "On the bed is she?"

"What?"

"You are glaring at your bed. Is she on it, then?"

"She? She who?"

"The Magnifikitten."

"The Magnifi—Magnifikitten?" Major Roth stared dumbfounded at Dillsworthy. "The Magnifikitten?"

"Yes. I do think The Magnificat is a deal better for a name, but your sister thought that was blasphemous. I, personally, do not think it is," he added, strolling toward the canopied bed swathed in heavy blue draperies, "but ladies, you know, must be bowed to in such things. Maggie, are you in there?" Dillsworthy elbowed his way past Roth and drew the draperies aside. "Maggie?"

"There," grumbled Roth, pointing in aggravation at a lump in the covers which wiggled the merest bit. "A moment ago that counterpane was leaping about as if a dervish had been imprisoned beneath it."

"No, really?" asked Dillsworthy, staring at the major, one eyebrow cocking significantly. "And Mags is generally such a sedate little being."

"Mrrr-pft," agreed the kitten in a muffled voice.

"Am I to understand that there is a kitten hiding under my counterpane and that it belongs to you, sir?" the major grumbled, although the grumbling part took him some determination because Dillsworthy's face had creased in silent laughter at the muffled mrr-pft and Dillsworthy's face creased in laughter was unaccountably difficult to grumble at.

"I am afraid so."

"Well get it out, man! Don't just stand there grinning like a fool. Get the thing out and then get the both of you out of my chambers at once! How did it get in here in the first place is what I should like to know."

"Perhaps," mused Dillsworthy, theatrically stroking his chin, "you opened your door when she scratched? Do not feel a fool if you did. I did exactly the same thing last night, went to the door, saw no one there, turned back around and crawled into my bed, and whop!"

"Whop?"

"Yes, whop, precisely. No sooner did my foot get between

the sheets than she pounced upon my toes. Rose straight up to the canopy, let me tell you.''

The image of this tall, thin, very ordinary looking gentleman in nightshirt and cap rising straight up into a canopy amused the major immensely, but he brought himself directly to order, refusing to let the smile that tickled at the corners of his lips rise on to his face. ''That is all well and good, Mr. Dillsworthy, but I want you to get that thing out of my bed.''

''No, Major Roth, you fail completely to understand. It was not well and good at all. My bed has a wooden canopy and I knocked my head against the thing with tremendous force. It was a considerable catastrophe.''

''You broke your head?''

''Broke the canopy. Dislodged it from its moorings. Thing came crashing down. Mags and I barely escaped with our lives, let me tell you.''

''Murryow! Murryow!'' agreed The Magnifikitten from beneath the major's counterpane, apparently jumping up and down in exclamation.

''Exactly, Mags!'' nodded Dillsworthy. ''Precisely!''

Major Harry Roth stared at the gentleman beside him, then at his blankets rising and falling with a thwack, thwack, thwack and another murryow. He rubbed a hand across the back of his neck. He cleared his throat. He turned away and then turned back again. He coughed. He hmmmed. He inhaled and held his breath. ''Who the devil are you?'' he asked on a gasp.

''Dillsworthy. Were you not listening yesterday? J. Tildon Dillsworthy, and this,'' he added, bending to fish beneath the major's covers and scoop out the oddest looking kitten Roth had ever laid eyes upon, ''is The Magnifikitten.''

A most overwhelming sensation arose in the major's stomach and flowed straight up through his chest and into his throat and behind his nose and up into his brain. It made his eye water and his ears ring. It made him sniff and snuffle and sneeze. He closed his eye and opened it again, but Dillsworthy was still standing there, his brown eyes aglow with enthusiasm, his brown curls fairly standing at attention with exuberant pride as he held the kitten up for the major's inspection and quite obviously for his admiration as well.

"Oh, do give over, Roth," Dillsworthy said at last. "You are going to laugh. You know you are. There is no stopping it once it has got so far as to set a person to sneezing and blinking."

"I n-never," gasped Roth. "I n-never—" and then he was holding both arms across his stomach, and bending forward and guffawing at the very top of his lungs.

Directly outside her brother's door Georgianna stared wide-eyed at the butler and her brother's valet. Parker and Arlesby stared back, open-mouthed. "Is that what I imagine it to be?" asked Georgianna.

"It is Major Roth, miss," whispered Arlesby hoarsely, "and he is laughing."

"He is truly laughing, miss," managed Parker, over a great lump in his throat.

Georgianna noted that a most suspicious sheen was rising in Parker's fine gray eyes and in Arlesby's haughty hazel ones. In a moment there might well be tears. One tear was already making its way slowly down Georgianna's own cheek. "I have wished for so very long to hear that sound again," murmured Georgianna unsteadily as a great tension lifted from her. "I thought Harry destined to remain in the dismals forever."

"Do you think I ought to go in to him now, miss?" asked Arlesby, tugging distractedly at his coat sleeves. "He will wonder, you know, why no one answered his summons."

"No, no, I think we should continue to do as Mr. Dillsworthy requested," Georgianna advised. "You shall go to

Major Roth when Mr. Dillsworthy has left him and not before."

Georgianna tugged a lace handkerchief from her sleeve and wiped several tears away. Harry was laughing. And not some mere titter either, but a series of whoops and guffaws that grew less inhibited and jollier by the moment. Whatever was occurring in her brother's chambers, whatever it was Mr. Dillsworthy had done and continued to do, she could never thank him enough for it.

How odd, she thought, that such an ordinary gentleman, and a stranger to boot, could walk into her home one day and announce that he intended to rescue Harry and then do precisely that. Of course, just because Harry was laughing this one time did not mean that he had shucked off the dismals completely and would be his old self from this moment on. Georgianna was not a peagoose. She understood well enough that the wall Harry had erected around himself was much higher and stronger than that. But this laughter, much like the anger that had flowed from him yesterday afternoon, was a chink in that wall into which a lever might be inserted. In time, with enough leverage, the entire wall might well come tumbling down.

Oh, but Harry's laughter was a wonderful sound! It made Georgianna's heart flutter and her hopes rise and she could barely refrain from hugging herself in glee right there in the corridor. If only Belle were here, if only Belle could share in the sudden hope surging through her!

"Dillsworthy, come out," laughed the major, staring down at the bottoms of Dillsworthy's boots where they stuck out from beneath the bed. "The fool kitten has already eluded you and is on her way to the top of the night table."

"Well snatch her up," called Dillsworthy in a somewhat

muffled voice as he began to crawl out from beneath the bed. "You are a cavalryman. Outflank her."

"I," stated Major Roth in good-humored tones, "am not the one who allowed her to escape."

"No, but it is your stocking she pounced upon and your stocking she is determined to tear to shreds. And it was you who teased her with it to begin with. Now she has got completely out of hand."

"Yes," grinned Major Roth, fondly observing The Magnifikitten as she padded triumphantly across his night table, tripping occasionally upon the long white stocking dangling from between her sharp little teeth. The Magnifikitten gave a throaty little brrr-pft and leaped clumsily to the floor. "Yes, Dillsworthy, she is completely out of hand."

"Brrrrr, pffff," commented the kitten quite happily, heading for a chair near the window. "Brrrr, brrrr, pffff!"

Dillsworthy scrambled to his feet, took a stand beside the major and watched as The Magnifikitten dug her claws into the chair and scampered up on to the wide seat, tugging the stocking up with her and then pouncing upon it and rolling about, tangling herself up in the thing with the utmost abandon.

"Well, she is quite a fighter," mused the major with a grin. "That stocking is three times her size, Dillsworthy, but I do believe she is going to subdue the thing."

"And quite possibly eat it," sighed Dillsworthy.

"No, she'll not eat it. Do you not know the first thing about kittens?"

"Not the first thing," admitted Dillsworthy with a sad shake of his head. "Do you?" he asked then, looking hopefully into the major's smiling face.

"Well, we had kittens when I was small. But they spent most of their time in the cellars or in the stables."

"Oh. Well, I cannot do that."

"Do what?"

"Send her to the cellars or to the stables. The cellars are absolutely frigid and my uncle's mews are three streets away. Besides, we have grown fond of each other, Mags and I, and a person does not send someone he is fond of away. At least, I do not," Dillsworthy declared with a decided glare in his straightforward brown eyes. "A person owes a sort of allegiance to those he is fond of and who are fond of him."

"But sometimes that allegiance demands that you send them away," murmured the major, his thoughts immediately traveling to Belle and Georgianna and his friends. "There are times, Dillsworthy, when one must send them away for their own good," he mumbled, collapsing into a chair by the fire.

"Balderdash," whispered Dillsworthy, running his fingers through his hair and sending his curls off in all directions, then placing his hands upon his hips and staring down at Roth. "I have been sent away twice in my life for my own good and there was not a bit of good came from it, let me tell you. It was all bad. Very, very bad, and it hurt like the devil too."

"But you got over it, did you not, Dillsworthy?"

"No."

"Oh," sighed the major, sadness once again swirling around him, his laughter all but forgotten.

"Mrrrgle," offered The Magnifikitten consolingly, abandoning the stocking and scaling the major as far as his shoulder to bestow a rough little kiss upon his ear. "Mrrrgle-waffs."

# Chapter Five

"And did Harry come down afterward?" asked Annabelle hopefully, taking her knitting from her bag and preparing to spend the remainder of the afternoon in the Roth's parlor as she had done any time these past few months.

"No, Belle, he did not come down," Georgianna replied, settling back to resume her own stitchery. "But he did laugh. Oh, you should have heard him laugh! It was the most delightful sound. And to think I have taken his laughter for granted all my life until this past March. What fools we are to think nothing of the laughter of our loved ones. We ought to give thanks for every chuckle, every smile. I gave thanks heartily this morning, let me tell you."

"I so wish I had been here," sighed Annabelle. "Do you think Dillsworthy will return this afternoon?"

"Oh, I cannot think so. Apparently he is quite busy with other things. There have been innumerable people running in and out next door and dashing off to here and there ever since he bid Harry goodbye. I have been peeking at them from the window," Georgianna confessed, a blush rising to her cheeks.

"Peeking at them? From the window? You, Georgie?"

"Yes. I cannot seem to help myself. Mr. Dillsworthy is a virtual enigma. And his staff—why, I have never seen a group of servants more boisterous and merry in all my life. Whatever it is that keeps them and their master rushing about, Belle, they apparently are enjoying it immensely. And Mr. Dillsworthy drove off in that atrocious hayer's wagon again, not above a quarter of an hour before you came. What can he be doing, Belle, driving about town in such a conveyance? It is most distracting to see him upon the box of a farmer's vehicle—and he all dressed to the nines. And the wagon was quite filled to overflowing."

"With what?" asked Annabelle, her head bent over her knitting.

"I cannot say. Covered up with a tarpaulin. But it was leaking bits of straw. Belle, can you not tell me more about Mr. Dillsworthy? How do you come to know him?"

"I have been thinking," murmured Annabelle, studiously keeping her gaze from meeting Georgianna's, "and I do not think I am supposed to tell anyone."

"What? But whyever not?"

"Because," whispered Lady Annabelle, "it is a very private thing and I do not know the rules and perhaps if I tell, Dillsworthy must go away."

Georgianna ceased her stitchery and stared in silent astonishment at her sister-in-law-to-be.


"It is not that I find Mr. Dillsworthy at all to my taste," Georgianna assured herself that night as she extinguished her bedside candles and snuggled down into the feather ticking. "It is merely that I am overwhelmingly curious about the man." Yes, curious, she thought, closing her eyes. I do not believe I have ever met anyone quite like him before, and now Belle will not so much as tell me how the two of them came to meet. "Sir Alfred's nephew," she murmured, turning onto her side and cradling her cheek upon one cupped hand. "Sir Alfred Edgerton's nephew."

Georgianna sat up quite suddenly and stared into the darkness. If the gentleman were indeed Sir Alfred's nephew, why had she not made his acquaintance before this? She had been on the town for two whole Seasons and she thought she had made the acquaintance of every acceptable gentleman in England. Did Mr. Dillsworthy *never* go about in Society then? Did he come to town *only* in winter when all of Society had gone to the country? And why had Sir Alfred never so much as alluded to a nephew in Kent?

Perhaps he was not Sir Alfred's nephew at all but an imposter come to—to—"To do what?" Georgianna whispered into the night. "To drive about in a hayer's wagon and run down innocent rose bushes? To infiltrate people's houses with the insidious help of The Magnifikitten? To make Harry bellow and laugh?" Yes, she thought, a smile curving her lips upward. Mr. Dillsworthy is some imposter come specifically to Green Street in the middle of winter just to make Harry bellow and laugh.

Truly, she was being a perfect peagoose. There was no reason to suspect that Mr. Dillsworthy was not Sir Alfred's nephew just as he said. Only she wished she had known. She wished she had known that Sir Alfred possessed such a nephew and she wished they had come to know each other during the Season—that Mr. Dillsworthy had taken her for drives in Hyde Park and escorted her to the opera and danced with her at the Presentation balls.

"What am I thinking?" Georgianna murmured, distractedly untying and retying her night cap. "To drive in Hyde Park with Mr. Dillsworthy? I am losing my mind." With a soft sigh, she lay back down and determined to put all thoughts of Mr. Dillsworthy from her mind and drift off to sleep.

In the establishment immediately next door, Mr. Dillsworthy was strongly wishing to drift off to sleep himself, but he was having a difficult time of it. "Drat," he muttered, propping himself up against his pillows and reaching over to strike a flint and relight his candle.

"Mrrr-pft?" queried the little lump on the bed beside him, raising a white and black and brown head to gaze up blearily.

"I am sorry, Maggie. I know you were asleep, but I cannot seem to do likewise."

"Mrrr," sighed the kitten, stretching.

"It is—it is—well, I do not know what it is, actually. I just cannot seem to settle down." Dillsworthy wiggled his feet between the sheets and ran a hand through his hair, dislodging his nightcap entirely. "And it does not help," he added, lifting the kitten into his arms and cradling her against his chest, "to have the house filled with the smells of baking. I have never been so endlessly hungry as I have these past few days."

With a tiny sniff, The Magnifikitten reached up and batted at Dillsworthy's chin. Then she stood upon his arm and stretching upward licked the precise spot she had batted, her rough little tongue setting Dillsworthy to chuckling.

"Yes, you are a charmer, are you not? Lord, whoever would have guessed that I would have a kitten in my bed? Is there nothing you cannot get me to do for you?"

"Mrrph," replied The Magnifikitten smugly.

"Mrrph, indeed," chuckled Dillsworthy. "Did you notice Miss Roth peeking from her window this afternoon, Mags? Like a curious little girl, she was. A peek here and a peek there. I laughed to see it. She is pondering the hay wagon, I think. And all the bustle. And you were very good," he added, as the kitten scampered to his shoulder and began to lick his ear. "I did not need to go looking for you once. You stayed on the box just as you ought. But you cannot go tomorrow. Tomorrow you must spend the day with Major Roth. She truly is very beautiful, is she not, Mags?" he added in complete nonsequitur. "Miss Roth is even more beautiful than Lady Annabelle."

"Yrrr-ow," agreed the kitten enthusiastically, abandoning Dillsworthy's ear and pouncing upon his strayed nightcap, engaging it in major combat.

"I only hope our assault upon her brother will prove successful. It cannot be easy for Miss Roth to constantly worry about him. And she does, Mags. Anyone can see she does."

"Pft-sss-pft," replied The Magnifikitten, paying not the least attention as she stomped up and down with all four feet upon the nightcap's tassle, squashing it into submission. "Pft-brrr-sss-pft!"

Major Roth had just settled into the chair by the window to sip his morning coffee and glance over the pages of *The Times* when a knock sounded upon his chamber door. "Who is it?" he called sullenly.

"Dillsworthy."

"Dillsworthy?" The major glared at the shining oak of the door. Dillsworthy? What the devil did the man want now? And how the deuce had he gotten into the house past Parker and then up the staircase all the way to the second story? "He did not get past Parker," the major mumbled, setting his newspaper and coffee aside and rising. "Parker allowed the man entrance. I'll have his hoary head for this."

It did occur to Roth that nothing required him to open the door to Dillsworthy, yet he had not quite managed to forget Dillsworthy's haunted whisper when he had spoken of being sent away. No, and he had not forgotten his own laughter and the forgetfulness that had swept through him at Dillsworthy's presence either. He had not once thought, for the brief time that the man had been in his chambers, of his missing fingers, his scars or the horrible travesty partially hidden by the eye patch.

"Well, what is it?" the major growled, flinging his chamber door wide.

"May I come in?"

"You have not got that wretched kitten with you, have you?"

"Uh, no," murmured Dillsworthy.

"Mrrrow," said a muffled little voice simultaneously.

Roth lifted an eyebrow.

"Be quiet, can you not, Mags. The major does not wish to see you, so I am telling him a bouncer and you are ruining it."

"Mrrrrr-oofwer?" queried the kitten, poking its head from the pocket of Dillsworthy's greatcoat.

"Oh, come in," mumbled Roth, waving Dillsworthy past him into the chambers. "And do take your coat off. Why did you not give it to Parker?"

"Parker?"

"You know very well that Parker is the butler. And I know very well that you did not enter this house without passing him."

"Well, of course not," countered Dillsworthy, shrugging out of his greatcoat and laying it across a lyre-backed chair near the doorway. "It is only that I do not wish to get Parker into trouble. He did tell me I ought not bother you."

"You *ought not?*"

"Well, he did put it a bit more strongly. But I did not listen to him, you see, and now he is doubtless downstairs quaking in his shoes. He is a magnificent butler, Major.

Truly. But I am a considerable handful when it comes to having my way."

Major Roth stared at the gentleman in the buff breeches and plum-colored morning coat and smiled the merest bit of a smile. "I begin to suspect that you may be," he allowed, waving Dillsworthy into the wing chair that matched his own. "A handful, I mean. Will The Magnifikitten remain in your pocket?"

"I have not the least idea," Dillsworthy grinned, sitting and crossing one knee over the other. "No," he amended, hearing a soft plop behind him. "She is out already. Are you growing a beard then?"

"Growing a—?"

"Will Lady Annabelle like it do you think? I attempted to grow a beard once, but I looked the devil in it. Rather like a wretched gravedigger is what Mrs. Duggan said."

"Who is Mrs. Duggan?" queried the major, settling back into his own chair and rubbing a hand rather self-consciously against the dark stubble on his cheek. "And how do you come to know Belle?"

"My cook. Mrs. Duggan is my cook. I do not know Lady Annabelle. Not really. We merely, ah, bumped into each other in church one afternoon and struck up a conversation. Well, I mean, when she discovered I was to be your neighbor, it was only proper, was it not, for her to welcome me to the neighborhood?"

"This is not *her* neighborhood," the major muttered with the lift of an eyebrow. "You have not got designs upon Belle, have you, Dillsworthy?"

"Lady Annabelle? Great God, no! Maggie, do not," added Dillsworthy, abruptly rising from his chair and dashing across the carpet, snatching up the kitten at the very moment that she took a hearty swipe at a delicately fashioned glass pitcher upon the major's bedside table and sent it tumbling to the floor. "Damnation, Mags, now he will never do it," Dillsworthy grumbled, stooping hurriedly to pick up the pitcher and the handle that had cracked off from it. "Look. You have broken the blasted thing."

"Never do what?" asked the major, grinning the merest bit at the kitten who was attempting to squirm from Dillsworthy's grasp.

"Well, I did have a plan," sighed Dillsworthy, placing the two parts of the pitcher back on the table.

"What plan?"

"It is—I was—that is to say—"

"Out with it, Dillsworthy."

"I thought perhaps," sighed Dillsworthy, gathering the kitten protectively against his chest, "that if I came here and—and we got to know each other better—that perhaps you would not mind to watch The Magnifikitten for me for the rest of today."

"You thought what?" Major Roth did not know precisely whether to bellow or to laugh. He did neither, electing instead to rise to his feet and face Dillsworthy head on. It was neither his intention nor his fault that one of his fingers apparently took it into mind to ramble gently over the space between The Magnifikitten's ears and then down the velvety length of her nose. "Dillsworthy, this is the outside of enough. Why would I even think to play nursery maid to your kitten? You have got servants. Leave it at home with them."

"They are all coming with me except Mrs. Duggan and she is much too busy to keep a watchful eye upon Mags."

"I see," nodded the major, who did not quite see, because where Dillsworthy could be off to with all of his servants except the cook he could not imagine. "Well, leave the kitten with my servants then."

"No."

"No? Dillsworthy I have made you an offer because you are a neighbor that I would not think to make to anyone else—damned if I would. And you will not take it?"

"Well, but, your servants will not take the time to play

with her, you know. And she is—that is to say—she likes *you*. And I thought, you know, that you *liked* her as well."

"Well, I do like her, Dillsworthy, but—Georgie! Georgie has always been fond of animals. She would be pleased as punch to play with the creature."

"She cannot," replied Dillsworthy. "She is to accompany me. I am in need of her assistance."

"Georgie's assistance? And just what is she to assist you with?"

"Well—well—it is a secret, actually."

"Oh, great heavens," sighed the major, "give the kitten here, man. I cannot think why you are so concerned about such a little ball of fluff, but I will do my best until you return. Which will not be too very late," he added with a frown.

"No," Dillsworthy replied with a shake of his head. "I give you my word. Not late at all. I shall return as quickly as possible."

"Off with you then," grumbled Roth, taking The Magnifikitten into his own arms and waving Dillsworthy toward the door. "You are not driving any sort of vehicle, are you? Dillsworthy? I shall not allow Georgie to accompany you if you are driving."

"No, no, we are going in my coach with Oscar at the reins. And Flower will ride inside with us to chaperone."

"Flower?"

"My clock maid," nodded Dillsworthy, snatching up his greatcoat and backing hurriedly out the door. "Thank you," he added as he backed into the hall and turned toward the staircase. "Extremely grateful."

Clock maid? thought Major Roth as he closed his chamber door and turned to set The Magnifikitten down upon the carpet again. What the devil is a clock maid? "I vow, Maggie, your master is the oddest piece of work I have ever met in my life and that's a fact. And how he has got

Georgie to offer him aid when she has not known him so much as seven days put together, I cannot guess."

"I am what?" asked Georgianna staring wide-eyed at the gentleman who stood donning his greatcoat in the doorway to the morning room.

"You are coming for a ride in my coach."

"I most certainly am not."

"Yes, you are," nodded Dillsworthy with certainty. "It is all part of the plan."

"What plan, Mr. Dillsworthy?"

"The plan to rescue Harry."

"Leaving Harry with a kitten and taking me off somewhere in your coach is part of a plan? Really, Mr. Dillsworthy, I do wonder about your sanity."

"No. It is a perfect plan. My coach will be out front in fifteen minutes. Can you be ready by then?"

"Certainly not," protested Georgianna. "Why I barely know you, Mr. Dillsworthy. And I most certainly cannot go jaunting about town with you in a closed vehicle."

"But we will have a chaperon, Miss Roth. I promised your brother so and I will keep my word on it. Please say you will. It is for Harry's sake."

Georgianna could not imagine for one moment where Mr. Dillsworthy could possibly be bound at eleven o'clock in the morning. Nor could she imagine why on earth her heart had given the slightest lurch at the thought of accompanying him. But he *was bound* somewhere and her heart *had lurched* and truly when he stared at one like that—all innocence and pleading—his most ordinary face took on a most extraordinary attraction. She had, in fact, the strongest urge to brush the soft brown curls from his brow and cup his cheek in her hand and assure him that she was his to command. Which is all complete and utter nonsense! she told herself in silence, watching as Dillsworthy lowered his gaze to tug on his gloves, then sought her face again.

"Well, since it is for Harry's sake," she whispered, her cheeks most unaccountably flushing a bright pink. What was wrong with her to blush as if she were a country miss asked out upon her first drive? Honestly, anyone would think she had never before agreed to accompany a gentleman anywhere—she, who had been The Incomparable for two Seasons running.

"Good," nodded Dillsworthy. "Good. In fifteen minutes then, Miss Roth. Shall I knock for you?"

"No, Mr. Dillsworthy," sighed Georgianna. "No need to knock. I shall step outside all on my own."

# Chapter Six

J. Tildon Dillsworthy, though he did not knock upon her door, came to meet Georgianna upon her doorstep, offering her his arm and escorting her most politely into his coach. "You look lovely, Miss Roth," he declared in a quiet and unaccountably shy voice as he took the seat across from her.

"Why, thank you, Mr. Dillsworthy," Georgianna replied, one warmly gloved hand nervously fingering the marabou trim of the fur cloak she had wrapped tightly around her. "And who is this, may I ask?" she added, smiling kindly at the very young person upon the seat beside her.

"Flower. Flower, say how do you do to Miss Roth."

" 'Ow do ye do, miss," smiled the young person with great good will. "I'm being Mr. Dilly's chaperon. I ain't never—have never—bin a chaperon before, but it must be me 'cause there ain't—isn't—no room for anyone bigger."

"Indeed," nodded Georgianna, Flower's heart-shaped little face and bright blue eyes fairly stealing her heart away. "Mr. Dillsworthy, what are all these boxes? My goodness, and it smells wonderfully like a bakery in this coach."

"They are, ah, things," murmured Dillsworthy, who was sharing his seat with innumerable cartons and crates and bandboxes. Several of the containers were stacked between Flower and the opposite door as well and filled the space between the floor of the coach and her feet. "Wave goodbye to your brother, Miss Roth. He is watching from his window."

"Harry? He is?" Georgianna peered upward from the coach window and was both surprised and pleased to observe Major Roth standing in the window of his chambers staring down at them. Beside him, tiny nose and two front paws pressed against one of the panes, The Magnifikitten stared downward as well. Georgianna raised one hand in farewell and Harry waved back as the coach moved into the street. "And where are we bound?" asked Georgianna pleasantly, the surprising warmth and coziness of the coach and the sweet smiling presence of Flower putting her in a most comfortable mood.

"To Leicester Square," Dillsworthy replied, setting his high-topped beaver atop the stack of boxes beside him. "To pick up Lady Annabelle."

"Belle? Where on earth do you plan to put her?" Georgianna smiled. "There is not enough space in here for a mouse."

"Yes, well, it is a bit more crowded than I thought it would be. But we shall contrive, Miss Roth. We shall contrive."

Major Roth watched until Dillsworthy's coach drove from sight, then turned from the window, stuffing his hands into the pockets of his breeches. Behind him he heard a tiny "mrrf" and a soft plop as The Magnifikitten ceased staring out the window and jumped to the carpeting.

"Just so," Roth mumbled. "They are gone off without us, Mags. You must adjust to being abandoned from time to time you know. You are a cat, after all, and you cannot forever be riding about in Dillsworthy's pockets."

"Mffle-brrr-mph."

"Indeed. It is not truly so terrible to be left alone," the major declared, beginning to pace. "I have been alone since March. Well, since June. That's when that confounded Dr. Mackenzie ceased to plague me. And I have enjoyed it, too. It is peaceful to be left alone."

"Mrrrow," The Magnifikitten commented, pattering along behind him and at every other step taking a swipe at the heels of the major's slippers.

"Well, perhaps I have not enjoyed it exactly. But it is not so very horrible. At least I am not forced to dress for dinner—and I know that my face will not keep everyone else from eating. Ouch," Roth chuckled at one enthusiastic and particularly well-aimed assault. "Enough, you little wretch." And turning about he bent to gather the kitten up into his arms. "If you are going to pace, Mags, you must learn to do just that and not add pouncing upon slippers in with it."

"Mrrrrrrr," agreed The Magnifikitten gazing contentedly up at him, blinking first one green eye and then one yellow eye.

"Heavens," murmured the major, stroking the kitten gently, "and to think I am concerned with the effect of my face upon the population. I vow you are the ugliest cat I have ever seen. You may have both eyes, Maggie, but they are disconcerting together to say the least. And there is not a wisp of fur upon you that matches any other wisp, and that's a fact."

"Brrrr-pft!"

"Brrrr-pft, indeed! Will you settle down here and allow

me to read my paper?" the major asked, sitting in the chair near the hearth, placing The Magnifikitten in his lap and picking up *The Times*. "Take a nap why don't you?"

But The Magnifikitten had not the least intention of napping, entertaining herself instead by batting at the edges of the major's paper and in the end launching herself full-force into the center of it the moment he turned the page. Unable to find purchase and being much too small to burst through the paper to the other side, she slid, instead, down the inside of the paper, through the major's knees and down onto the carpet where she sat for a moment peering dazedly up at him. Then she turned her back upon the man and scampered off across the chamber where she hunkered down under a cricket table and made elaborate preparations to pounce upon a most ferocious dust mote glittering in the sunlight from the window.

The major, peering out from behind *The Times*, studied her as she hugged the carpeting with her front end while her little rear stuck preposterously up at attention. A wide smile lit his face. "What a gudgeon you are," he murmured. "You will never catch a dust mote. You need something a sight more solid to scramble with. I wonder if I have not got something—" he added, setting his paper aside, rising and wandering into his dressing room.

Dillsworthy, having rearranged a number of boxes, handed Lady Annabelle into the coach and entered behind her, taking Flower up upon his lap. "There," he said, "that is not so very bad, is it?"

"Oh, not so very bad at all," laughed Georgianna, giving Belle's hand a squeeze, "so long as we do none of us breathe, Mr. Dillsworthy."

Flower giggled but Lady Annabelle smiled only faintly.

"Belle, dearest, what is it?" asked Georgianna. "Oh, my dear girl, you have been crying!"

"N-no, I h-have not," Belle replied very quietly. "It is merely that—merely that—Oh, Dillsworthy!" she sobbed suddenly. "What am I to do? Devon says that if Harry does not alter his attitude this very day, I must cry off. He says he will put the notice in *The Times* himself so that everyone knows our engagement has ended."

Georgianna closed her eyes, all laughter gone from her. Of course she had known all along that it would come to such a pass. Lord Lackenshire could not be expected to go on forever allowing his sister to remain betrothed to a gentleman who would not even step down into his own parlor to speak to the girl. But Harry—poor Harry—he would be devastated at this final blow.

"Do not look quite so desolate, Miss Roth," urged Dillsworthy, fishing his handkerchief from his pocket while attempting to keep Flower from falling off his lap. "Here, my lady, dry your eyes. Lord Lackenshire has not done anything as yet, has he? No, he has simply said that the major must change by tomorrow, which gives us an entire day to rescue Harry from himself. And we have already begun to do it, too."

"We have?" Lady Annabelle asked tearily.

"Indeed. We are well begun. At this very moment The Magnifikitten is preparing the way."

"How is she doing that?" asked Georgianna, discovering herself oddly bolstered by the confident tone of Mr. Dillsworthy's voice and the knowing gleam in his straightforward brown eyes.

"Unless I am much mistaken, Miss Roth—and I am not—Mags is already cheerfully providing your brother with any number of things to think about besides himself and his wounds. She will not give the major a free moment in which to loathe himself."

"He does not loathe himself," protested Georgianna.

"Yes, he does. That is why he will not come out of his chambers. He loathes the very sight of himself and thinks everyone else will loathe him as well—or pity him, which is equally as bad. And he thinks the beautiful lady he loves will be bitterly disappointed in him."

"I do not care a fig how Harry looks," sobbed Lady Annabelle, swiping at her tears. "I would not care if both his ears were chopped off as well."

"Mr. Dilly," called a voice through the hatch, "what now?"

"To Fretting Dog Lane, Oscar. Everything up to and including myself will be frozen soon if we do not hurry. Lady Annabelle, do not cry any more," he added. "Your brother is fond of Harry and only impatient with him. And besides, we do not allow puffy eyes in this coach."

"No," agreed Flower. "Mr. Dilly don't 'low puffy eyes."

"I should say not. I require something else entirely, do I not, Flower?"

"Uh-huh. Smiles."

"And what else?"

"Singing."

"Exactly."

"S-singing?" whispered Annabelle through her tears.

"Singing?" queried Georgianna.

"Indeed. And I do hereby require that both you and Lady Annabelle take part. Begin, Flower."

"God rest ye merry gen'lemen," began the child in an enthusiastic soprano.

"Let nothing you dismay," Dillsworthy's clear and thoroughly delightful baritone entered the lists.

"Remember Christ our Saviour," joined in the driver's voice from above. "Was borned on Christmas day."

"To save us all from Satan's power when we were gone astray," sang the three of them with so much exuberance that a little sweep upon the corner they were passing joined in as well and a hackney driver bound in the opposite direction added his voice.

"O tidings of comfort and joy, comfort and joy. O tidings of comfort and joy."

Georgianna knew she ought to be embarrassed. Really, persons of quality did not go about singing at the top of their lungs as they traveled the streets of London. But one glance at Belle revealed that Belle's tears had ceased to flow and most inexplicably had been replaced by a beaming smile. Georgianna's determination to maintain proper decorum wavered.

Then Belle's pure, sweet alto joined in the second verse and Mr. Dillsworthy, not pausing for a moment in the song gave Georgianna the most audacious wink. Oh, he is such a—a—scamp, thought Georgianna, feeling a smile rise to her own face. Thank goodness that we are so hemmed in by boxes that no one is likely to recognize us. Belle and I both should be ostracized for such unladylike behavior else. And with a little shake of her head, Georgianna added her clear soprano to the chorus and giving Belle's hand a squeeze, continued on into the third verse.

Mr. Dillsworthy, however, was apparently not to be satisfied with the singing of merely one song. No. No sooner had the final note of "God Rest Ye Merry Gentlemen" faded than his rich baritone led them into another melody. And then another and another. And outside the coach windows, glistening in bright sunlight, snow began to fall, dancing on the wind, a sparkling curtain of frozen lace. And something deep inside of Georgianna warmed and the warmth spread all through her and she rode through the streets of London in the midst a dream, all her fears for Harry and Annabelle becoming buried and forgotten beneath the purely ethereal experience of Mr. Dillsworthy's soothing voice and reassuring smile. For a moment she paused in her own singing and was surprised to hear a beautiful echo of song trailing along behind them like a choir of angels following in their wake.

But after a time the sun began to dim and the snow lost its celestial glow and a mass of dingy gray buildings rose up about the coach and its occupants. "Where are we?" Georgianna asked as they came to the end of a delightful round of "Deck the Halls" and before Mr. Dillsworthy could begin another carol.

"Deep in the innards of London, Miss Roth," Mr. Dillsworthy replied quietly. "We are almost there now."

"Almost where, Mr. Dillsworthy?"

"It is not as though you or Lady Annabelle will be in the least bit of danger. And if it offends your sensibilities to be here, well, it truly cannot be helped and I can only hope that you will find it in your hearts to forgive me."

"Mr. Dillsworthy," Georgianna persisted, raising her voice as the coach drew to a halt, "where are we?"


The Earl of Lackenshire stomped directly past Mr. Parker and took the stairs two at a time all the way to the second story, where he stalked angrily down the corridor, spurs jangling, and threw open the door to Major Roth's chambers. "Where the devil is she?" he bellowed, and then stared wide-eyed at the sight of Major Roth sitting flat upon the carpet, his legs stretched out before him, tugging at one end of a cravat while a kitten scrambled wildly after the other.

Roth looked up immediately, and then hurriedly gained his feet. "Devon? Where is who? Georgie?"

"What the devil are you doing, Harry? Where did that thing come from? Good gawd that is the ugliest creature I have ever seen. Do you mean to tell me that Georgie is not at home either?"

"Either? Who else is not at home?"

The Earl of Lackenshire entered the chamber and closed

the door behind him. He had not actually seen Harry since that gentleman had given orders that no one was to be admitted into his presence in early June. And before that, Harry had been in bed and swathed in bandages. The difference in appearance between this gentleman and the gentleman Lackenshire had known was considerable.

"Cease staring at me like some nodcock, Dev. I realize that I am not pleasing to look upon. Why are you here?"

"Belle has run off," replied Lackenshire gruffly.

"Run off? Oh, surely not, Dev."

"Well, she has not packed her bags or anything of that sort, but she ran from the house without even her maid to accompany her almost two hours ago and has not returned. I thought she had come here, but Parker vows he has not seen her and now you tell me that Georgianna is missing as well."

"Mrrrrow!" inserted The Magnifikitten excitedly, making a bold leap at Harry's leg in an attempt to scale him like a mountain.

"Ouch!" Roth cried, and reaching down plucked the kitten from the kerseymere of his breeches and scooped her up into his arms. "Georgianna is not missing," he informed Lackenshire with some asperity, rubbing at his leg. "She has gone off on an errand with Dillsworthy."

"Who?"

"Dillsworthy. Sir Alfred's nephew. From Kent. He is spending the winter next door it seems."

The Earl of Lackenshire, his dark curls much like his sister's curling about his face, his blue eyes wide in disbelief, opened his mouth then closed it again without uttering a sound.

"What?" asked Roth. "I swear Devon, if you do not cease staring at me like that I will blacken both your daylights for you. What did you do to make Belle run off without any escort whatsoever? You must have done something. She is generally a most circumspect young lady."

"I—I told her I had decided she must cry off from your engagement. Well, you will not even see her," added Lackenshire defensively. "You have refused to see her for months and she has been in agony over it. But Harry—"

"What?"

"Sir Alfred does not have a nephew, Harry, in Kent or anywhere else."

"Mrrrow-pft," murmured The Magnifikitten stretching up to place two tiny paws upon Harry's shoulder and licking at the lobe of his ear. "Mrrrow-pft-burrrr."

# *Chapter Seven*

All contemplation of himself, his scars, even the disgust Lackenshire must feel at the sight of him drained from Major Harry Roth's thoughts as quickly as the blood drained from his face. "An imposter? Are you certain?" he asked, hurrying toward his dressing room. "How do you know, Dev?"

"Because my father and Edgerton were friends all their lives, Harry. Sir Alfred is an only child. He cannot have a nephew if he is an only child."

"No. Most definitely not," Roth growled, slipping into a uniform jacket that had become much too large for him and crossing to tug at the bellpull. "Arlesby, my greatcoat," he ordered as his valet poked his head in at the door. "And my gloves and my cap. Send word to the stables to saddle Nuisance and have him at the front door as soon as possible," he added, tugging on his top boots and then buckling on his sword. "He has taken Georgie. They drove off in a coach shortly after eleven, Dev. And he would not say where they were bound. It was a secret, he said."

"Indeed," declared Lackenshire. "And if Georgie were already in the coach, Belle would not have hesitated for a moment to join them. She was in need of comforting and your sister would be just the person she would seek to give it to her."

"Damnation! Why did you not go after Belle immediately? How could you let her go running off alone?"

"Well, you let Georgie go off with a man you did not know from Adam," replied Lackenshire defensively. "Besides, I was—disconcerted—to say the least. You have been breaking Belle's heart bit by bit since June, Harry, and if she has her way, she will allow you to go on breaking it forever. It was difficult enough to tell her that I intended to call the thing off. It was all I had on my mind. It did not occur to me to go after her because it did not occur to me that she would leave the premises without proper escort, much less run off with some villain."

Lackenshire grabbed the greatcoat from Arlesby's hands and helped Roth to shrug into it.

"If that scoundrel has harmed either one of them, I'll have his gizzard for dinner," thundered the major, spinning about on his heel. "To horse, Dev!"

"But where do we ride, Harry? You said yourself that you have not the vaguest idea where this Dillsworthy person may have taken them."

"No, but I'll wager his cook knows," growled Harry, stalking toward the doorway.

"His cook?"

"Mrrrow!" interjected The Magnifikitten abruptly, leaping from the shaving stand and dashing after Major Roth.

"No, you may not come," declared the major. "Arlesby, grab that creature and hold onto her."

"Mrrr-sppt-ssss!" hissed The Magnifikitten as Arlesby reached for her. "Sssss-pttt!" And she dodged between Lord Lackenshire's legs, then between Roth's, then spun about and leaped as high as Harry's thigh where she clung perilously with all four sets of claws.

"Dratted cat!" the major exclaimed. "It's no wonder Dillsworthy was forever carrying you about. You are like to cripple a man when you are threatened with being left behind, ain't you?" With a modicum of care, Roth peeled the kitten from his breeches and stuffed her unceremoniously into the pocket of his greatcoat.

Lackenshire stared.

"What?"

"You stuffed that kitten into your pocket, Harry, like it was a handkerchief."

"She likes pockets. Why would Dillsworthy lie? How did the blackguard get into Sir Alfred's residence in the first place then if he is not his nephew? And who the devil is he?" the major fairly bellowed, leading the way down the staircase.

"A villain," growled Lackenshire from behind. "Out to ruin your sister and mine as well. Possibly thinking to hold them for ransom or some such."

"Well, he'll not get away with it," Harry responded, stomping past an amazed Parker and through the door the butler held wide, clattering down the outside stoop, spurs jingling, and stepping over the tiny wall between his residence and Dillsworthy's. "If he lays one finger upon Georgie or Belle, I shall strangle the scoundrel with my own two hands!"

"Not before I horsewhip him to within an inch of his life," muttered Lackenshire, stepping over the wall after Roth and matching him stride for stride as they headed for the kitchen entrance of Sir Alfred Edgerton's town house.

Roth raised a gloved hand and thumped impatiently upon the kitchen door.

"Why are we here? Why do we not go around to the front and pull the bell, Harry?"

"Because Dillsworthy mentioned that the only servant at home today would be the cook. And the cook will be in the kitchen. Now what did he say the woman's name was? Diggins? Duggale? Duggans? Duggan, that's it. Mrs. Duggan."

"Yes? What is it?" queried a husky voice as the kitchen door opened inward. The face that met theirs shocked both Roth and Lackenshire into instant silence.

Georgianna could not believe her eyes. No, nor her nose either. "What is this place, Mr. Dillsworthy?" she asked as that gentleman lifted Flower from his lap and opened the coach door. "I have never smelled such vile smells in all my life nor have I ever seen such squalor. It is appalling."

"Yes I expected you would think so. That it is appalling, I mean. That is the one thing wrong with the plan, but I thought you would not mind so very much because you are not required to leave the coach, you know."

"You are not stepping down into the street, Dillsworthy?" asked Lady Annabelle. "Only see those persons across the way. Certainly they are thieves and cutthroats."

"Belle is correct, Mr. Dillsworthy," Georgianna added, catching at Dillsworthy's sleeve as he descended from the coach. "It cannot be at all safe to walk about here."

"Flower, look there," Dillsworthy grinned, ignoring both their warnings and stepping down to the cobbles then swinging the child from the coach as well and pointing toward the flagway opposite them.

"Da!" Flower called excitedly. "Da, it's me! It's me, Flower!"

Georgianna watched in amazement as Dillsworthy lowered the little girl to the cobbles and Flower fairly flew into the opening arms of a most intimidating man in a ragged surtout.

"Hey, Henry," Dillsworthy called. "Did you miss her then?"

"Aye. Ever' minit o' ever' day," laughed the man, catching the child up and twirling her about in his arms.

What on earth? thought Georgianna. He knows that man by name? How can he come to know such a person by name? And then she noted that other people were separating themselves from the dingy buildings and bursting excitedly from broken doorways and popping out from dark, narrow alleyways, all of them advancing rapidly upon Mr. Dillsworthy and the coach. And in a moment Mr. Dillsworthy was surrounded by them and they were speaking all at once and laughing and shouting. Georgianna could not believe her eyes. Who were these people? And what had Mr. Dillsworthy to do with any of them? Her heart stuttered as the mob pressed in about him and she reached for Belle's hand, squeezing it tightly.

And then appeared a number of people whom Georgianna did recognize. "Mr. Dillsworthy's servants?" she murmured.

"They have been following us in that dreadful hay wagon ever since we turned off from Bridge Street," Belle informed her. "Did you not hear them singing along with us, Georgie? I expect I was foolish to fear for Dillsworthy. I know I was," mused Belle. "See, he is laughing and shaking their hands."

"Apparently," whispered Georgianna, horrified. How could a plain Mr. Dillsworthy, Sir Alfred Edgerton's nephew from Kent, possibly know these—these—persons? He could not. He would not. Something was dreadfully wrong.

Major Harry Roth and the Earl of Lackenshire stood open-mouthed before a tall, exquisite woman in cap and long white apron with a bit of flour upon one cheek.

"You are Mr. Dillsworthy's cook?" Harry managed at last in disbelief.

"I am called Mrs. Duggan," the woman informed him with the slightest tilt of an elegant brow. "And you, sir, are?"

"R-Roth," stuttered the major.

"Our neighbor! Mr. Dillsworthy is not at home, but I expect you know that or you would not have come to the kitchen door. No one is at home but me. Mr. Dillsworthy required all of the others elsewhere."

"Where?" asked Lackenshire, slowly finding his tongue in the face of such regal and unexpected beauty.

"Yes, where have they gone?" echoed Roth, uneasily rubbing a hand against the back of his neck.

"Fretting Dog Lane," smiled Mrs. Duggan whose perfect teeth absolutely glistened in the sunshine.

"Bedamned," whispered Roth. "The Devil's Elbow."

Mrs. Duggan, her deep blue eyes glittering with quiet amusement, nodded. "Indeed, sir, the area is oft called so."

Whatever color remained in Roth's face drained from it that instant.


"What is it you need?" Lady Annabelle asked as Dillsworthy stuck his head back inside the coach.

"The packages, my lady," Dillsworthy answered stretching to seize two bandboxes from the floor. "Do not disturb yourself. I can get them."

"Oh no, Georgie and I shall be pleased to hand them out to you," Lady Annabelle assured him.

"Yes, of course," murmured Georgianna, gazing suspiciously down at the gentleman. "Does it matter which ones come first?"

"Not at all. Nor does it matter to whom you give any of them," he added, lifting a bandbox in each hand. "Except for these two. Tyre,'' he called, passing the boxes on to that gentleman, ''see these get as far as the Limping Dragon, will you? The one with the blue riband is for Granny Orange. And the other for Meadow Lil.''

''Aye, Mr. Dilly. I'll see they get them.''

Granny Orange and Meadow Lil? Georgianna handed a small carton across to Belle who handed it down to Dillsworthy. Granny Orange and Meadow Lil? Two very distinct images popped into Georgianna's mind at the very mention of those names. But they popped out again shortly as the crowd around the coach became a veritable mob and Georgianna had all she could do to pass the boxes and crates and cartons to Annabelle fast enough to fill the waiting arms outside the coach. Mr. Dillsworthy himself had disappeared into the throng and when the final band-box was passed off into the street, Georgianna peered out of the window in hopes of discovering where that gentleman had gone.

''Why, he is lighting fires.''

''Who is lighting fires?''

''Mr. Dillsworthy, Belle. See, just there. He is striking his flint over that iron barrel. Now why would he be doing that right out on the flagway?''

''It be fer the ones what don't got no place ta take cover,'' answered a voice from beneath the window. Georgianna looked down to see a boy, no older than ten, leaning against the coach. ''I'm Scotty,'' the boy introduced himself with a tip of his cap. ''This year I'm Mr. Dilly's stable boy.''

''This year?'' asked Georgianna.

''Yes, miss. Last year it were my brother, Ted. But he has got himself a position at Tattersall's now, leadin' the horses about the rings. So this year it be my turn to work in Mr. Dilly's stables, an' nex' year 'twill be Arnie's turn most like. We brung enough wood on the wagon ta keep the fires burnin' all day an' the whole night. And tamorrow we will bring more. We brung the barrels day afore yesterday an' the coal fer the ones what gots a place inside las' night. My Ma gots a place inside," the boy finished proudly. "Mr. Dilly made sure-certain she did."

"He did?"

"Oh, yes, miss. Him an' Mr. Sneed had a ter'ble row about it. 'Cause Mr. Sneed, he do not like my Ma above half. But Mr. Dilly, he won out in the end like he mostly does."

"Sneed?" asked Georgianna, the significance of Mr. Dillsworthy's intimate acquaintanceship with these people, which had faded somewhat from her mind while she had been busy with the boxes, returning full force. "Mr. Dillsworthy is familiar with a person named Sneed?"

They rode like demons, Major Harry Roth and Lord Lackenshire, ignoring the slippery snow, weaving recklessly through traffic, passing drays and hackneys and squeezing between carriages at the gallop. And when the way was clear they gave the horses their heads and clattered over the cobbles at a full run, until they reached the warrens of ramshackle houses and squalid alleys that stretched behind the London wharves where they slowed considerably.

"Do you know which one is Fretting Dog Lane?" Lackenshire queried, bringing his mount up beside Roth's.

"No, not precisely. It's behind the bull pit, if I remember correctly. Near the bend of the elbow."

"This way then," nodded Lackenshire spurring his horse forward.

He was the biggest, ugliest, most intimidating spectacle of a man Georgianna had ever seen. "Whoever is that?" she gasped.

" 'Tis Mr. Sneed!" exclaimed Scotty. "It means they be

comin' then. I got to go." And he was off at a run toward
the place where Dillsworthy was just then kneeling upon
the walkway helping a group of children to open one of
the crates.

"Sneed," hissed Annabelle in a most un-Annabellelike
tone. "Oh, what a devil he looks. And he is stomping
toward Dillsworthy!"

Sneed, bedecked in the most outrageous cloak of pea
green satin lined with marabou fur, his boots like great
tree stumps, had come to a halt above Dillsworthy, grabbed
him by the back of the collar, and tugged him to his feet.
Around them, Scotty and the other children shrieked and
scattered.

"Already?" gasped Dillsworthy.

"Passin' the Limpin' Dragon when I come," growled
Sneed. "Be here in no more'n three minits now. Ye sure-
certain, Dilly?"

"Yes."

"How dare he!" Georgianna declared angrily, forgetting
her doubts about Mr. Dillsworthy as the great, ugly Sneed
hoisted that gentleman above his head. "How dare he!"
With a great deal of indignation and no rational thought
whatsoever, Georgianna threw open the coach door and
stepped down into the street, followed directly by Lady
Annabelle.

"Unhand Mr. Dillsworthy this moment, you great lout!"
Georgianna cried, hurrying across the cobbles toward the
two. "At this moment, sir, do you hear me!"

"Georgie," whispered Annabelle, catching at her sleeve,
"you do not need to help. I am certain Dillsworthy is quite
capable."

"Capable? Capable of what? Why that man is three times
Mr. Dillsworthy's size at the very least, Belle. And he has
caught him by surprise as well," grumbled Georgianna,
refusing to come to a halt and forcing Belle to step most
quickly to keep pace with her.

"Yes, but none of that matters because Dillsworthy is an angel, Georgie."

"I do not know why you insist upon referring to that gentleman as an angel, Belle," sputtered Georgianna. "But even so, an angelic character is not what is needed at this point. Do not you dare to shake him like a dusty rag!" exclaimed Georgianna, close enough to lay a hand upon Sneed's arm. "Drop Mr. Dillsworthy at once, sir!"

"D-drop him?" stuttered the man, turning to look down his exceedingly bulbous nose at Georgianna and Annabelle.

"No, Sneed, do not drop me," managed Dillsworthy in a rather strangled voice.

"Release him at once," demanded Georgianna. "Already Mr. Dillsworthy's servants are gathering to present you with a proper comeuppance for your brash and vulgar behavior."

"Huh?" asked Sneed.

"Drop him, sir," Georgianna repeated. "I command you to do so at once."

"No, Sneed, do not drop me," coughed Dillsworthy over what sounded to Annabelle suspiciously like a laugh.

Lady Annabelle looked Sneed up and down, studied Georgianna for one moment, then walked around them both to get a look at Dillsworthy's face. "I knew you were laughing," she said, her hands going to her hips. "You ought not to laugh, Dillsworthy. Georgianna is attempting to save you."

"I do not require saving," choked Dillsworthy.

"And so I told her, but Georgie will have it that you do."

"If you do not drop him, I shall be forced to call in the constables," threatened Georgianna, forced to tilt her head back to scowl straight up into Sneed's enormous dark eyes. She was concentrating so determinedly upon the great bully that she did not notice the sudden clattering of horses hooves upon the cobbles, nor Annabelle's little gasp.

"Oh, well then," sighed Sneed, who did hear the clattering and knew precisely what it was. "I be right sorry, Dilly, but the lady says if I don't be droppin' ye, she be callin' in the constables. What kin I do?" And with a wide smile, Sneed lifted Dillsworthy higher into the air and tossed him into the gutter.

# *Chapter Eight*

"What the devil!" exclaimed Major Roth, he and Lackenshire riding into Fretting Dog Lane just as Lady Annabelle cried out in alarm, Georgianna placed a well-aimed kick upon Sneed's knee and Dillsworthy bounced unceremoniously from a stack of empty bandboxes into the wet gutter. Roth jerked his mount to a halt and leaped from the saddle. He picked Georgianna up, set her aside and landed Sneed a facer. As Sneed sank to the flagway, the major wrapped Lady Annabelle in his arms, and pushing aside her little fur cap, kissed the top of her head and then her brow and then her eyes and her nose and at the last her lovely, cupid's bow lips. "It is all right, my love," he whispered. "You are safe now. Not one of these villains shall lay a hand upon you, Belle. I vow it. There is no need to be frightened any longer."

Georgianna stared open-mouthed at her brother, then she turned to see Lord Lackenshire sitting his horse contentedly beside the empty hay wagon, a wide smile upon his handsome face. And then she heard Mr. Dillsworthy groan the tiniest bit and turned to see him sitting up in the gutter. All around her the street was crowded with silent people standing very still.

"You are not to cry, dearest," she heard Harry murmur into the silence. "I do not know what all this is about, but I shall get to the bottom of it immediately. And if Dillsworthy or that wretched giant has so much as laid a finger upon you or Georgie, they shall pay dearly for it."

"Oh," sighed Lady Annabelle happily, resting her head upon his shoulder. "Oh, Harry, I am not crying because I have been harmed. I am crying because I am so very happy."

"Because you are happy?"

"Oh, yes. Because you have abandoned your chambers at last and have come riding all the way to this odd place like the brave soldier that you are. And because you hit Mr. Sneed in the face which is just like your old self, surely. And because you are holding me in your arms just as you were used to do. You *are* going to marry me, are you not, Harry, now that you are yourself again? You will not allow Devon to put an end to our engagement?"

"I—I—Belle, my dearest girl, look at me. You cannot possibly wish to be leg-shackled to a man who is lacking an eye and two fingers and is scarred from tip to toe besides."

"Mrrrow," interrupted a muffled but angry little voice, and the right side of Major Roth's greatcoat began to wiggle and jump about most disconcertingly.

Annabelle giggled.

"What?" asked Major Roth. "Belle, I am perfectly serious. You cannot possibly wish to connect yourself with—"

"Mrrrr-pft-pfff!" interrupted The Magnifikitten again, more loudly, struggling up to the top of Major Roth's pocket, sinking her claws into the sleeve of his greatcoat and climbing onto his arm, balancing shakily. "Mrrrr-brrr-pft!'' she announced, angry but triumphant, on a little wobble.

"Oh, Harry!" Annabelle's laughter trilled sweetly through the afternoon. "Do you not think that kitten the sweetest, most wonderful kitten in the entire world? She has ridden all this way in your pocket and is certainly nonplussed at the shaking she has taken and yet anyone can see how proud she is of herself."

"I had forgot all about her," muttered Roth, glancing down at the disheveled little animal and striving to hold his arm as still as he could so as not to send the kitten crashing to the flagway. "And yes, dearest, she is sweet and a scamp to boot and I have grown fond of her, but we are not speaking of—"

"And you do not think that she is ugly or disgusting?"

"Well, odd-looking, but one grows accustomed to that. I have not thought what an eyesore she is since she clambered across my bedside table with my stocking in her—but I am a man, Belle!" exclaimed Harry, abruptly grasping her meaning.

"The man I love," smiled Belle encouragingly, plucking The Magnifikitten from her unsteady perch and cradling the little creature in her arms. "And I have grown accustomed to your appearance, Harry, in the space of time since first you came riding up. You have long since endeared yourself to me, you see. And even if you do not have two eyes," she added, touching his chin gently with one finger, "at least you do not have one green eye and one yellow eye."

"I—I love you, Belle," murmured Harry. "More than anything. And—and—if you are certain—"

"Oh, I am quite certain, Harry."

"At last," bellowed Lackenshire cheerfully from the back of his horse.

"Three cheers!" yelled Scotty. "One for the major an' one for Mr. Dilly an' one for The Magnifikitten!"

"Hip-hip-hooray!" roared the crowd with great enthusiasm. "Hip-hip-hooray! Hip-hip-hooray!"

Georgianna, tears of happiness streaming down her cold cheeks, noticed in wonder that Mr. Sneed had regained his feet and was one of those cheering. Mr. Dillsworthy had regained his feet as well and coming up beside Georgianna, he wrapped a reassuring arm about her shoulders. "Your brother will be all right now, Miss Roth," he whispered, his lips very close to her ear. "It is the first step back into the world that is the most difficult. And Harry has taken that step like the hero he is."


Tears stood in Georgianna's eyes as she gazed from the parlor window into the lamp-lit night. It was Christmas and the sun had set hours ago and she had not so much as seen Mr. Dillsworthy since they had departed Fretting Dog Lane all those days ago. He had offered his coach to her and Belle and Harry and Lord Lackenshire, set his groom the task of returning the gentlemen's horses, abruptly placed a kiss upon Georgianna's cheek and sent them all off without him. The tenderness of that kiss had lingered as no other gentleman's kiss had ever done. As unexpected as it had been and as impetuously given, it had opened the door to a chamber of Georgianna's heart that not even she had known existed. But that chamber was empty and ached to be filled.

"Georgie?"

That voice brought a smile to her lips and she turned to see her brother standing in the doorway, clean shaven, his hair trimmed and combed into a perfect Brutus, and fitted out in evening dress that Weston had provided him in less than a week.

"What is it?" the major asked, striding across the carpeting toward her. "You look as though you have lost your best friend."

"No. It is nothing, Harry. You look splendid."

"As do you," the major replied with a twinkle in his eye. "Are you hoping for a glimpse of Mr. Dillsworthy? I thought him such a great villain for a short while, and what a very ordinary gentleman he turned out to be after all."

"Oh no, Harry, he is not ordinary," Georgianna replied. "He is the most extraordinary gentleman I have ever met. Only think what he did for us when he did not know us in the least."

"Indeed," chuckled Harry, wrapping his sister in his arms and gazing out the window over her shoulder. "He laid siege to this house; set that wretched kitten to plague the devil out of me; convinced Dev to tell the most outrageous clankers; and carried you and Belle into The Devil's Elbow."

"It was his plan," replied Georgianna, the smile upon her lips at last reaching her eyes.

"The most outrageous plan ever conceived. Damnation, even Dillsworthy's cook was in on the thing and expecting me to come and ask where he had gone!"

"Lord Lackenshire says she is quite beautiful."

"Ravishing."

A little piece of Georgianna's heart stuttered to a stop. "Who is Mr. Dillsworthy?" she asked in a confused little voice quite unlike her own. "I know that he is truly Sir Alfred's nephew—that Devon lied to you about that—but how is it that Sir Alfred's nephew comes to know such odd people as Mr. Sneed and the others and to have such a thing as a clock maid and a cook who is ravishing? And why has he not come to see us even once since—since—"

"We shall be forced to ask him," drawled Harry, taking his sister's hand. "It is time to go, Georgie."

"But where are we going?"

"To a Christmas party, my girl. I told you that."

"Yes, but you did not tell me where, Harry."

"How remiss of me," smiled the major, donning his greatcoat. "We are going next door, Georgie, to Mr. Dillsworthy's."

J. Tildon Dillsworthy paced the length of his Uncle Alfred's ballroom in nervous splendor. His coat was of Bath Superfine and cut to perfection. His waistcoat was red in deference to the holiday and a ruby glittered in the pristine white of his neckcloth. His black boots shone with the brilliance of polished ebony and his brown curls had been combed ruthlessly into place. None of which, he was well aware, made him any the less ordinary than he had always been.

A great lump formed in Dillsworthy's throat as he heard the distant ringing of the doorbell and he coughed to clear it. He coughed again. And again. Bedamned, but the blasted lump would not begone! And then he heard footsteps ascending the stairs and all rational thought escaped him. In a moment they would appear and Miss Roth would discover him amidst pine boughs and holly and mistletoe—an ordinary gentleman who had always been contented to live an ordinary life but who had conceived, in a matter of moments it seemed, a most extraordinary tenderness for a woman whose lineage and beauty must place her quite above his touch. His stomach churned with the sheer futility of his situation.

And then Lady Annabelle fairly swooped into the ballroom and flew into Dillsworthy's arms. "Dev says that you are not an angel and that you are an ordinary gentleman and that I am to call you Mr. Dillsworthy from now on," she whispered as she hugged him in the most unladylike fashion. "But you will always be an angel to me." And standing upon her toes, she placed a most enthusiastic kiss upon his speedily reddening cheek.

"Enough, Belle, you are putting Mr. Dillsworthy to the blush," laughed Lackenshire, stepping forward to shake Dillsworthy's hand.

"I would quiz you about such familiarity with my fiancée, but your ears are already burning," grinned the major, taking Dillsworthy's hand as Lackenshire relinquished it. "I do thank you," he added, "for everything."

"You are very welcome, I'm sure," Dillsworthy responded. "Miss Roth," he added as the major drew his sister forward, "it is kind of you to attend my little party."

Georgianna curtsied quite properly as the gentleman bowed over her hand and then looked up to search his face with questioning emerald eyes. She heard the front bell ring at a great distance. There was the sound of any number of guests arriving. Myriad feet climbed the staircase and a plethora of voices murmured in the corridor, but none of that caused her to take her gaze from a face she suddenly found decidedly endearing.

"Miss Roth, I must—" Dillsworthy began, releasing her hand. And then the rest of his guests burst into the ballroom.

"Dilly!" called a gruff voice. "There you are! Happy Christmas to you, my boy!"

Georgianna turned to see the giant of a man called Sneed striding forward, both arms outstretched. In a moment he was clasping Mr. Dillsworthy to his bosom with great good will. Behind him a multitude of men, women and children came buzzing and laughing and chattering into the ballroom. All of them were dressed in their finest clothes, though some were threadbare, some were patched and others had obviously been tailored to bodies quite unlike the bodies that now displayed them.

"Are you not going to introduce me to your friends, then, Dilly?" asked Sneed with hearty good cheer. "Jeremiah Sneed," he said, offering a hand the size of a meat cleaver to Major Roth. "And you are Roth, of course. Dilly has long since told me all about you. You've a punishing right, lad."

"You went down on purpose, did you not?" grinned Major Roth, grasping the hand and giving it a hearty shake. "It occurred to me much later that I could not possibly have sent you to the cobbles with one punch."

"Aye, lad, but it was a punishing right regardless. Felt it for an hour afterward, I did. And this gentleman will be his lordship," he added, extending his hand to Lackenshire.

"And this is my sister, Lady Annabelle," smiled Lackenshire, drawing Belle forward.

Sneed smiled widely and bowed quite properly over Belle's little hand and then he turned to Georgianna and enclosed her hand in both of his. "And you, my dear, must certainly be the beautiful Miss Roth who has stolen my stepson's heart away."

Four very aristocratic jaws dropped in astonishment.

In a small alcove above the dance floor an odd assortment of musicians began to play and with a significant flourish, Mr. Sneed placed Georgianna's hand upon his arm and led her out onto the floor. "Come, Dilly," he called over his shoulder in a most pleased voice. "It is time to begin the party. Granny Orange awaits you. Grande Promenade, my boy. Grande Promenade."

Georgianna danced the evening away in the arms of footmen and fireboys, stovers, fishermen and sweeps. Large and tiny, wide and tall, boys and men, they approached her one after the other, leading her with smiles and laughter through reels and country dances. Belle, too, skipped and hopped and twirled to the music and Lord Lackenshire and the major quite merrily followed suit, leading out mothers and grandmothers, flower girls and scullery maids and even Mr. Dillsworthy's ravishing cook—whom Lord Lackenshire led to the floor any number of times.

Supper appeared in three separate rooms simultaneously and Mr. Dillsworthy's guests sat down whenever they pleased to lobster patties and pheasant and ham, a side of mutton and a rack of ribs liberally interspersed with boiled potatoes and green peas and pears. Wine flowed for the adults and milk for the children. And in each room a most magnificent Christmas pudding was cut and passed with innumerable smiles.

It was not until very late indeed that J. Tildon Dillsworthy begged the favor of a dance with Miss Georgianna Roth. "I ought to explain, I expect, about Jeremiah," he murmured, his hand resting lightly upon her waist. "He is a very large man with a very large mouth."

"Really, Mr. Dillsworthy. Such a way to speak of your stepfather."

"Well, but it is true. With Jeremiah there are no secrets. I ought not have spoken a word to him about it. But I found that I had to speak to someone. The thing of it is, I have developed a—a *tendre*—for you, Miss Roth. I know I am quite ineligible," he inserted hurriedly before Georgianna could utter a sound. "You do not need to tell me that. And I would never have mentioned it at all, except that Jeremiah—"

"When did it happen, Mr. Dillsworthy, that you developed this *tendre* for me?" Georgianna asked, fighting to keep a smile from her face.

Dillsworthy's straightforward brown eyes lit with remembered laughter. "When you ordered Jeremiah to drop me. I knew for certain it was love then. You were so very beautiful and quite magnificent and I could not help but admit to myself that I particularly wished to have you for my wife."

Georgianna missed a step in the dance and would have tumbled backward had Mr. Dillsworthy not pulled her close within his arms. "Your wife, Mr. Dillsworthy?"

"Do not fret, Miss Roth. I am aware that we barely know each other and even if we did, you are quite above my touch. I do not aspire to such heights as an earl's niece when I am rational. My mother was Sir Alfred's sister and my father no more than the second son of a baron. When he died, my mother married the Reverend Mr. Sneed."

"Mr. Sneed is a clergyman?"

"Indeed."

"And these people are his—"

"Flock. My mother is dead now, but Maeve and I return to London every winter. To help in whatever ways we can."

"Maeve?"

"My stepsister. I thank God she came to me when Duggan died. She will have it that she is my cook, you know. But she is only my cook because she wishes me not to starve to death. And because she enjoys feeding everyone each winter."

His stepsister. The ravishing cook was his stepsister. Georgianna wished to raise a finger to Mr. Dillsworthy's very serious lips and to tickle them upward into the beguiling grin that she knew hid therein.

"Tell me about Flower," she said instead. "What is a clock maid?" And she was instantly rewarded with the grin she sought.

"Why, a clock maid is in charge of clocks. She must dust and polish and wind them. Henry had lost his position and I did have a number of clocks in Kent that needed tending, Miss Roth, so—"

"So you took the responsibility for Flower until he found another position and you convinced them both that she was needed," finished Georgianna for him, her very soul filled with an admiration for this gentleman that all of the beaux in all of London had never raised in her. "You are remarkable, sir."

"Me? Remarkable?" Dillsworthy's face held such a look of surprise that it set Georgianna to giggling.

And then, most abruptly, Dillsworthy stumbled in the midst of a twirl and tilted precariously backward. Georgianna attempted to hold him upright but it could not be done and Mr. Dillsworthy hit the floor with a thump pulling Georgianna down on top of him. The music ceased to play. The other dancers ceased to dance.

"Mrrr-ow-rrow!" exclaimed The Magnifikitten into the encroaching silence, extricating herself from between Dillsworthy's legs as Georgianna rolled aside. With multi-colored fur standing uprighteously on end, The Magnifikitten stomped directly up to the center of Dillsworthy's waistcoat, leaving a little trail of Christmas-pudding-footprints. "Brrr-pfff, brrr-brrr-pfff!" she exclaimed, jumping up and down excitedly upon Dillsworthy's stomach. "Mrrr-ow-brrr-pfff!"

"She is attempting to inform you, Dillsworthy, that she discovered the ring in the Christmas pudding and that I took it from her," laughed Major Roth, offering his hand to his laughing sister and tugging her to her feet. "And I warn you, sir," he added as Georgianna scooped the kitten from Dillsworthy's stomach, "that if you persist in compromising my sister by rolling about on the floor with her in this manner, I shall force you to use that ring to marry the girl."

"Indeed, Dilly," chuckled the Reverend Mr. Sneed helping his stepson to his feet, "and I shall perform the ceremony."

"Oh, I should like that, Mr. Sneed," Georgianna declared, her eyes twinkling mischievously.

"You should?" asked Dillsworthy, astonished. "You should like to be married to me?"

"Well," nodded Georgianna, "I do think it bears thinking upon. Perhaps we ought to continue our dance, Mr. Dillsworthy.''

"Indeed," concurred the major putting a fond arm about his sister's waist, "and Sneed and I shall set The Magnifikitten upon him a second time when you have definitely decided that you want the fellow."